Acclaim for **KENT HARUF**'s

THE TIE THAT BINDS

"This is strong stuff, and marvelous writing."
—John Irving

"Haruf's voice . . . resonates across the plains."
—*Los Angeles Herald-Examiner*

"There are people in this novel—individuals so deftly sketched that the reader knows how they look, sound and think."   —*The Oregonian*

"Haruf writes in the tradition of Hamlin Garland and Willa Cather about the constricted lives and obscure destinies of small farmers on the Great Plains. . . . He knows his people and knows the quality of their lives; and with a simple, engaging style he makes the reader care about them."
—*Library Journal*

"A powerfully eloquent tribute to the essential dignity and tenacity of the human spirit."
—*Booklist*

KENT HARUF

THE TIE THAT BINDS

Kent Haruf's *The Tie That Binds* received a Whiting Foundation Award and a special citation from the PEN/Hemingway Foundation. He is also the author of *Where You Once Belonged* and *Plainsong*, a finalist for the National Book Award. He lives with his wife, Cathy, in Colorado and Illinois, and teaches at Southern Illinois University at Carbondale.

THE TIE THAT BINDS

A Novel

KENT HARUF

VINTAGE CONTEMPORARIES

Vintage Books
A Division of Random House, Inc.
New York

for Ginger and Mark

FIRST VINTAGE CONTEMPORARIES EDITION, MAY 2000

Copyright © 1984 by Kent Haruf

Library of Congress Cataloging-in-Publication Data on file.

Vintage ISBN: 0-375-72438-9

Author photo © Cathy Haruf

www.vintagebooks.com

Printed in the United States of America
10 9 8 7 6 5 4 3

THE TIE THAT BINDS

· 1 ·

Eᴅɪᴛʜ Gᴏᴏᴅɴᴏᴜɢʜ isn't in the country anymore. She's in town now, in the hospital, lying there in that white bed with a needle stuck in the back of one hand and a man standing guard in the hallway outside her room. She will be eighty years old this week: a clean beautiful white-haired woman who never in her life weighed as much as 115 pounds, and she has weighed a lot less than that since New Year's Eve. Still, the sheriff and the lawyers expect her to get well enough for them to sit her up in a wheelchair and then drive her across town to the courthouse to begin the trial. When that happens, if that happens, I don't know that they will go so far as to put handcuffs on her. Bud Sealy, the sheriff, has turned out to be a son of a bitch, all right, but I still can't see him putting handcuffs on a woman like Edith Goodnough.

On the other hand, I don't suppose Bud Sealy ever intended to become a son of a bitch at all. As late as nine days ago he was sitting on a barstool at the lunch counter in the Holt Café. It was Friday afternoon; it was about two-thirty, that slack time that comes every day for him when he's got all his paper work filled out, when there isn't a thing more for him to do except wait for the high school kids to get out of school so they can begin to race up and down Main Street or drive out onto U.S. 34 and cut cookies on the blacktop. So Bud had time. He was relaxing. Already he had eaten his butterscotch pie and Betty had cleared his plate. Now, while he waited for his second cup of black coffee to cool, he was turned around on the barstool so as to front the men who sat opposite him in the booths. The men had come in earlier in their town pants and adjustable caps. Two or three of them had slapped him on the back like they do, and they had all taken their places on the other stools or in the nearby booths so they could hear the talk and keep current.

Most of the talk that afternoon was Bud's. He was telling them a story. I believe most of the men had heard this particular story at least twice before, though I doubt that any one of them would have thought to stop him from telling it again, since the one thing they all had too much of was just that—time. I mean two or three had already retired from the work they had never gotten around to beginning.

At any rate, the story Bud was telling that afternoon had to do with how there was this guy at the National Western Stock Show who was walking around in public with a piece of pink thread tied to himself, like what it was tied to was one of the agricultural exhibits in the pavilion hallways. He was sort of displaying himself to folks. That is, until the police collared him and took him to jail for indecent exposure and creating a nuisance. They booked him. A few weeks later when they stood him up in front of a judge—an old man with wire glasses and no hair to speak of—the judge says to him: "Son, I'm going to ask you just one question and I want an answer. Son, are you crazy?" And the guy with the pink thread says, "No sir, I don't believe so." And the judge says: "Well then, are you just half crazy?" And the guy says . . .

But Bud never got to say this time what the guy says, because just then someone walked into the Holt Café that neither Bud nor any of the other men knew. He asked which one of them was the sheriff. One of the boys pointed to Bud.

It turned out this new man was a newspaper reporter from Denver. He had just driven into town. At the police station they had told him that he might discover the sheriff at the Holt Café, and he did. So I date it about then, a little after two-thirty on a Friday afternoon in April, that Bud Sealy started seriously to become a son of a bitch. Because in a few minutes Bud and this Denver man went out to the town's cop car; they drove off up Main Street, and I don't guess they had driven long or far before Bud gave him the fifty-pound bag of chicken feed that had been knifed open and laid in easy access for the six or seven chickens, laid just inside the chicken coop where it wouldn't get wet or snowed on.

That was not enough, however. That did not satisfy him. The man from Denver wanted more than just chicken feed. So Bud turned off onto one of the residential streets and drove a block or two under the budding elm trees risen along the curb, and then on Birch Street or Cedar he gave him the dog too, told him how the old milky-eyed dog, which had never been tied up before, had nevertheless been tied up that particular December afternoon three and a half months ago and again within easy reach of several days' food and water.

But that still was not enough. Chicken feed and an old dog must have only whet the Denver man's appetite. Besides, I suppose he was beginning to crowd Bud now, shove him hard for more. Then too, maybe by this time Bud was beginning to see something in it for himself. Perhaps Bud imagined that having his name appear on the front page of a Denver newspaper would somehow insure his twenty-year-old investment at the local county polls, as if it would permanently close an insurance policy with us that would make us want to go on marking that X beside his name come the first Tuesday in November. Because with his name featured prominent in the big city papers and on the front page, no less, we'd be proud of him, take pride in one of our own's managing such a thing, and then he wouldn't ever have to do any more storytelling in the Holt Café in order to collect from us. All he would have to do would be to enter his name on the proper election papers at the appointed time and see to it that it was spelled right, and then—why hell—just go on paying his wife's doctor bills and sending those tuition payments to the state university in Boulder, where it looked like his kid was never going to amount to a goddamn or even to graduate.

But I can't say for sure that's how Bud was thinking. What I've suggested is based only on what I know about him after these fifty years of seeing and talking to him about once every week. No, all I know for sure is that his cop car was out in the country a little later that same afternoon and he and the Denver man were still in it, still talking, still licking up to one another like they were a couple of dogs discussing the fresh joys of a bitch in heat. Only they were not discussing copulation, nor love and the weather, nor even the price of fat hogs at the sale barn in Brush. It was more than that. I believe it was a lot more, because it was then and there, with corn stubble on one side and green wheat on the other, that Bud Sealy emptied himself. He gave him Edith Goodnough.

He told him how in December Edith had sat there quiet, rocking herself and waiting, while over there across the room from her, Lyman, her brother, had lain on his cot asleep, snoring against the wall. Bud didn't have to tell that. There was enough without any of that. It's just a good thing the son of a bitch didn't know about Lyman's travel papers and pumpkin pie, because if he had, he'd have thrown them in too. Sure as hell.

4

Myself, the next afternoon when he came to me, I didn't give him a thing.

T HIS WAS EIGHT DAYS AGO. Saturday. First I hear the tires on the gravel grind, then the car door. It's too early in the afternoon for it to be Mavis and Rena Pickett returning from town, so I look up from the squeeze chute where I'm doctoring cows, and, at the time, when I see the Denver plates, I still think it must be one of these state farm agents come out to talk fertilizer. Even when I see he's wearing a tie and yellow pants I think it is, because nowadays some of your young farm agents are starting to dress like that, like they think at any minute they're going to be called on to play Ping-Pong. Anyway, here he comes, walking over towards me away from his car. He gains the corral, finds the gate, fiddles with the bar latch, but then it looks as if he can't figure out how to work it, because he starts climbing. It doesn't do the hinges a lot of good. He climbs up on it anyway, and at the top, with the gate shaking back and forth underneath him, he swings both his legs over, then he drops down into the corral beside me.

"I'm looking," he says, "for Sanders Roscoe."

I turn back to the cow. I shoot her and she bawls, then I release the head catch on the chute and she goes out, already running, crow-hopping with her head down and kicking up fresh cow manure. A piece of it the size of a half dollar splats onto his shirtfront next to his tie.

"You found him," I say.

He doesn't look to be much more than a kid, but I haven't seen a lot of his face yet. Right now he has his head ducked down, studying his shirtfront. Then, while I watch him, he takes an Eversharp pencil out of his shirt pocket and begins to flick with the point of it at that little splat of manure. When he's got it all off pretty good, so that it appears as if maybe he's just spilled him some brown gravy there, he clips the pencil back inside his pocket and sticks his hand out. His hand's like that toilet paper they say on TV they don't want you to squeeze. Soft.

"Mr. Roscoe," he says. "I'm Dick Harrington. With the *Post*."

"That so?" I say. "I hope you're not selling anything."

"No," he says. "The *Denver Post*. It's a newspaper. Maybe you've heard of it."

"Sure. I've heard of it," I say. "But we keep it out on the back porch where we scrape our boots, so we don't have to track cow into the kitchen." Then I throw my head back and laugh. "It saves throw rugs," I tell him.

But he doesn't think that's real funny; he looks at me like How can I be so dumb and live? Guys like him think they drive the 150 miles out here due east from Denver and when they get here we don't know anything. They think they have to educate us poor dumb country bastards. They think we don't know what the *Denver Post* is. We know all right. We just don't give a damn.

But now he's busy with his hands again. It seems like his hands are always flat busy, like he can't let them rest. He reaches behind him into the back pocket of his pants and removes his billfold, opens it, and fingers out a little white card. I study it. It has his newspaper's design at the top and his name printed underneath that—only the card says Richard—with a phone number below his name to call him at his office if anybody wants to call him at his office. I hand it back to him.

"You can keep it," he says.

"No," I say. "It'd just get lost around here."

"Well," he says. "Well . . ."

But then it's like he doesn't know how to go on. He looks over across the corral to where the three or four cows I've already doctored are pushing one another butt up against the fence, facing him with their eyes rolled back to white and looking like for two bits they'd either bust down the fence behind them, or, if that didn't work, race him headlong across the corral to that gate he couldn't figure out how to open, and escape that way. So, for about two minutes, those cows and him are watching one another, staring at one another across that thirty feet of corral space and fresh cow manure that separates them, until all of a sudden that one cow I haven't doctored yet decides she has to bawl. And then it's like he's been jerked hard by the sleeve; he turns back in the other direction, quick, to face her. She's still caught inside that narrow alley that leads into the chute; you can see her between the alley rails. Her eyes have got plenty of white showing, too, and she's beginning to get a little antsy from being left by herself, but at least there's that much—there's that fence—separating him and her, and besides, crowded into the alley the way she is, she can't back up enough to collect herself for a good jump, even if she wants to jump over in his direction. Which she surely doesn't. Only I don't believe he knows that.

"Mr. Roscoe," he says. "Isn't there some place else we can talk?"

"Oh," I tell him, motioning at the cows, "you'll have to never mind them. They just haven't seen many yellow pants before. Give them a little more time—they might get used to it."

He looks doubtful over at the cows again. I have to admit they haven't changed much. They still look like they flat want to run or fly or get loose somehow. They're still facing him with their eyes rolled back and their butts jammed up against the fence as tight to it as they can get.

"Well," he says, turning back to me, "if I can, I'd like to ask you some questions. Can I ask you a few questions?"

"Depends," I say.

"On what?" he says.

"On what you're asking."

So then he asks me, and what he asks shows he's not even a state farm agent, that he doesn't even amount to that much. It shows too that yellow pants or no, the joke's over. Because what he asks is:

"You're a neighborly sort of man, aren't you, Mr. Roscoe?"

"I can be," I say, because I know what he's driving at now; I know what's coming.

"I mean," he says, "you know all the neighbors around here."

"Maybe. Some of them."

"Edith and Lyman Goodnough, for instance?" he says. "People tell me you knew them better than anyone else did. That you did things for them. Is that true?"

So there it is. It hasn't taken him long. And I say, "Didn't all these people you say you talked to at least tell you how to say their name—while they were telling you the rest of it?"

"You mean it's not Good-now?"

"No."

"What is it then?"

"Good-no."

"Okay," he says. "Suit yourself."

Then he reaches behind him again to dig in his back pocket. He draws out a little spiral notebook and writes something into it with that Eversharp pencil he used a little while earlier to flick the cow manure off his shirt. When he's done scribbling he says, "They used to live down the road from you, didn't they?"

"It's still theirs," I say. "Nobody else has bought it from them yet."

"Yes," he says, "and I already know it's located down the road from you."

So he's starting to talk that way now, like he's sure of himself, because with that spiral notebook and that pencil in his hands he's forgotten he's standing on top of cow manure inside a work corral where, thirty feet away from him, some fresh-doctored cows are still on his side of the fence, and they would just as soon run through him as have to look at him any longer.

But he goes on. He says, "I've been told that you were the first one there that night, last December. That when the others arrived they found you already waiting for them, and then you didn't want to let them go inside. You tried to prevent them. Why is that?" he says.

"You tell me. You know all about it."

"Look," he says, "Mr. Roscoe. I'm just trying to get what my editor sent me out here to get. And I don't think I like it any better than you do. But I think I know how you must have felt about—"

"You don't know a damn thing," I tell him.

"All right," he says. "All right then, forget that. But listen, let me just ask you this. Let me ask you: you agree it was deliberate, don't you? You don't think it was just an accident."

I don't answer him. Here he is, standing in front of me in his yellow Ping-Pong pants; he's not more than an arm's length away from me, and for what he's trying to get me to commit myself to saying I ought to swing on him. But I don't. I just look at him.

So he says, "But we both know that, don't we? I just want to know what you think of it."

I've had enough of him now. More than enough. I say, "You want to know what I think?"

"Yes."

"I think it's none of your goddamn business. I think you better go on back to Denver."

"Mr. Roscoe," he says, saying my name this time like he was saying shit. "I've already talked to the sheriff, Bud Sealy. And he told me—"

"No," I say. "No, you better go now." And I take a step towards him. He looks surprised, like he's just opened the wrong door and come up on something he never expected. He backs up a couple paces.

"It'll all come out anyway," he says. "I'll find out from somebody."

"Not from me you won't."

I step towards him again and look at him close up, a foot away from his face. His moustache is thin under his nose and he's got pockmarks along the side of his jaw. He could use a haircut. But—I'll give him this much—he doesn't back up anymore, even if he is just a kid, so I'm through playing with him now. I walk around him over to the corral gate and open it by throwing back the bar latch and holding it for him.

He walks over towards me, and when he's just about to pass me to go through the gate I take his little notebook out of his hand and rip the top page out of it, the one he wrote something on while he was talking to me. Then I give the notebook back to him. His face looks like somebody just slapped him.

"What are you doing?" he says. "You can't do that."

"Son," I say, "get your ass off my place. And don't you ever come back here. Understand? I don't ever want to see you again."

He starts to say something more; his mouth opens beneath the moustache, then it closes. He turns and walks away from me over to his car. He gets in and for a minute watches me through the window. Then he turns the key;

the car moves, spraying gravel out behind him as he leaves. I watch him out the lane onto the road back to town. When I can't see him anymore I look at the scribble on the piece of paper I took from his notebook. It reads: *Sanders Roscoe—fiftyish—heavyset—obstinate—Goodnough's neighbor—Good-no.* Then I tear it up and drop it underfoot. My boot heel grinds it into the cow shit until it's disappeared, gone, turned into just brown nothing. The damn squirt.

But it didn't do any good. He found out anyway. It got into the papers anyway. He must have talked to Bud Sealy again and some of those others in town. They put it on the front page. That's why they're talking of trial now. His damn newspaper account sparked this trial talk.

Some of it was even right. Some of what they threw on the front page between those two pictures of Edith and Lyman was even the truth, because I guess even a Denver newspaper reporter can walk into the Holt County Courthouse and copy down the date from a homestead record, and then, after he gets that straight, drive on out to the cemetery and read what it says on the three headstones that are standing there side by side in brown grass, away off at the edge of the cemetery, where there's just space enough left over between that last stone and Otis Murray's cornfield for one more grave. Because yes, he managed to get that much straight. And after he got it, his paper managed to arrange it clever on the front page.

They had Edith's picture over here on the left and Lyman's picture opposite it, over here on the right, with both of them staring into the middle so that they seemed to not only be looking at one another but to also be studying what was between them. And what was there, between them, like it was some kind of funeral notice or maybe just the writing on the inside cover of a family Bible, was this:

ROY GOODNOUGH BORN, CEDAR COUNTY, IOWA, 1870
ADA TWAMLEY BORN, JOHNSON COUNTY, IOWA, 1872
R. GOODNOUGH & A. TWAMLEY, MARRIED 1895
GOODNOUGHS, HOMESTEAD, HOLT COUNTY, COLORADO, 1896
EDITH GOODNOUGH BORN 1897
LYMAN GOODNOUGH BORN 1899
ADA TWAMLEY GOODNOUGH DIES 1914
ROY GOODNOUGH DIES 1952

And then, finally, below that there was just one more date, that last one, the one that was the reason for there even being a story on the front page at all:

FRIDAY, DECEMBER 31, 1976

So that much of it—that much of what that Denver reporter found out and that much of what his paper printed—was right. But that wasn't all of it. That wasn't even all of that much. It didn't touch on the how; it never mentioned the why. And even when it went on to repeat what Bud Sealy must have told him about those half-dozen chickens and that old dog and Lyman asleep on his cot while Edith rocked, even then it wasn't complete. For one thing, it left out Roy's stubs. For another, it didn't say a word about Lyman's wait, nor his Pontiacs and postcards and twenty-dollar bills. For still another, it didn't tell how Edith herself waited, first for one to die and then for the other to come back, and what she did with him when he did come back, and how, finally, she ever managed to live through those years of travelogue. It never mentioned my dad.

But then, to tell truth, I don't guess that Denver reporter could have written about those things, even if he'd have wanted to, because nobody told him about them in the first place so that he could go on and write them up after he was told. I wouldn't tell him. I would have been the one to tell him too—Bud Sealy was right about that. But I wouldn't. By God, I would not.

But listen now, if a person didn't want to print it up in some damn newspaper or throw it all over the front page between two pictures that were arranged so the people in the pictures had to stare at what was printed between them like it was a thing to be ashamed of—no, if a person just wanted to sit down quiet in that chair across the table from me and, since it's Sunday afternoon, just drink his coffee while I talked, and then if he just didn't want to rush me too much—well, then, I could tell it. I would tell it so it would be all, and I would tell it so it would be right.

Because listen:

· 2 ·

Most of what I'm going to tell you, I know. The rest of it, I believe.

I know, for example, that they started in Iowa, like the papers said.

I believe, on the other hand, that he must have seen flyers talking about it. Maybe he saw notices in the Iowa papers and government brochures too, all talking about it, saying there were still some acres of it left out here and if he proved on some of it, stayed on it, it was his to homestead.

He was twenty-five. He had married late. Ada had married later—for a woman, I'm talking about, since this was eighty-two years ago and she was already twenty-three. But things like age and time would have bothered him in a different way than they did her, because the pictures I have seen of her show that she was a small thin woman with eyes that seemed too big for her head—one of those women with blue veins showing at both temples. A woman like that—tight strung, nervous, too fine altogether for what was wanted of her—never should have married somebody like him, and she paid for it. He was a hard stick. He was all stringy arms and legs, with an Adam's apple like a hickory nut that jugged up and down when he chewed or said something, and I don't suppose he was much more than just getting used to having a woman in his bed before he was already thinking something like: *Here I been married a half year already, but I'm still at home. I'm still shoveling corn to another man's hogs, still spooning soup at somebody else's dinner table. Jesus God.*

He was a mean sort of private man, I know from personal experience with him, and more muleheaded even than he was private. He hated like the very goddamn to be dependent on anyone for anything. So I believe there had to be something like those flyers, and I believe he had to have seen them.

On those cold wet Iowa nights then in that first winter of their marriage, with his brothers and sisters sleeping in the bedrooms next door and his folks snoring from another room down the hall, I picture him standing beside a kerosene lamp. I picture him reading those flyers and notices and government brochures till he had them by heart, while in the room with him Ada would have been lying thin and straight in their bed under some thick homemade quilts, lying there waiting for him with her hair already combed out and braided, trying to stay awake for him because she no doubt believed a new wife would do that or should at least try to. And still—because I know that's the way he was—he must have gone on night after night the same. Gone on standing there beside that damn foul-smoking lamp, reading and planning and shivering in his long sag-butt underwear, with his red feet itching from the cold and his stringy arms and legs gone all to goose bumps and pig's bristle by the time he finally blew out the lamp and crawled into bed beside Ada—not to sleep yet, you understand, or even to raise Ada's flannel nightgown so he could rub his calloused hands over her thin hips and little breasts—but just to wake her again, wake her so he could tell her one more time how, by God, he had it all figured.

Well, he had it all figured—he always did—but I don't

suppose that cold-feet, goose-bump, being-wakened-in-the-night sort of thing could have gone on for too long, because even Ada would not have put up with it forever. She would have gone back home to her mother in Johnson County, claiming whatever they called incompatibility in those days, and then Roy would have fumed and claimed foul and begun to rage something about a wife's duty. And maybe that would have been the best thing for both of them; at least it would have been the best thing for Ada, because then she might never have had to leave Iowa. But, like I say, that goose-bump business must not have gone on for too long, not to the point where Ada left him, anyway, because come the next spring, the spring of 1896, I know they both left Iowa in a loaded wagon and moved to the High Plains of Colorado.

They drove across western Iowa and ferried across the Missouri River, then they crossed all of Nebraska. They couldn't have made more than twenty miles a day, and they probably came alone, since there hadn't been any real wagon trains for thirty years, and maybe by the middle of the second week Ada had stopped looking out the back of the wagon. Anyway, they got here, and when they got out here to northeastern Colorado, what did they find? That happens to be one of the things I know; I know what they found, but what I don't know is what they expected to find. It depends on what kind of lies those flyers and government brochures told. But if they expected to find some more of Cedar County, Iowa, some kind of extension of that country they had left three or four weeks earlier, then they never should have thrown any bag of seed or any plow or foot-pedal sewing machine into any wagon; they should have stayed put, because this country wasn't like that. It wasn't any of that deep-black-topsoil country with forty inches of annual rainfall and good drainage and plenty of hardwood close by—burr oak and black walnut—for lumber and fuel. What this country was was sandy, and it was dry, and for the most part it was just flat, with only some low sand hills running off in a north-easterly direction towards the Nebraska Panhandle. There were almost no trees.

Even now there are not many trees here, although people in towns like Holt have full-grown trees that were planted by early residents sixty and seventy years ago in backyards and along the streets—elm and evergreen and cottonwood and ash, and every once in a while a stunted maple that somebody stuck in the ground with more hope for it than real experience of this area would ever have allowed. In the country we have a few trees now, too, of course, standing up around our houses, and you can tell where somebody lives, or used to live, because of those trees, but we are more interested in windbreaks. The 1930s taught us windbreaks, and the government wants to encourage it.

Every spring now the soil-conservation office tries to sell us red cedar, blue spruce, ponderosa pine, Russian olive, Nanking cherry, cottonwood, lilac, sumac, plum, and honeysuckle—thin saplings at nine dollars for a bundle of thirty or fifteen dollars for a bundle of fifty. For another twenty cents per tree the government will send out somebody to plant them for us. Last spring it was an old man on a tractor plowing a furrow so that a young woman riding a tree planter behind the tractor, with a bundle of saplings in a box beside her and her feet raised onto stirrups to be out of the way, could poke the saplings down between her thighs into the plowed furrow almost like she thought she was giving birth. This particular young woman enjoyed getting as much sun as she could all over her body, and the folks down at the soil-conservation office are still trying to figure out how much to charge us for watching her do that.

But then I was talking about what it was like in this country in 1896 when Roy and Ada rode here in a wagon from Iowa to homestead, and I said there were almost no trees here then, and that's true. The only trees in this country at that time stood along the rivers and the creeks, and there were only two each of those. To the north was the South Fork of the Platte River and about one hundred and fifty miles to the south was the Arkansas River; in between were the two creeks, the Republican and the Arikaree.

What they found when they got here then—and I don't believe Ada ever got over the shock of it—was a flat, treeless, dry place that had once belonged to Indians.

It was a hell of a big piece of sandy country, with a horizon that in every direction must have seemed then—to someone who didn't know how to look at this country and before Henry Ford and paved highways diminished it just a little—to reach forever away under a sky in summer that didn't give much of a good goddamn whether or not the bags of corn seed Roy was going to plant in some of that sand ever amounted to a piddling thing, and a sky in winter that, even if it was as blue as picture books said it should be and as high and bright as anybody could hope for, still didn't care whether or not the frame house Roy was going to build ever managed to keep the snow from blowing in on Ada's sewing machine. There just wasn't a thing in the world concerned enough to care whether Roy's corn did anything more than shrivel, and there wasn't a thing tall enough or wide enough anywhere between Canada and Mexico to stop the snow from blowing.

No, Ada never got over the shock of this country. There was too much of it, and none of it looked like Iowa.

But Ada wouldn't have left Iowa at all if this had still been Indian country. She wasn't the kind of woman to dare that much. Somehow she would have blocked Roy's

homestead plans, and she would either have found a way
to endure Roy's cold feet or she would have gone home
to her mother, like I've already suggested. But whatever,
she would have stayed in Iowa, which was established
country by that time, and feeling at home she would have
gone on attending church circles and making little forays
to town to buy thread for doilies and gimcracks for the
house, and if that had happened, if she had stayed in Iowa,
that dark lost look, which pictures of her show, might
never have taken root in her eyes. But the Indians were
gone. She didn't have that ready excuse nor good reason
not to come. She had to follow her husband, if what he
proposed to do seemed even remotely reasonable, and after
all, by the beginning of the last decade of the last century,
this country was already starting to fill up with homesteaders; there wasn't much homestead land left. So Ada
came.

But Roy now, I suppose Roy would have come anyway,
even if Indians were still here. He was about enough of a
fox terrier to trot into a territory that belonged to somebody else, and once he got there, raise his hind leg to it,
claim it for his own, without thinking twice about prior
claims or possible consequences. But Roy never got the
chance to prove that either. Colorado had already been a
state for twenty years by the time he got here; the Indians
had been gone for at least that long; and the little piece of
land he claimed was signed over to him in a local government office.

But all right, by late spring in 1896 the Goodnoughs
got here in their wagon from Iowa, and if they were dis-
appointed, if what they found wasn't what they expected
to find, having read those flyers and government brochures, still they stayed; they didn't go back. They unhitched the wagon, and then, no doubt, Roy stuck Ada
in the ramshackle boardinghouse in town to bide her time,

to wash the dirt out of her hair and write another long miserable letter home, while he rode out on one of the workhorses to look this country over. I don't suppose that took him very long. He was in too much of a hurry; he was too muleheaded; he wanted to get some seed in the ground; and he might even have known that if he didn't do something quick, then Ada might somehow wake from her dream and daze, sit up and look around her, and then just take off, walking if she had to, with her small chin and her big eyes pointed east. So, in a hurry, he looked this country over, finding the expanses of bluestem and buffalo and sand love and switch grass and prairie sand reed, which still stood belly high on his Belgium, locating those areas that still remained after other, earlier homesteaders had staked their claims and done their chopping and busting.

He found what he thought he wanted seven miles south of town. There was already a house and a shed or two and a couple of pens, just a half mile west of the corner of the quarter section Roy intended to claim for himself, but in the house there was only a six-year-old boy living alone with a black-eyed silent woman. And I believe Roy picked that place because he thought that boy and that half-Indian woman who lived there, a half mile up along what wasn't even a wagon track yet, would never last, in fact, could never last. With time then, and not very much time at that, he believed he would be able to take over that other place that was already started, because there wasn't any man around. The man who should have been there had disappeared three years earlier. On a Saturday morning he had gone to town—to the three stores, the boardinghouse, the saloon and graveyard and fifteen or twenty wood houses that meant Holt then—and he never came back, and never wrote either, since the six-year-old boy couldn't read yet and because the pipe-smoking woman he left behind never would be able to read. It would just be a waste of pen and paper and a two-cent stamp to do something like compose a letter and tell why.

Anyway, you understand, because it was that particular quarter section of grass a half mile east of that other house that Roy picked for his own, decided in all the world was his, that's the reason why I know what I do about him, and also about Ada and Edith and Lyman, because, of course, the six-year-old boy living in the house was John Roscoe, and John Roscoe lasted.

Well, the Goodnoughs lasted, too. And things—at least at first—went along about like you would have expected them to. Roy filed his claim, put his horses to pulling a sod-busting plow, planted his bag of Iowa seed as best he could in the rough ground, bought a cow or two to stake out on the nearby grass, and then turned finally to throwing together a frame house for Ada. She'd been living under a tarp till then, which was tied to the side of the wagon and which had to be untied any time Roy decided he needed to haul something, living almost like she was some kind of nomad Arab but without even that much permanence or experience at it. She had to cook over an open fire and try to coax a few beans and peas and maybe a couple of zinnia plants to grow in the corner of the plowed sod Roy allowed her to call a garden. It wasn't easy. To water her little garden and even to have something to drink but never to have enough left over to take a bath in, Ada had to walk a half mile one way with two yoked pails across her thin shoulders and fetch water from that other place where the boy and the woman lived and owned a windmill that pumped water.

But that other woman apparently took some interest in her. Or maybe she felt something like pity towards her— like maybe you would towards some dog that had been dropped off out in the country and not some strong mongrel dog that would manage to live anyhow, but a toy poodle, say, or a Pekinese, that belonged in the parlor— because I know for a fact that at least once the woman walked out to Ada, where Ada was stooping beside her two pails at the windmill and horse tank, splashing water onto her wrists and face, and said:

"Don't you want to take a bath?"

Ada looked at her. She did something with her mouth that was meant to be a smile and then quick looked east to where she could just make out Roy walking behind his horses in the field, and turned back.

"If it wouldn't be any bother."

"Come into the house."

So I know that Ada took at least one more bath that summer besides the one she had taken in the boarding-house in town. When she was dressed again, she said:

"But don't tell him. He won't want to know I took a bath in somebody else's house."

Well, Roy never knew that about his wife. And I suppose there were a lot of other things he didn't know or understand about her, but he did build her a house. He had the first part of it completed by fall. Later there were other rooms added on, a new kitchen and a back porch and also what turned out to be a parlor, but the first square two-story part of the house was raised late that summer. And he was a good rough carpenter, I'll say that for him.

He had to buy the lumber in town, in Holt, and haul it home in his wagon, and then he had to nail it together himself. Ada helped him to lift the wall frames into place and steady them while he tacked them down, but for the most part he did all the work himself, since he had picked a place to live where there wasn't another full-grown male anywhere near, and anyway he wouldn't have asked for help if there had been. They bought a few sticks of furniture to go along with Ada's sewing machine and moved into the house sometime before time to pick corn.

Roy's dryland corn didn't do very well that first year. There wasn't much to pick. There was too much sagebrush and soapweed and too many grass roots to contend with, and even in his hurry the corn had still been planted late; the corn seed was still in the bags when most of what rain we get here falls in the spring. So his corn didn't do very well, and I don't suppose Ada was doing very well, either. By corn harvest I believe she was good and sick, because sometime in August of that summer Roy had found enough sap and energy and time too to get her pregnant, so that on the night of April twenty-first in the following spring, after she had managed somehow to get through that first long High Plains winter, Ada gave birth to a girl she named Edith.

Roy was going to do that by himself, too, of course. He was going to boil the sheets, rotate the head, slap some breath into the baby, and sew Ada up afterwards with needle and thread—without help from anyone. I don't know, maybe he had read some flyers and government brochures about that too, but things in this case didn't happen the way he expected them to, either. Because sometime that night, after Ada had been in labor for two or three days with her thin brown hair sweat-stuck to her face and her white thighs gone as rigid as sticks, Roy caught one of his workhorses and galloped that dark half mile west to the other house and woke the half-Indian woman. When her face appeared in one of the upstairs opened windows he yelled up at her:

"Goddamn it, I can do it. But she wants you. She wants you to come over there."

He was sitting down there on that bareback excited Belgium, yelling up into the dark towards a dark face he could barely see.

"I could do it myself, but now she says she has to have you there. But I'll make that right too, goddamn it. You wait and see."

The woman in the upstairs window watched him on his horse in her front yard.

"Don't you hear me?" he yelled. "Don't you understand a goddamn thing I'm telling you? She wants you over there."

But the woman was gone by now, leaving him yelling up into the dark where there wasn't even a silent face in a window to hear him yell and rage. The woman had gone to wake her boy, who was seven now and had been since February twenty-fourth. She told him to get their saddle horse ready; she was riding over to the Goodnoughs' to set things right and she would be back in the morning. And I guess Roy understood that he had done enough yelling for one night when he saw the boy go out the back door towards the corral, so he galloped back home again.

The woman got there a few minutes later. I can't say exactly what she did or how she did it, but I'm certain she got Roy out of the room where he was less than no help, and then I believe she was able to get Ada revived enough to make another effort. Maybe she made some tea or something hot with herbs in it, or maybe it was just her voice and hand, but anyway she delivered the baby girl and Ada got some rest. And afterwards she must have made a couple of things plain enough that even Roy understood them, because two years later in June, when again it was Ada's time, Roy didn't wait until his wife had been in labor for two or three days and had turned to frazzle before he decided it was time for him to start howling in the dark. No, he came in broad daylight, knocked at the front door, and asked if the woman would come. So Lyman's birth went easier, smoother, without the galloping horse and the yelling. This was 1899.

24

Well, Roy had a girl and a boy now, and I don't suppose he ever expected much from Edith (more than just constant work, I mean) or ever thought much of hoping something for her either—he wouldn't have; she was a girl, a potato peeler, an egg gatherer—but he might have expected more from Lyman, so he probably wasn't real thrilled with the way Lyman turned out. And it wasn't that Lyman didn't work hard enough—he did, in his loose, mechanical, dry fashion—and Lyman sure as hell didn't leave the farm very often until it was almost too late for him to ever leave it at all. But he just didn't like any of it; he never really got his hand in. Lyman was too much of a lapdog even to suit his father.

But at least with both a boy and a girl on hand now to help, Roy could believe enough in tomorrow to begin adding on to his original quarter section, and he did. God only knows he was frugal enough. In fact, he was about so tight as to be able actually to squeeze blood from the turnips Ada grew in the family garden. As for his farming, he would do things like go on tying his machinery together with baling wire and patching it up however he could, rather than do anything as rash as to buy something new. Before he would do a thing that crazy he had to be dead certain that baling wire and goddamns wouldn't work anymore. He never spent five cents on himself or his wife or his kids, and what he made he saved, and then about once every eight or nine years he would suck in his belt, spit, and then finally buy another quarter section of nearby Holt County sand for Lyman to help him sweat over. So in time, Roy acquired quite a lot of land. He had some Hereford cows with calves on grass, and a few Shorthorns to milk, besides the wheat and cornfields to till and plant and harvest.

Meanwhile, Edith and Lyman were growing up out here seven miles from Holt, and they were about all each other had. As kids, Edith says, they slept together in a double straw-tick bed in one of the upstairs bedrooms, and wrapping their legs around one another to keep warm they told themselves stories about what they were going to do when they were big enough and free enough of the farm and their father to do those great things. Well, they never did them. But during the days when they were kids, in the few hours left when they weren't hoeing beans or milking cows or churning butter or shoveling shit out the milk-barn window, they played those games farm kids play behind haystacks and deep in tall cornfields. In the winter they went to school a little bit.

When Edith started school in 1903, when she started riding the three miles farther south to the converted chicken house with the foul two-hole privy behind it, riding on one of the played-out workhorses her father still kept and whose back was so broad that riding him her legs stuck straight out sideways, the boy who lived down the road from her was already in his seventh and next-to-last year of school. I believe he was a help to her—John Roscoe was—and I believe he took care of her. I know they rode to school together, the thirteen-year-old boy with stiff black hair and the six-year-old girl in high-topped shoes that had been her mother's, and I know every school day for two years they rode home together. He also protected her during lunch hour and recess, never mind what the other kids said about *Johnny has a girl friend*, *ain't she sweet*, *when she takes her boots off*, *he tickles her feet*, because I believe that's when and how what later happened—nineteen years later—started. With just that much.

Then that ended. The two years were up; he had finished the eighth grade, so for quite a while John Roscoe and Edith Goodnough didn't see a lot of each other except during harvest, even if they lived just a half mile apart.

26

Neighboring families don't visit much when one of the neighbors is Roy Goodnough.

Anyway, Lyman was old enough to start school then, so Edith rode double on the broken-down workhorse to school with him. But that didn't last very long, either. Lyman only went to school for four or five years, and Edith herself never finished the eighth grade. That has always bothered her, too. I believe she thinks things might have ended different than they did if she had finished the eighth grade.

"But what was I going to do?" she says. "He wouldn't allow it. It was a waste of time."

By "he" she means, of course, Roy.

WELL, then, what more do I need to tell you about those fifteen years that passed between the last two times Ada wanted the woman down the road to come? Just this, I suppose: in the pictures taken of Edith and Lyman between 1899 and 1914, Edith is a beautiful girl, with her mother's big eyes and brown hair and enough of her father in her to make her stand up straight and face the camera full on. Also, in one of the pictures I've seen in the Goodnough family album, Edith has her arm around Lyman. He is standing there almost as if he's been tucked into the folds of her long skirt, like he's some kind of wet-combed cocker spaniel. Lyman looks scared and half protected at the same time. I don't think he felt that way just when somebody was taking his picture.

But it was about Ada that I wanted to tell you now. I've already said how this country was a shock to her, how she had to live under a tarp for three or four months after already living in a wagon for three or four weeks, and how as thin as she was she still had to carry water in yoked pails for a half mile every day until her husband found time to dig their own well. She wasn't made for that kind of life. And even if she had been, she was still married to a man like Roy Goodnough. She was bound by law to a hickory stick.

So in the same family album, while Edith and Lyman are growing up, their mother, Ada, seems to be sinking down. In one picture after another, she looks smaller, shorter, thinner. Her cheeks suck into bone, her thin brown hair turns to sparse gray. By 1913, in what must be the last picture taken of her, she stands barely as tall as Roy's shoulder, and he was no more than five feet eight himself. In the picture I'm talking about, Ada looks like she might be her husband's mother. About all you can make out of her face in the grainy photograph is her big eyes, staring not at whoever it was that held the camera, but away, off towards something in the distance.

Then in 1914, in August, in the hottest month of the year in Holt County, she got sick. They say it was the flu, and people did die of the flu then. But I believe, and Edith says, that it was more than just a virus bug that killed her. It was all those years of looking east; it was almost two decades of being married to Roy. Once, when her own mother died, she had gone back home to Johnson County on the train, and she had stayed so long after the funeral that Roy had had to go out and bring her back. She never went a second time. Now, on the High Plains of Colorado, she lay up there in the second-story bedroom, with the windows open to catch any breeze there was, sweating and burning up with what maybe only one of her family still believed was just flu fever. So it was almost the same story again. It was almost like the two times she had delivered babies there in that same bedroom. Only it was August this time, and instead of her arms and legs going rigid as sticks, she seemed as weak as water now. She didn't make much of a bump under the sweat-soaked sheets. She didn't move.

On the second or third day of this, she told Roy, "I want her now."

"What?" he said.

"I want her to come. I think it's time."

"Now, damn it, Ada . . ."

"Please," she said.

Maybe Roy thought she was talking out of her head, that it was just fever talk, but when she seemed worse by the middle of the afternoon when the sun was the hottest, he drove the half mile west to get the pipe-smoking half-Indian woman. She was an old woman now, though her eyes were still clear and black, and her hair was still the same straight brown; her hair never did get very gray. But she had some trouble mounting the stairs, so that Edith had to help her. When she was led into the room where Lyman and Roy stood against the wall, she first pulled the blinds on the windows and then sat down on the wood chair beside the bed.

After a while Ada opened her eyes. She fumbled her hand out from under the bedsheet towards the older woman. "I thank you," she said.

"Do you want anything?"

"I thank you for coming."

They stayed that way the rest of the afternoon. Later, Roy went out to feed and milk the cows, while Edith continued to smooth the bone-thin yellowing forehead with a cool washcloth and Lyman went on staring at his mother from his place against the wall, like he was rooted there, like he didn't dare do anything else but stand and stare at his dying mother. Ada slept for several hours that way, with her loose hand held by the other woman, who also managed to sleep some, sitting up in the chair beside the bed. The old woman's head rocked back above the top of the chair, and her dark mouth dropped open a little.

At six Roy said they should eat. So he and Edith and Lyman went downstairs to the kitchen where Edith warmed some potatoes and green beans, sliced some bread, and made a fresh pot of coffee. When the food was on the table in front of him, Roy said grace and began to eat.

Between mouthfuls he said, "You didn't tell me that red-faced cow was going dry."

"What?" Lyman said. He was pushing his beans around on his plate.

"She's damn near dry. You never told me."

"I forgot."

"What else have you forgot?"

"Nothing. I don't know."

"Never mind, Daddy," Edith said. "Not now."

"We need the milk," Roy said.

After supper, Edith put the dishes to soak and took a plate of food and a cup of coffee upstairs to the old woman. They found that she was awake now, smoking one of her scarred briar pipes. She had raised the blinds again, and the blue pipe smoke drifted out the opened east window. She didn't want the food. Beside her, Ada still lay silent in the bed, like a thin wax child.

"Did mother say anything?" Edith asked.

"No."

"Did she wake again?"

"No. She's resting. She's getting ready."

"I believe she does feel cooler now, don't you think? Maybe the fever's broken."

"It hasn't."

The old woman put her pipe away in her apron pocket and they went on waiting. Gradually it grew darker in the room, but Edith says she remembers there wasn't much of a sunset that evening. She had hoped there would be; she thought her mother might like to see one, that it might make her feel better. There wasn't, though. There weren't any clouds to make a sunset. It was just hot.

When it was completely dark in the room, so dark they could barely distinguish the yellow face from the white pillow, Roy fumbled over to the chest of drawers in the corner and lit a lamp on top of it. The lamplight cast wavering shadows, and then the millers, those small dusty moths this country has more millions of than it needs, came out from the cracks in the wall and fluttered around the lamp, bumping against the hot globe and singeing themselves. One of the millers landed on Ada's forehead and left its smudge of dust there, so it must have been that, when Edith brushed it off, that woke her again.

Ada seemed to rouse for a minute then and to look dimly around her. When she seemed to have each person in place, her thin lips moved.

"You make him. Tell him."

"What?" Edith said. "Would you like some water?"

"I want him to take me to Johnson County. I want to sleep beside my mother."

"Yes. All right."

"You make him."

"Yes."

She didn't say anything more. She went back to sleep, as if she hadn't said anything at all, or as if she had said all there was to say. Sometime before midnight she died. Edith says they didn't know for sure what time it was she died; they couldn't set the exact minute. They weren't able to tell when she stopped breathing, because her breath was so soft at the last anyway. They just knew for certain that she was dead when Hannah Roscoe put Ada's hand under the sheet again and then went downstairs and walked home by herself.

31

By the lamplight, Edith washed the child-sized body, combed the hair into place, and put on the Sunday dress. The next day Roy buried her in the Holt County Cemetery northeast of town.

"You know what mother wanted," Edith said. "You were there."

"No," he said. "She was sick then."

"You heard her say so."

"I want her here."

"But mother didn't like it here. She hated it. This wasn't her home."

"Your mother's dead. You're the mother now."

"What do you mean? I can't replace mother."

"You will."

Ada's was the first of the three Goodnough graves that have been dug so far, over there in the brown grass beside the fence line that separates the cemetery and Otis Murray's cornfield. Ada lived to be forty-two.

· 3 ·

Edith was seventeen when her mother died. Lyman was fifteen. They were a year older when the next thing happened that fixed it for them. It wasn't enough that their father was Roy Goodnough or that their mother died early; there had to be at least one more thing to clinch matters, to fix them forever, to make Edith and Lyman end up the way they did—two old people, a sister and a brother, living alone out here in a yellow house surrounded by weeds.

It was an accident that did it. It was during harvest, and Roy Goodnough must have hated harvesttime.

No—that's not quite right. Like the rest of us, he must have loved it too, because it meant the end; it meant the accomplishment of what had been started months before with plowed sand and bags of seed. Also, he must have worried about it, like we all did and still do, stewed in his juice over it, stepped out the first thing in the morning, even before he had his pants buttoned good, to search the sky for clouds in the hope now that it wouldn't rain, or worse, that if there were clouds, then he would detect no sickly green, because that kind of green in clouds meant hail.

But at the same time he was loving it and worrying about it, he must have hated it too, because at harvesttime Roy had to ask someone for help. He couldn't do it alone.

He could operate the header himself, but even with Edith driving the team of horses pulling the header barge and Lyman leveling the wheat off in the back of the barge, he still needed one more person to stack the wheat once the barge was full and ready to be unloaded. So he had to ask John Roscoe, down the road a half mile, to do that.

John Roscoe was twenty-five in 1915. I've already said about him that he lasted. But he was able to last not so much by farming himself, like Roy did, as by adding more grassland to the original claim his mongrel father had filed ten years before he ever went to town that Saturday morning and disappeared. Calving time was the worst: you had to get up at three o'clock in the morning in a March blizzard to pull a calf that was trying to come breech; but usually one man could manage a small cattle operation. He also farmed some, though, in a small way. His mother cooked dinner and washed clothes, smoked her pipe and rocked herself to sleep in the afternoons beside the stove in the living room. Anyway, it was John Roscoe that was helping the Goodnoughs harvest their wheat that July in 1915.

I don't suppose it was as hot then as it had been the previous year, when Ada died in the upstairs bedroom, but it was hot enough. The sky stayed clear, bright, high, and the heads of the wheat had filled and turned tan, ready to be cut. They had already cut most of it in the preceding five or six days, and Roy believed he could finish today, or at the latest, tomorrow.

So on this Thursday morning late in July, while Lyman milked and fed the six or seven Shorthorns they kept for milk cows—because they gave more milk than their Herefords—Roy slid the sickle bar out the end of the header to sharpen the blades. Edith had to help him after she had cooked breakfast and washed dishes; she had to hold the end of the long sickle bar while he sat on the narrow iron seat, pumping the foot pedals of the grindstone like he was some overgrown kid racing to hell on a tricycle. He ground and honed both cutting edges of each blade, those triangular-shaped serrated blades called sections that were riveted along the length of the sickle bar. A few of the sections had been nicked by rocks, but he didn't bother replacing them. That would take more time; he wanted to finish while the weather held. He ground the nicked serrated edges down smooth so that they shone like just-honed knife blades.

Lyman came over and watched as his father sat pumping on the grindstone.

"You turn the cows out?"

"Yes."

"Did you put a cloth over the milk cans?"

"Yes."

"There was a gob of flies dunking in it yesterday."

"I know. I couldn't find the cover cloth."

"We wouldn't need no cloth if you hadn't lost the god-damn lids. But you never looked for the cloth either, did you? It was hanging on a nail in the kitchen."

Lyman looked quick above his father's bowed head at Edith. Lyman made a face.

"But go on now," Roy said. "Get the horses in and harnessed. We're late already."

Lyman looked once more at Edith and ambled off in his hard high-topped shoes and loose overalls towards the horse pasture. Then Roy was finished with the sickle bar. Edith went in to prepare something for lunch for the four of them; they would eat at noon in the shade of the wheat stack. It saved having to go to the house.

When Roy had the sickle bar slid into the front of the header and bolted in place so that the sharp section blades, set between iron spikes called guards, would move back and forth, slicing the wheat off close to the ground, Lyman walked six horses up to the back of the header, where Roy harnessed them, three at each side, alongside a heavy iron pole. Then Edith hitched two more horses to the wagon, to the header barge, and they drove rattling out of the yard towards the wheat field. When they entered the field they could see John Roscoe standing on the stack far over there in the corner, waiting for the first load. They stopped the horses so that the header would be ready to begin cutting where they had left off the night before at the near end of the field.

"I suppose Roscoe's been waiting there for a hour," Roy said, "without a goddamn thing in the world to do except wait on us."

"He doesn't have his shirt off yet," Edith said.

"It ain't hot enough. He wants to get burned. He thinks fried skin looks pretty."

"I don't think he'll burn," Edith said. "He's too brown."

"That's the Indian in him."

"Daddy," Edith said.

"What?" he said. "You know it well as anybody."

"Just the same, I don't care—"

"You damn God better learn to," Roy said. "Get the barge in place."

Roy engaged the gears and chains on the bull wheel, and then he climbed up into the seat at the back of the header, between his two teams of horses.

"Giddup," he said. "Go on now."

The six horses moved, lunged forward, pushing the heavy rattling header. The engaged gears and chains turned the reel at the front that came around and laid the wheat down onto the sickle bar, to be cut off by the slicing knife-sharp sections. As the wheat was cut it fell onto a platform beneath the rotating reel, and then it was carried by a canvas belt off to the side and up another canvas belt through a chute and out, falling into the header barge that

Edith drove alongside. Lyman was in the back of the barge where the cut wheat on its dusty stalks fell around him and on him, made him itch and sweat and scratch, while he forked the stuff around in the barge to level it off. Edith could hear him cussing miserably, insanely, behind her, but not so loud that Roy would hear.

"By Jesus," he was saying. "Oh, you dirty son of a bitch. Get over there. Hog shit in a bucket."

They finished that first swath through the length of the field, then Roy disengaged the gears on the bull wheel, pulled the lever to the tiller wheel, and the header made its neat square turn, with three of the horses walking slow, almost backing around, while the other three horses walked out fast at an angle, to point the header back up the field. The gears were engaged again, and the Goodnoughs started another swath.

When the header barge was full, so that Lyman stood up higher now on top of the cut wheat with his high-topped shoes full of bits of chaff, Roy stopped his six horses.

"Well," he said, "go pitch it off. And don't take all day jabbering."

Lyman crawled up onto the front seat of the barge, and he and Edith drove over to the corner to John Roscoe, where the stack was. On the way Lyman took his shoes off and dumped the chaff out. When they stopped at the stack both of them got into the back to pitch the wheat off with their three-tined wheat forks.

"Shoes bothering you again?" John Roscoe said.

"Son of a bitch," Lyman said. "Trade with me. I'll stack this stuff."

"Can't. Your old man wants you right where he can see you, getting your nose full of it."

"Son of a bitch," Lyman said.

"Why don't you ask Edith? Edith, whyn't you crawl back there and relieve your little brother? Be good for you to do some real work for a change."

"You should have heard him," Edith said. "My, my."

"Needs his mouth washed out with soap."

"Lye soap this time," Edith said.

"Oh, dirty bastard," Lyman said. "Oh, horse piss too."

Then John Roscoe and Edith laughed and Lyman grinned like a cocker spaniel. They went on working that way throughout the morning, while the July sun rose higher and hotter in the sky and the dust behind the machinery hung in the air like clouds of gnats. Roy sat up there hard on the seat at the back of the header with the horses on either side of him. The horses lunged against the harness to get the header moving again, to push the heavy machine forward to cut another swath of wheat after it had been stopped at the end of a square turn or after stopping to wait for Edith and Lyman to come back with the emptied barge. Then with the header in motion, the six horses walked steadily up the field, pushing the weight and noise of the machine ahead of them. The horses were dark with sweat along their necks and shoulders, where the collars rode, and along their flanks. White foam, like soap lather, worked up between the big muscles on the insides of their back legs. Flies bothered their eyes and underbellies, so that as they walked, straining against the harness, they tossed their heads and switched their long harsh tails.

Roy sat grimly between them, watching straight ahead, the tiller-wheel lever stuck up between his legs. In the header barge Lyman was covered all over with sweat-stuck chaff and wheat hulls; his cheeks and neck and arms were covered with it, and he had almost stopped cussing. He was too tired, too hot. Only Edith, in her thin work dress and flat-brimmed straw hat, clucking to her horses from her seat at the front of the barge, seemed at all comfortable in the morning heat and dust. Occasionally, she looked up at John Roscoe across the field on the wheat stack. She could see that his bare back shone wet in the sun, then she would turn back again to be sure that she had the barge in position to catch the falling wheat. She shredded several heads of wheat and chewed the hard kernels to make wheat gum while she sat rocking on the wood seat, watching the rise and fall of the horses' rumps ahead of her.

At noon they finished a swath at the end of the field nearest the stack and stopped. They unhitched the horses, then at Roy's command Lyman mounted one of the horses and led the others along the fence line and then across the road to the tank at the Roscoe place, since they were working in the west field that day, which was closer to the Roscoes' than it was to their own place. At the tank beside the corral, the eight horses pushed in beside one another, snorted into the water and drank. Lyman climbed down then and held his head under the pipe that ran water from the windmill, the same pipe and windmill you see there now, the one his mother had walked a half mile to with her yoked pails three years before he was born. I don't suppose Lyman thought about that, though, or remembered it if he knew it at all. He held his head under the running water, which was so cold it numbed his face, and wished he could take his overalls off and climb into the horse tank like a little kid, his father be damned.

When the horses had stopped drinking and had begun to sniff at the water or to raise their heads to look around them with dark eyes, sighing and shuddering a little like horses do when they've been worked hard and seem to look off away towards something you yourself do not see, cannot see, then Lyman mounted again, dripping water from his head and shoulders down into his pants, and led the big horses back across the road to the stack. On the north side of the stack Roy and Edith and John Roscoe sat in the shade, eating.

"Feed 'em," Roy said.

Lyman tied the horses to the header and along the side of the barge. John Roscoe came over and helped him fit the nose bags onto the horses' heads and slip the straps behind their ears to hold the bags with barley in place, while the horses swung their heads suddenly and stamped their feet to ward off flies.

"You fall in the tank?" John Roscoe said. "Head first?"

"I wish I did," Lyman said. "Ain't it hot?"

"Going to get warts on your dinkus that way, boy. There's toads in that horse tank."

"Hell, too," Lyman said.

They went back and sat down in the shade then, and ate the fresh peas and beans Edith brought, and the salt pork and thick slices of bread and cold boiled potatoes and Dutch apple pie, and drank buttermilk in tin cups. When they were finished Edith put the things away and Roy got up to oil the gears and chains on the machinery and to examine the section blades. Then Edith and Lyman and John Roscoe lay down with their straw hats over their faces and talked to one another up through the sweaty crowns of their hats.

"Ludi Pfeister and his crew going to thresh for you again this year?"

"I don't know," Lyman said. "Pa don't tell us nothing one way or another."

"He is," Edith said. "I wrote the letter to him in Kansas."

"I thought him and Ludi had a little argument last fall."

"They did," Lyman said. "Ludi thought the wheat hadn't sweat enough. 'Too wet to thresh,' he said. Pa said, 'Thresh it anyhow.' "

"Ludi's all right. He's got to think of his thresher, though."

"Daddy's right, too, sometimes," Edith said.

"I'm just talking, Edith. I never meant nothing."

"I know," she said.

The sun speckled through the straw weave of their hats, and they could hear the horses stamping and rattling their harness. Lyman lay between Edith and John Roscoe; the wet back of his shirt and overalls was caked now with sand. They could smell the cut wheat, dusty and heavy in the air, and the sharp green smell of the sagebrush across the fence line in the native pasture that belonged then to the Roscoes and still does. Lyman went to sleep in a little while, breathing slow, regularly, like a small boy, but I believe his sister and my father must have stayed awake together, thinking about one another across Lyman's overalls, with the sun speckling down onto their faces. I know I would have.

"Get up," Roy said. "Come on."

Because the horses had finished eating, you understand. The horses had rested enough, and all the gears and chains were oiled, and he wanted to get back into the wheat field. So they began to work again like they had all morning, only it was hotter now.

Roy was up on his seat between the horses, sitting up there ramrod stiff in the sun, with the reel ahead of him turning and the sharp section blades along the sickle bar cutting the wheat off close to the ground, and then the canvas belts carrying the wheat off and up through the chute to drop into the header barge Edith drove alongside so Lyman could level it off in the back. My father stayed on the stack, forking the wheat level and even all around him, and I believe they would have finished too. I believe, if what I remember about that afternoon is everything that I was told about it, that they would have finished cutting that field of wheat before dark, and then all Roy Goodnough would have had to do was to let it stay there in the stack sweating for a couple of months until it was dry enough for Ludi Pfeister to come along with his crew and threshing machine and thresh it for him.

But late in the afternoon, along about five o'clock, the header stopped working. It jolted hard, lurched, and then passed over several rods of wheat without cutting them off.

"Goddamn it, back up," Roy shouted. He sawed at the lines to the horses, pulling them back. "Now stand still," he said.

The horses stood there, nervous, high-strung, hot, bothered by flies, while Roy climbed down to see what had happened. They had just made one of the square turns at the end of the field next to the barbwire fence separating Roy's wheat from the native pasture across from it. So maybe that's where they picked up the wire. Or maybe a piece of the heavy wire Roy always tied his machinery together with finally broke and fell into the teeth of the section blades. But I don't suppose it matters where it came from, because he had it, all right. He had wire stuck hard between two blades and another piece running across the top of the sickle bar and then down where it was stuck between two more blades, so that the whole business was stopped dead from cutting wheat. He blamed Lyman. He blamed my father.

"You, Lyman," he yelled. "Goddamn you."

And the horses lunged forward then, thinking he wanted them to start up again. They pushed the header towards him where he stood in front of it, cursing.

"Whoa. Goddamn it. Stop now."

"Pa," Lyman called. "Do you want me to hold them? Pa, do you want I should—"

"No. Stay in the barge. You and that Roscoe have done enough. Can't even fix a goddamn fence without you have to spread wire all over goddamn hell."

"But you told me—"

"I know what I told you. I told you to help him fix his fence, for him helping me last year. But that don't mean you have to spread it all over a man's wheat field, does it? Does it? Answer me."

Lyman didn't say anything. What was he going to say?

"Answer me."

"It's not Lyman's fault," Edith said. "You know it isn't."

"You shut up," Roy said.

"It's not John's fault, either."

"Stay out of this, I said. Answer me, boy. Does it or not? I want to know."

"No, Pa," Lyman said. "No."

"No, by God, it don't," Roy said. "But I got it just the same, don't I? Roscoe's fence wire stuck in my header. Goddamn it, anyway. Son of a bitching kids."

But my father was twenty-five and no kid that summer, and it might just as well have been Roy's own wire stopping the teeth—wire he used to tie up his damn machinery with instead of ever buying something new or even forking over the two cents that would buy the bolt that would fix it. But that didn't matter to him: he knew he had fence wire stuck in his header and now he couldn't cut wheat.

He bent down in front of the header, under the wood bats of the reel, and began to pull at the wire with both hands, working it back and forth, sawing at it to either break the wire or get it free somehow, and he managed to get one piece out that way. He stood up panting then, glaring at Edith and Lyman, then he bent down again and started on the other piece of heavy wire, bending it back and forth, trying to saw through it with the sharp serrated blades, but it wouldn't come, and he went a little insane with the heat and the salt sweat running into his eyes, and the wire wasn't coming. He pulled at it, sawed at it and it wouldn't come, and he went on bending it, sawing at it viciously—then it came so suddenly, snapped so fast, that he stood up too quick and banged his head hard against a reel bat.

"Goddamn it," he yelled, loud and fierce. "Goddamn it, to hell."

And that's what did it. It was that, his hot angry insane yelling, that did it for him. And I suppose it's only right too: the voice that he hardly ever used at all except to tell somebody what to do with or to curse you with, to damn you, the voice he just didn't seem to know how to use in any way that was kind at all—his own angry insane voice fixed him. Because, you understand, the horses were hot. The horses were high-strung, nervous, jittery now with his yelling at them and with his sawing at the lines. Besides, they were used to being started by his yelling, and they couldn't anyway distinguish his giddup from his god-damn.

And it was goddamn, he yelled. Goddamn it, to hell.

So the horses lunged forward. The six workhorses threw themselves hard into the harness, and the header moved, jolted forward. It was free of wire now. The long bat of the reel came around, hit him hard, a blow across the nape of the neck. It dropped him onto his hands and knees. He braced his fall, but his fingers caught in the sharp blades of the sections. He had honed them that morning himself on the grindstone; they were knife sharp. Now his fingers were in them, between the bright blades, and his fingers were being mangled, torn to bone and bits, broken, cut, sliced. And he was yelling. All the time he was yelling, cursing, screaming, his feet kicking out wild behind him, the header was still moving forward, jolting in the rough field, with Edith and Lyman running alongside, yelling at the horses, the horses wild with the noise and still lunging forward in the harness, shoving the header at him, carrying him forward with it, cutting wheat with his fingers. It was insane, insanity, it was hell. The bats of the reel were cracking him down again and again, and still the wheat was being cut all around him, and his fingers were in the blades, being cut, sliced, hacked, and then it was over. It was done. That fast. He was torn free from his fingers and carried off to the side by the canvas belt.

They got the horses stopped. John Roscoe had seen what was happening. He had jumped down from the stack and had come running across the field, and he and Lyman had stopped the horses finally. Now Edith was helping her father crawl out of the header. It was bad. He had a long open cut above his eyes, another in the hair at the back of his head; one of his pants legs was ripped from cuff to thigh and showed deep bruises and cuts all along his leg; he was covered all over with blood and wheat chaff. But it was his hands that frightened you. He held them in front of him, out away from his body, as if they were exhibits. His hands were gore now, raw meat, hamburger. All the fingers and the thumb on his right hand were gone, chopped off. The thumb and the first three fingers on his left hand were gone too, just ragged meat and splintered bone, leaving his little finger alone on that hand, alone of all his fingers, uncut. It was ridiculous. His little finger on his left hand didn't have a scratch on it. It was a mockery. He held his hands out in front of him, staring at them, as if he had finally gone insane entirely, while his ruined hands throbbed blood, dripping the blood off the jagged stumps of his fingers, down into the wheat stubble and sand at his feet.

"Oh Daddy," Edith cried. "Oh God, Daddy. Come on, we've got to get to the doctor. Can you walk? Oh God, come on, though."

Roy seemed almost to wake up then. He seemed almost to come out of his wild fascinated daze. "I ain't leaving," he said. He wasn't yelling anything now; he was just talking, high, in a kind of old man's shocked whine. His fingers were gone. "I ain't leaving," he said. "They're mine."

"What? No, come on. What are you talking about? We've got to hurry. Help me."

"I ain't leaving them here. They're mine. They ain't yours, are they? They ain't yours."

"No, please. Oh God. Help me, John."

John Roscoe took Roy's arm and tried to lead him away, tried to get him to walk towards the road. But he pulled his bloody arm free.

"They're mine, goddamn it. I tell you, they ain't yours. I told you, didn't I?"

"Yes, you told us," John Roscoe said.

"They ain't yours."

"No."

"They're mine. I told you already."

"Yes, all right. We'll find them."

"Give them to me. I want them all."

"We'll find them," John Roscoe said. "Lyman, go get my car started. Bring it here."

"Oh Jesus," Lyman said.

"Hurry up, goddamn it. Run."

Lyman turned and ran stumbling across the wheat stubble to get the car. He fell down, jumped up again, and ran on. Edith and my father stood with Roy Goodnough beside the header. His hands and arms were twitching uncontrollably now, dripping blood all the time. He held them out in front of him. His face was bloody from the wound above his eyes, and there was more blood running down the back of his neck.

"I told you," he said. "I already told you so."

"He's going to die," Edith said.

"No, he isn't. Not yet."

"I'm afraid he's going to die, though."

"Stay with him. I'll look if I can find any of his fingers. Jesus Christ Almighty."

"Give them to me. They're mine. They ain't yours."

"Yes, Daddy. Hush now."

"I want them."

"Yes, I know."

"They're mine, I told you."

"Oh, please be quiet. Please, Daddy."

"They ain't yours. They're mine."

JOHN ROSCOE found two of the fingers and one of the thumbs. The thumb was still stuck in the section blades. The two fingers he found in the sand and stubble behind the header, but he couldn't find any more. Edith held them in her lap on the way to town, sitting in the back seat of the old Model T Ford behind her father. They looked like thick bloody sausages in the handkerchief on her lap, except that they had black hair on them between what would have been knuckles and they had fingernails on the ends. There was still dirt under the nails. Edith brushed the sand and wheat chaff off them: the fingers were very stiff. Roy sat in front of her with his head fallen on his chest. He was mumbling to himself, and his bloody hands dripped blood steadily onto the floorboards of the car.

"I'm afraid he's going to bleed to death," Edith said.

"I don't know," John Roscoe said. "He's getting weak."

"Daddy," Edith said. "Daddy, can you hear me?"

"I told you," Roy was saying. "I told you, didn't I? I told you."

"God in heaven," Edith said. "At least he's still alive."

"Yes. We'll be there soon."

47

Lyman sat beside his sister, staring forward at the back of his father's head, without saying a word. They drove as fast as they could in the Ford on the dirt road going north to town.

Holt didn't have a hospital yet; there wouldn't be one for another fifteen years. They stopped the car on Main Street at the storefront that was the doctor's office, next to the harness and general store that has since become a Coast to Coast store. They got Roy Goodnough out of the car, and my father and Edith supported him under the arms and walked him inside. Doc Packer wasn't there.

"Go find him. Quick."

"I can't," Lyman said. "What if I can't find him?"

"Just look for him. Hurry up. Goddamn it, ask somebody."

"But Jesus," Lyman said. Then he ran out onto the sidewalk.

I don't know whether or not Marcellus Packer was the first doctor in Holt, but he was one of the first. He was a short man, and fat, with a walrus moustache like you see in pictures of Teddy Roosevelt. His moustache was always discolored from tobacco juice, even as an old man, when I was taken to him as a kid with mumps. He parted what hair he had in the middle. Lyman found him in the dark beer saloon on the corner, talking to some of the men at a table.

"You got to come," Lyman said.

"What's wrong, boy?"

"It's Pa."

"What's wrong with him? Slow down. Stand still a minute, can't you?"

"It's Pa."

"Where is he?"

Lyman ran back onto the sidewalk in the sun and up

the block to the office. Packer followed him, taking short quick steps under his big stomach, on up the sidewalk and into the back room of the office, where Edith and my father had Roy seated on a chair with a bucket on the floor between his feet to catch the blood.

"Good God, man," Packer said. "What happened to you?"

"They ain't yours," Roy said. "They ain't yours neither."

"What's he talking about?"

"He got caught in a header," my dad said. "He was trying to pull some wire out. The horses spooked."

"He's so weak now," Edith said. "He's been bleeding all the time."

"I can see that. Help me get his shirt off him. That cut over his eyes ain't so bad, but them hands of his . . . good God."

They cut his shirt and long underwear off along the sleeves so they wouldn't have to touch his hands yet. He sat there in his ripped pants dripping blood into the bucket. Then they moved him over to a table.

"Pick up his feet," Packer said. "There now, there. Lay him down. Hold his arms for him. Get another bucket, boy, if you ain't going to help lift him, so he don't bleed all over my floor. Over there in the corner. There now, that's better. Hold him still now while I try to wash some of this blood off him. Jesus God, he's lucky he don't feel nothing."

"They ain't yours," Roy said.

He was lying back on a table with his arms held out to the side, and Doctor Marcellus Packer was washing one of the stumps of his hands with alcohol. "I told you they're mine," he said. "I told you so."

"What's he talking about? Hold him still."

49

"You might as well give them to him, Edith. Do you still have them?"

"Yes."

Edith reached into the pocket of her dress and handed the handkerchief to Doc Packer.

"What's this?" he said. He looked at the two fingers and the thumb in the bloody handkerchief. "What do you expect me to do with them things?"

"He had to have them," Edith said. "But we couldn't find the others, and John looked all over. He wouldn't leave without them."

"You wasted your time," Packer said.

He shook them off the handkerchief into one of the buckets. They looked like they might be blunt fish nosing one another in the bucket.

"I ain't no Jesus Christ," he said. "Hold him still now. This is going to hurt. Maybe you think I'm some damn circus magician?"

In the end about all Doc Packer could do was to trim the stumps of Roy's fingers and thumbs a little bit so they wouldn't be so sharp, then he stretched the ragged flaps of skin over the ends and stitched them up into hard welts. Roy still had the one uncut, unscratched little finger on his left hand, and he damn near died. He probably should have died, too, but he didn't die. He lived for another thirty-seven years with those cruel, raw-looking hands. He could crook his arms under a bucket and hold a fence post while you tamped in around it, and he learned to push a button through its hole so he could get his shirt on by using that one little finger, but he couldn't milk a cow or work a fence pliers or drive a tractor. He couldn't do any of those things that mattered. So he was snookered all right. He was fixed. Now he was dependent on other people, and he hated it.

But if their father was fixed, Edith and Lyman were fixed even worse. They were stuck now on that sandhill farm. How were they going to leave him, the way he was? They couldn't leave him. Not that way, they couldn't. It was hell for all of them. They were all fixed.

· 4 ·

But if Edith and Lyman had been city kids, things might have been different. City kids, even in 1915, had some opportunities to escape which farm kids didn't have. City kids could take off and walk ten or fifteen blocks or jump on a trolley car going across town and end up as far away from home as if they were in another state entirely, another country even. Then they could make their mark, or not make it, and start their life over or end it, but whatever happened, at least the ties would have been cut, the limits of home would have been broken.

Or if Edith and Lyman had been country kids living now, alive and howling in the 1970s, things might have been different too. It's TV and movie shows and high school and 3.2 beer and loud music and paved highways and fast cars (and what goes on and comes off too in the back seats of those cars, until maybe Bud Sealy shines his flashlight in through the side windows)—it's all those things and more that country kids have now, and you can't tell a farm kid from a town kid, even with a program. They're just about all the same, all alike in their cars, driving up and down Main Street every Saturday night, honking and howling, in Holt, Colorado.

But Edith and Lyman didn't have those things, those chances and opportunities to escape. They were farm kids in the second decade of this violent century, and they were stuck. Their mother died early, like I've already said; their father was Roy Goodnough, and even if he was a raging madman sometimes, even if he yelled too much at them, he was still their father. And then—to clinch matters, to turn that heavy vise a few more turns to the right—they had to see him get his hands ruined. They had to be right there when it happened; they had to witness it all, watch his hands being ground to hamburger; they had to run for help, get him to town, carry what was left of his fingers wrapped up in a damn handkerchief, and then one of them had to hold an arm in place, and they both had to watch while Packer did what little he could to rectify the bloody mess of his hands—and all the time he was still talking about I told you so, I told you, didn't I?

So when I say they were stuck, I don't mean they were stuck just a little bit. I don't mean they were just sort of stuck the way you might be if you stepped into some mud and you were able to get out of it if you made the effort, and once you were out of it about all the loss you'd have to show was that you might have to leave a pair of good new shoes behind you in the mud. No, I mean they were deep stuck. I mean it was like they were stuck clear up to their chins, almost up to eye level, and no real effort was even possible. They might manage to wiggle their arms a little bit now and then, they might turn their heads a few degrees, but they couldn't get out no matter what, and about all they could see in any direction around them, when they did manage to turn their heads a little bit, was just more mud. More of the same. Or, in their case, more sand and more work and duty and obligation.

So Edith went on, of course, cooking and cleaning and mending and washing clothes and ironing. Also, she still had the garden to manage: to plant, hoe, water, can, and pickle. Also, she had the wood to cut and carry in, the stove to stoke, the chickens to feed, the eggs to gather and clean. Also now, every morning and every night, on top of all those other duties she had to do the milking.

Have you ever milked cows? No, I suppose not. Well, milking cows is all right if there isn't any way you can get out of it, but it's not quite the fun times old pictures make it out to be, with some bare-armed milkmaid sitting down beside some nice brown and white Guernsey cow under an oak tree and over there not far away is a blue stream bubbling and everything looks lazy and fine and somehow it's always summer. No, you get up—Edith got up—every morning in the dark, never mind if it was blizzarding out, never mind if she was still exhausted. She got up, threw on a dress and a coat and went outside to find the five or six Shorthorns in the cow pasture. She walked them through the gate and into the barn, set the head catch to hold them there, hitched up her skirt and coat to climb up the ladder to the loft, threw down some hay into the manger, climbed down again, set the T-shaped milk stool in place, sat down with her head close to the cow's flank to keep from getting hit in the face too much by the stinging shit-filled, eye-blinding tail, washed the tits off with a wet rag, pulled some first squirts of milk from each tit to further clean them and to check for mastitis, squeezed the bucket between her knees, and then, finally, milked the cow out enough to still leave some for a calf to suck and survive on. And then she did the same with the next cow, and the next, and the next. And all the time she was talking quietly to them to keep them calm enough that they would let the milk down and not kick the bucket away from her.

When she was finished milking, she turned the cows out to pasture again, and then carried the buckets of milk into the house to the back porch, where she ran the milk through the separator, turning the crank by hand. Afterwards, sometime during the day, she had to find time to make butter and to get the sour cream ready to take to town to sell. I believe they did that once a week, took the cream and eggs they didn't need into town to Bishop's Creamery opposite the railroad tracks.

But you understand, don't you, that what I've told you so far was just the morning milking. Because she had to do it all over again late in the afternoon before she cooked supper; twice a day she had to do it, every day in the week. You also understand that what I've said about milking cows is based on the shaky assumption that everything would go right. I mean, that's how it was supposed to be. But, of course, it didn't always go that way. There were many days when whatever could go wrong, did go wrong. A cow stepped on her foot. Another one kicked the bucket over. One of them turned up sick and had to be doctored. Or maybe they just didn't want to come in from the pasture in the first place. Who knows what an old speckle-faced cow is thinking? Or if she's thinking anything at all? Well, some people claim pigs are smart, and maybe they are, but nobody I know has ever said that about cows.

But the worst part of milking was always that constant stinging foul tail. Now a shit-filled tail is bad enough. Struck across your eyes or snapped into your mouth, a shit-filled tail will do for starters, and it happens all the time. But you don't know what bad is, you haven't experienced the full benefit of stink and outrage, until you've had a fresh cow (especially an old raw-boned bitch of a one that you hate anyway) come in to be milked for the first time after having a calf, and when she gets in she has a three-day-old afterbirth hanging down out of her because she hasn't cleaned out right. So there it is, that damned stuff is hanging down out of her, swinging there between her back legs; it's shit-soaked, juicy, buzzing with flies, and the rottenness of it is so putrid, so God-awful, that it's all you can do to keep from throwing your guts up. But you've got to milk her, don't you? That's what she's there for. So you set the bucket down, perch your butt on the milkstool, and you pray or hope or cross your fingers, you make all kinds of impossible promises: if only you can just get her milked without having to taste any of that putrid foulness. And by God, yes, it looks like you're going to make it. Yes, that's right, you're going to make it. So easy now, easy Mama, easy. That's right. And Jesus, yes, you've almost got her milked out enough to call it good—when bang, oh holy shit, oh Christ on a crutch, she hits you with it all, all of that blood and shit and juice and unbelievable outrage, right across your face. It covers your eyes, your nose, your mouth. You can even feel some of it dripping down the back of your neck. Oh brother, help me. Son of a bitch. Then you can't hold it any longer: you throw up, all over yourself, all over the damn cow, all over the milk bucket. You throw up until you're gagging on acid bile, your stomach hurts, and you're groping for air.

Well, it happened to me once. Once was enough. It made me want to kill something. But I suppose it happened to Edith Goodnough a number of times. It had to. Edith milked cows twice a day, every day of the week, all those years.

Bᴜᴛ Lʏᴍᴀɴ, meanwhile what about Lyman? Because, after all, Lyman was stuck, too. I mean, he sure as hell wasn't any sixteen-year-old kid from the city. He was just a tall big-boned mop-haired farm kid, with raw wrists and patched overalls and high-topped shoes, and he seemed to stumble about in a kind of daze, like he had lost something and couldn't remember what it was he had lost, let alone know where to look for it. Lyman was stuck out here on that same sandhill farm, stuck in the same way his sister was. He was caught in the same vise, smothered in the same mud hole with just his chin (weak and pointed like his mother's) sticking up above it, and I don't believe Lyman was even able to get his head up enough to look around him, to see that there wasn't a thing in the world out there but more of the same.

Roy saw to that. Roy, with his destroyed hands and his hard eyes, kept Lyman's nose buried in it. It was like Lyman was just some ass-whipped mongrel dog that Roy kept at heel on a short chain, and any time Lyman got any notion otherwise, then his father would give him a sharp jerk to make him remember and pay attention. Because that's the way it was for a long time: Roy kept Lyman's nose buried right there at home. He made damn sure that Lyman never had time enough to hatch up any escape plans; he saw to it that Lyman spent all his brain and all his muscle and all his sweat right there planting those quarter sections of corn and wheat, planting the same corn rows year after year and then cultivating that corn and handpicking it, planting the same wheat fields and disking and harvesting, and in between times when he wasn't working corn or working wheat, then he was exhausting himself with raking the same hayfields and stacking the same haystacks.

So, for a long time, Lyman stayed there working. And it wasn't that there was anything particularly unusual about that—everyone in the country worked, worked hard too—but what made it worse for Lyman, the thing that must have made it seem like he had one of those barbed goat heads, one of these poisonous sandburs, buried forever in the back of his neck was the fact that all the time, every day, he was being ordered around. There was never any letup. It was Roy who decided everything. Roy ruled it all. If Lyman had had any say-so, if he had had any choice in when to plant the corn or where to stack the hay or how many acres of wheat he was going to plant, then it

57

might have been all right. But he didn't. He might just as well have pissed against the wind as to suggest anything to Roy.

For a long time then, while Lyman worked that sandhill farm, about all he could manage to do was to wait and to hope too, I suppose, hope in his dog-eyed dazed fashion, hope that someday somehow some kind of barn door or pasture gate would get left open just enough to let him squeeze through it, so that once he made it through and got his overalls unstuck, then he could take off and start running. And by God, never look back. Not even long enough to see if something was gaining on him.

Well, Lyman didn't need much, you understand, but he sure as hell did need something.

THINGS went on the same for about seven years, and then it was Edith who made the first attempt to get out. Or at least for one summer she seemed to encourage the possibility of it. And if you've understood what I've said about her—or more to the point, if I've managed to make it plain enough—then it shouldn't surprise you that it was Edith who made the first attempt to break free. Of the two of them, she was the one who had the sand. Besides, by 1922, when Edith was twenty-five, she must have been just about as beautiful as any woman can be. And I believe she still is, in her own clear-eyed way, and no more so than now, when in four days she will be eighty years old and still lying there in the damn hospital bed, waiting to get well.

But in the summer of 1922 she must have been just about perfect. She was slim and quick, with brown eyes and brown curly hair. She was woman breasted. She had strong hands. She was uncomplaining with plenty to complain about. She was . . . but hell, I don't know how to describe women. Only look here, this is more what I mean: she was quiet and focused and there for you in a way that didn't make you feel awkward or clumsy even when you were worse than both of those things, as failing on your feet as a newborn colt, as drunk as a just-dropped calf. She made you want to hold her there in the front seat of that car on that country road, hold her, put your arm around her, kiss her, breathe her hair, talk to her, tell her all those things you hadn't told anyone else before, all those things beyond the jokes and the surface facts of yourself, things you yourself didn't know for sure you felt or thought until you heard yourself telling them to her in the dark in the stopped car with your arm around her, because somehow it would be all right if she heard them and they would be true then. Edith Goodnough must have been something that summer.

But, Christ, what a waste of life. It makes you sick to your stomach. It makes you want to do anything else in the world but think about her.

You SEE, Edith and my dad, John Roscoe, went out together that summer. And if you think about that for a minute you'll understand at least one of the reasons why I feel about Edith the way I do. For six or seven weeks that summer, Edith and my dad went spooning or sparking or whatever it was people called it then when two people drive out together in an old Ford car with the windows rolled down and the dark air blows in on them, carrying that green smell of sage in with it. Driving in the car, they turn towards one another now and then, and then more and more often as the evening fades; they laugh a little bit about something that may seem funny to them only, while the stars have begun to snap overhead, and behind them there's only that dust billowing up in the road after the car has passed.

So Edith and my dad went to a few dances together. They went into town to a movie or two. They ate supper once in Norka, the next town west of Holt. But mainly they drove along the country roads in the sandhills in my dad's old Ford, talking and laughing a little bit. It must have seemed enough to be together and to be moving, and almost always they had Lyman with them in the back seat.

Maybe that's the reason why Roy let them go. With Lyman along to stick his head up between them from the back seat, it may have seemed all right to let Edith go out driving with my dad. I suppose he thought Lyman would put a halt to any funny stuff. Not that Lyman would say anything to anybody—Lyman didn't do much talking in his life, except maybe to Edith—but he did always seem to be there. You'd be working on something in the machine shed or visiting with someone on Main Street, and then you'd look up and there Lyman would be, standing off a little ways, cleaning the dirt from under his fingernails with a jackknife, and you couldn't be sure how long he'd been standing there or how much he'd seen or heard, but there he was all right, waiting like a stray dog to see what developed. So maybe that's the reason why Roy allowed that six- or seven-week vacation, that brief lessening of his hold on the vise that summer, but that's only a guess. It sure as hell wasn't like him. Maybe he just wanted to see how far it would go, to kind of test the water. Or maybe he already had in mind what he was going to do next.

Another thing I can only guess at, concerning that summer, was why it took my dad so long. He was already thirty-two. He was still young, of course, still in his prime—strong, tough, black haired, the kind of man dogs and horses will come up to for a scratch and a pat without his ever having to whistle or snap his fingers. But for at least ten years there hadn't been any reason to doubt that he would make a good go of ranching. He had been well established for quite a while; he had things in control. So maybe he was just waiting. He was a country boy too, after all, and every fall during harvest he was still there helping the Goodnoughs, watching Edith, talking to her some and joking with Lyman, while he himself drove the header now that Roy couldn't.

Then his mother, my grandmother, died. That was in the spring of 1922. When he came in for supper one evening, he found her dead in the rocking chair with tobacco ashes spilled out onto her black dress, and he buried her up on that little rise north of the barn. He stuck her briar pipe under her hands on her chest. Edith was the only other person there. Together they shoveled the sand in onto the wood box.

"There ought to be a tree or bush, though," Edith said. "Even if it's just the thought of it, she ought to have some shade."

The box was covered now. My dad was mounding the sand on top and packing it with the flat of his shovel.

"I mean in July and August," Edith said. "I don't like thinking of her up here then."

"Be a awful long way to carry water."

"A bucket or two every other day," she said. "We could take turns."

"What kind of tree?"

"A cottonwood. They grow fast, and if there's any wind you can hear the leaves washing and turning in it. Unless you'd rather it was something else."

"I believe she liked cottonwoods. She never said."

"You could get one from along the Arikaree."

"I'll get one this afternoon," he said. "I guess we're done here now."

They stood on the rise looking at the mound of damp sand, with the switch grass and brome and sagebrush around it. They could see the house south of where they stood.

"Do you want me to leave now?" Edith said. "I will."

"No. Why would I want that?"

"Maybe you want to be alone."

"I'll have that as soon as I go down to the house," he said. "No. No, you look okay there. You might even look pretty if you didn't have all that wet sand on your shoes."

"Go on," she said.

"And your big nose wasn't peeling."

"Go on, you," she said. "But John, she was a good woman, wasn't she? My mother thought so. She made a difference for my mother."

"Sure, she made all the difference. But I'll never forget how that son of a bitch left her."

"Nor you either. He left you too."

"Never mind me. I always had her. But she never had anything—just a six-year-old kid and a homestead he hadn't even got started good yet. The son of a bitch. I don't know how she stood it."

"Some people can't," Edith said. "She did though. She was as strong as anything."

"She shouldn't of had to be that strong. That's what I mean. He just left her out here—with me and a milk cow and one horse. Can you believe that? Hell, he even took the other horse."

"I'll help you water the tree tomorrow," Edith said.

So maybe that's what he was waiting for: his mother to die and Edith Goodnough to suggest some shade for her. Anyway, he planted a cottonwood and they took turns watering it—or watered it together, more like—each of them carrying a bucketful up to the rise in the evenings, and later he built a fence around it, and then they began going out together in his Ford car with Lyman along in the back seat for the ride.

It was called the Gem Theater then. It was on the other side of the street and north a block and a half from the theater we have now, the Holt Theater. There is a marquee out front above the double-door entrance to the Holt Theater now, so people can see what Blaine Fisher is showing for their enjoyment on the weekend, but you can only read what is showing if you are driving south on Main Street, because Blaine only changes the words on the north side of his marquee. I suppose he figures that's enough ladder climbing for him, with his big stomach and his skinny legs and high blood pressure. Blaine leaves the other side of the marquee always the same: ENJOY FRESH HOT POPCORN. It makes you wonder now how fresh it is and how hot, considering how many years he's been advertising it that way.

As for the old Gem Theater, I can't remember whether it had one of those things above its doors or not—probably not—and it wouldn't have had sound by 1922, either. But my dad and Edith and Lyman must have had some fun there just the same, with the lights in the auditorium darkened and the heads on the screen flickering bigger than any human head could be, and then before they were ready for it, that guy with the pencil moustache was tying the little blond to the railroad tracks, or strapping her down good to a buzz saw, and she was looking Help me right at Lyman chewing his popcorn and right at my dad and Edith holding hands on Edith's lap, and all over that pretty lipstick mouth she had that big scream screaming "Help." Some things were simpler then.

But it was late in the summer, after one of those two or three nights in town at the picture show and after a dish of ice cream at Lexton's Confectionery, that what started right, ended wrong, and it stopped whatever else might have happened later. They were in the car going south towards home. Lyman was asleep in the back seat with his head shoved up against the side. When they got to the corner where they had to turn east to come the mile off the highway to the Goodnoughs', they woke Lyman up and Edith asked him if he would walk the rest of the way, not quite home, she told him, but wait for her before he got home so they could go into the house together.

"For a favor to me," she said. "Will you?"

"Don't forget John," he said.

"Yes. For him too. What's wrong, though?"

"Nothing," Lyman said. "What if Pa finds out?"

"He won't. Here, you can take my coat to lie on in the grass."

"But what if he does?"

"I don't know. Will you do it?"

Lyman got out of the car then and spoke in through the window to Edith, so close that his breath moved her hair. "Don't forget to pick me up," he said.

"We won't. And thank you, Lyman. But don't you want my coat?"

"No. Lay on it yourself."

"Don't say that. Why would you say that? What's wrong with you?"

"Nothing's wrong with me."

"What's wrong, though? Something is."

"It better not take very long," Lyman said. "That's all I know."

Then he turned to walk alongside the road in the dark, away from the car. My dad and Edith drove a mile or two farther south on the highway and then turned west into the sandhills.

"He's tired all the time," Edith said. "Did you see him back there? He's going to have a stiff neck tomorrow."

"Lyman's all right," my dad said. "He needs to get out more. Needs a girl himself to go riding with. Even if she has to eat as much ice cream as you do. Chocolate and nuts all over it, like she wasn't never going to have another chance at it. Just howdy, mister, and forget the napkins; I ain't got time to be fancy."

"Oh, be quiet, you," Edith said. "I only had one dish of it."

"Yeah, just a little old triple decker."

"But I like ice cream. And it was strawberries, not nuts."

"Good. I'll have Lexton bring you a gallon of both next time. Make him stack them on top his head like a trained monkey. He's got that nice flat bald spot, just right for juggling things on it."

"He doesn't either. And it's not flat like you say it is—it's ridged."

"Why, it is too. Flat as a pancake. It's where his ma hit him with the shovel."

"She didn't do any such thing."

"Well, she did. Banged on the head with a shovel. 'Now behave yourself,' she said, 'and quit picking them britches, or I'll bang you again.'"

"I'll bang you on the head with a shovel," Edith said, "if you don't be quiet. Now hush, and see if you can keep this car out of the ditch."

"I'm just trying to get you some ice cream, Edith. I don't want you to go home hungry."

"I'm sick of ice cream. And I don't want to go home yet."

"Good," my dad said. "I don't either."

"But I can't imagine any of this for him," Edith said. "Can you?"

"Who? Bernie Lexton?"

"No. Lyman. I think I'm the only woman he's ever talked to. Besides mother, I mean."

"Poor bugger."

"Yes. And not the way you mean it, either."

So they were alone now. It was one of the few times, and the car was stopped on the country road. On both sides of them, since it was a piece of sandhill country and too steep for plows, they had all those sunflowers and all that sage and soapweed and blue grama grass, and I don't know whether or not they had the moon. But I hope they did, a full moon, because Edith Goodnough deserved to be seen in that pale blue light at least once in her life, and anyway I know they had the high stars snapping clean for them, and all that country was quiet too. So my dad must have held her then, and kissed her—and not one of those first nose-positioning, chin-bumping kisses, but where you've gone past that part already and you've learned to make a good mixture of your mouth with hers, and it tastes good and you both want more, and then you have more. So he must have kissed her, and been kissed in return, and I'm going to hope they got out of the car then. I'm going to believe they did that, believe they stood out into that pale blue quiet and then together walked away from the car, up the hillside, until they found a hollow in the grass and lay down on his coat and talked quietly, almost in a whisper, though there was no need for whispering, while he unbuttoned her soft blouse and she watched his eyes, and his eyes showed that he knew he was being given a gift, and the only thing he was afraid of was that his hard work-calloused hands might somehow harm such smooth blue whiteness, and all the time on her part she wasn't afraid of anything, but was just waiting and watching him still, his dark eyes, and then she had one hand warm on his neck and the other alive in his black hair. And I'm going to believe that it was as beautiful as sometimes it can be, when you're right with one another, when together it's good for you both, because Edith deserved that too.

AFTERWARDS they must have talked a little, still quietly, in a sad whisper now. Edith must have said, "What's going to happen to us, John? What am I going to do now?"

"Why, we're going to get married."

"But I don't know that."

"We're going to get married. We'll have a fine time."

"I don't know that at all."

"I'm asking you, though. Right now. Is that what you're waiting for? I'm too comfortable and easy to get up on my knees, but you know I want us to be married."

"That's not what I mean. I mean how can I?"

"Why hell, girl, you just say yes now, and a little later you say 'I do.' What else is there?"

Edith must have sat up then, moving up off his arm where she had been lying while he made circles in her brown hair with his fingers. She must have begun to put her blouse and skirt on again.

"I mean," she said, "there's Lyman."

"Well, damn Lyman," my dad said. "He's old enough. What is he—twenty-four, twenty-five? He's old enough to manage by hisself, ain't he?"

"Lyman was twenty-three," Edith said, "June sixth. But it's not a matter of age, you know it isn't. It's him, it's the way he is, and it's me too. I've always had to be there for him—against Daddy."

"All right, yes, I know that. I've seen it all often enough. But Jesus, Edith, you'd only be a half mile apart even so."

"It's not a matter of miles either."

"Well, what then? Hell."

"It's Daddy too. Don't you see that? Think about him, the way he is. His hands."

"I don't want to think about him. He's a dried up son of a bitch. Even before his hands, he was."

"That's not fair."

"It's a fact, Edith. He's no good to anybody, let alone to hisself."

"But that doesn't seem to matter," she said. "Does it? I can't help that. All I can help is . . . I can help about mother."

"But for godsake, Edith. Your mother is dead."

"I know that. That's what I mean. When mother died I had to take things up into my own hands. And you know it doesn't matter if I wanted to or not: sometimes now I don't even know what it was I might have wanted once. I can't recall. It's been too long; it will be eight years in August since mother died. But anyway, these things and these people here are mine now. I've taken them up. That's all there is. And besides, what would Lyman do?"

So what was my dad going to say to any of that? He was lying there in sandhill grass, watching her while she talked and while the light shone pale on her fine face, and I suppose he must have known that he couldn't win any fight against the memory of any frail little woman, even if that woman was just skinny and tiny and homesick and even if she had been dead for close to eight years. But perhaps he still had reason to hope—I suppose he did— so perhaps he changed targets and aimed instead at Edith's obligation to Lyman, because maybe he still thought he could at least win a fight against a twenty-three-year-old

shuffling, shambling brother. With humor then my dad
must have said something like:

"All right, hell then. If he has to, Lyman can come live
with us. I'll cut him another hole in the outhouse."

"What? Don't be silly."

"He can have his own Sears, Roebuck catalog too. We
won't bother it none. We won't even notice if he uses all
the pages except the ones with corsets and women's socks
on them. He can spend all the time he wants to out there—
we won't care."

"You are good for me," Edith said.

"Why sure. Old Lyman will be as happy as a dead sow
in clover."

Edith felt about in her hair to see if she had all of the
grass combed out. "Give me another kiss," she said. "And
stop all this talking about outhouses and dead sows."

THEY WENT HOME THEN, out of the sandhills where,
for a while, they had been alone in the sage and the blue
light, then north on the highway to the corner and east
almost a mile, before they got to the Goodnoughs', to find
Lyman. They didn't find him, though, not right away.
They had to stop the car and look for him along the road-
side in the tall grass, and they didn't find him until they
turned the headlights of the car on again. Even then they
didn't find him immediately. He was lying on his side,
rolled into himself like a kid, asleep with spit dribbled onto
his chin. He was a good fifteen feet off the road. Edith
brushed him off.

"Are you awake now?" she said.

"Where's Pa?"

"In the house. Come on. Can you get in the car?"

My dad drove them into the yard and squeezed Edith's

hand before she got out. Then he drove the half mile home, and Edith and Lyman walked into the house together. Roy was waiting for them in the kitchen. He was sitting at the kitchen table in his work pants and long underwear, with his raw hands and one good finger resting on the white enameled wood in front of him. Some things weren't any simpler then than they are now.

"Get upstairs," he told Lyman.

Lyman looked at Edith. He was fully awake now and aware, but he went upstairs anyway. The barn door had just banged shut again for him.

"You're done with that," Roy said to Edith. "That's enough of Roscoe."

Edith stood on the other side of the table, waiting, watching her father feel his little finger over the bad nubs of his right hand. His finger looked like a claw raking dead meat.

"I seen him stop the car," Roy said. "I seen the lights on the road go off and come on again. But that's done with."

"I'm twenty-five," Edith said.

"That don't mean a diddle."

"John's thirty-two."

"That don't mean a goddamn, either. He's a half-breed bastard, and you're done with him."

"He's not either."

"He is if I say he is, goddamn it. And you're his whore. Now get to bed. You must be all wore out after tonight."

"Shut up, Daddy. You don't know what you're saying."

Roy stood up then; the chair banged down behind him onto the wooden floor. He reached across the table at her with his finger, but she stepped back.

"You don't tell me to shut up," he yelled. "I'm your father. I'll say any goddamn thing I please. I told you to go to bed. Now get."

"I will go to bed," Edith said. "But I won't listen to you say that."

"This is my house. I built it. I'll say anything I want in these rooms. Do you understand me?"

"It's my house too. And Lyman's. And it was mother's before she died."

"I wish she could see you now. She'd hate the damn sight of you."

"No, she wouldn't," Edith said. "She would not."

"By God, don't tell me, you goddamn—"

But Edith walked past him then—he was insane, wild-eyed, stump waving—and went into the living room and up the stairs to the bedroom. He was still yelling at her: "You're done with him, you hear me? Goddamn sow to a Roscoe, you're done now. You're through. You whore. You hear me?"

THE NEXT DAY Roy used more than just his voice. In the afternoon while Edith was snapping beans in the kitchen and Lyman was mowing hay in the field, Roy Goodnough kicked the chopping block over with his boot and pushed it rolling with the heels of his hands across the yard into the barn. There he righted it again under a crossbeam in the center alley of the barn. The chopping block was a sawed-off stump of an elm tree, with deep ax marks and dark dried blood on it where the slack heads of chickens had been chopped off. Over the crossbeam above him Roy looped a hemp rope and tied a full-handled ax to the rope so that the ax would fall and cut deep into the block.

He experimented with it twice, pulling the ax up almost to the crossbeam to give it enough weight to do what he wanted it to do when it fell. Then he pulled it up one more time and clamped the rope tight between his right elbow and his ribcage. The ax hung ready above him in the dusty horse-shit air. He waited until it was still, no longer swinging. A speckled pigeon watched it all from a high perch in the barn rafters, and then he laid his one finger down on the block and released the rope. The pigeon blinked a pink eye when the ax fell, thunking through his finger into the block.

Only it didn't just cut his finger off. Maybe he moved a little when he released his elbow-hold on the rope and then saw the ax falling and falling, taking too long to fall. Or maybe he hadn't experimented enough. Whatever went wrong, the ax chopped through the top knuckle of his hand, splintering it bad as it smashed through bone and joint and gristle. But it must have still been satisfactory.

He pinched up the twitching finger from the block like it was just a chicken's head, pinched it up between his two hand stumps and carried it bloody into the house to the kitchen and dropped it into the bowl of snapped beans on the table in front of Edith. At first she didn't move, didn't speak. It bled a little among the beans. Then she looked up from the bowl at her father.

"You might have saved yourself the trouble," she said. "I already decided last night I couldn't leave this house."

She got up and went to the bandage box she kept in a kitchen drawer and poured alcohol over his hand and wrapped it to stop the bleeding.

"You'll probably get infection," she said. "I suppose you should see Doc Packer again, but I'm not going with you. I've been there once. And I might have married John Roscoe. I might have married him. I don't care what you say. He wanted me to and I might have. Oh yes, God in mercy, I might have. Oh damn you."

But she was crying then. There wasn't any sound to it. It was past the point where the puny sound of a human voice can make any difference. She walked out of the house away from her father towards the hayfield to tell Lyman, with the unregarded tears falling onto the breast of her blouse. After that, I know of only two other times in her life that Edith Goodnough allowed herself to cry. Neither was at the death of her father.

· 5 ·

W HAT's 365 times 20? Something over 7,000, isn't
it? Well, that's how long it was. That's how many days.

For over 7,000 days, for almost 20 years, nothing happened to the Goodnoughs. After Roy chopped his last
finger off with the ax, nothing happened to the Goodnoughs—or *for* them either—until almost two decades of
slow days had passed. Days that must have seemed as
cruel as stillbirth; the pointlessness of them, the sameness,
one slow day grinding slow into the next, with no letup
and no relief, nothing to look forward to and even less to
look back on. Not even those small things the rest of us
use to mark the passing of time—what we mean when we
say "But you remember, don't you?"—because Edith and
Lyman didn't have even that much that was worth re-
calling about last Christmas, never mind the day before
yesterday. I believe even the Great Depression, when it
came in the thirties, must have seemed like just more of
the same to them, or if it was different then it was only
slightly worse, because then they stopped going into town
once a week to sell eggs and sour cream during the depression, to make a little money.

So it only surprises me that Roy didn't start in on his
toes the same way, chop his ten toes off, nine all at once
in the header or hay mower or corn picker and then the
last one by itself in the barn with an ax—just for a little

variety, I mean. To keep the knack of it fresh. Hell, the old bastard could have yelled Lyman in from the hayfield and made Lyman take the damn things into the house and dump them into the bean bowl or the kitchen sink. Chopped his own ears off, too, for all I know or care. Except I guess even Roy knew he had done enough that one afternoon.

Because Edith never went out riding with my father again. She and Lyman went on working like they had before. Of course, when those six or seven weeks of that summer ended for Edith, she wasn't the same. It was as if the reason for her to have female hips and soft breasts was gone. She got so she was more what you really mean is thin when you say a woman has a good body, that she's slim. She didn't laugh as easy. Something bright went out of her brown eyes. Her quick gestures became deliberate movements, like there was nothing now to hurry about, and it was at that time that she and Roy stopped talking to one another any more than they had to. Oh, she took care of him—I don't mean that. She buttoned his shirt for him now that he no longer had even one finger to use to poke a button through a hole, and she mashed his potatoes and cut his meat into bites so he could still eat his food by lifting a fork to his mouth between his clenched stumps, and she tied his shoes. But she didn't have much to say to him and she paid less attention to whatever he said. So there must have been a lot of quiet around that kitchen table for all those years, with about all the talk being just Roy's orders and farm questions and Lyman's mumbled grunts of obedience and short answers and pass the pepper and ain't there any more gravy; and then in December of 1941 it must have got to be almost dead silence.

Bᴜᴛ ɪ'ᴍ ɢᴇᴛᴛɪɴɢ ᴀʜᴇᴀᴅ of myself. Or if you want it for a joke, I'm forgetting myself.

Because in fact there were a few things happening in the house down the road a half mile west, in this house here where you and I are sitting away a Sunday afternoon.

For one thing my dad just about quit. He damn near quit on himself, quit giving a good goddamn about anything. When he and Edith ran into each other on Main Street—it was a couple of days later, on Saturday afternoon—when Edith told him what had happened that other afternoon and that she wouldn't leave the house ever, my dad wanted to kill Roy Goodnough.

In front of Nexey's Lumberyard, across the street from Bishop's Creamery, my dad said, "I'll kill him."

"It'll be all right," Edith said. "It has to."

"I'll chop his head off."

There were people on the sidewalk, men in overalls and caps, women in silk stockings, kids sucking horehound candy and bouncing sticks on sidewalk cracks, all walking past and then stopping ten yards away to watch with their mouths held shut and their eyes wide open. They didn't want to miss anything; they would want to talk about it later.

And my dad was saying, "I'll kill him."

And Edith was still saying how it would be all right.

Well, it wasn't all right, and I believe he could have too—could have killed him. If somehow he could have gotten away with it, it might have been the best thing. Does that surprise you? To think that murdering an old stump-handed man might be an answer? But of course it wasn't, and he didn't. That sort of thing only happens on TV. Nobody I know has killed anybody, and you can never mind what they say this approaching trial is about. Whatever the lawyers in their ignorance say about it, I know it isn't murder.

So instead of anything similar to that, my dad, John Roscoe, who's been dead now for nearly twenty-seven years, and I still can't stop thinking about him at least once every day while dehorning a calf or mashing my thumb purple with a claw hammer (still it's his voice saying, "Smarts pretty good, don't it?"—it's still his voice I hear in my head, measuring things, setting standards, his voice and way of looking at things: "But life *ain't* fair, Sanders," he told me once)—my dad, for about three years after he and Edith stopped going out together, went a little crazy.

He began to work like an immigrant during the day and to drink at night like there was no tomorrow. He was going on anger and disbelief and about four hours of sleep. He bought more cattle. He went in debt for another section of grass. He hired one of his cronies to help him. The crony was a short, squat, blocky character named Ellis Burns, who looked like a fireplug with a two-day-old beard, or, when they were working cattle in the pasture, like a fat monkey on a circus horse. He moved Ellis into the house with him and did nothing fancy. They fried meat and opened cans, mixed it together in a black frying pan, and boiled coffee. They rinsed last night's supper off the two plates and the two forks and sat down to eat. And Ellis Burns never did lose weight.

"Damned if I know why," my dad said. "I worked his ass off too. Maybe it was the beer."

They went out drinking four or five times every week. They couldn't go to town to the dark saloon on the corner of Main and First streets, since this was in the time of Prohibition: the saloon was boarded up for a while and then somebody opened it again as a café. They had to drive instead to Leon Shields's place, a run-down farmhouse east of town, set back a mile off the highway amongst some trees. Some rough characters showed up there, so I've been told, but as far as I know it never got busted. Apparently Leon Shields had the sheriff, one of Bud Sealy's predecessors, gripped hard by the short and curlies, or at least Leon had him tucked deep into his back pocket. I believe Leon knew something about the sheriff and another man's wife that wasn't public knowledge and that the wife's husband didn't even know about. Besides, I suppose there must have been the usual exchange of quiet-money, to sweeten it all. Anyway, it was that unpainted farmhouse surrounded by trees that my dad and Ellis Burns would drive to, during those three years. They stayed there drinking homemade beer and playing cards all those nights, until finally along about two o'clock Leon would say, "That's all, boys—Mama's waiting on me," and then start turning the lights off so that at the card table in the back Ellis Burns couldn't tell now whether it was a jack of clubs or a ten of spades that he still had hopes of drawing. Ellis would say, "Now, damn it all, Leon. I was just about to win a hand."

"No, you wasn't, " Leon would say. "I'm saving you money."

"Hell, too. Turn them lights back on."

"Nope. I'm going upstairs to play with the kids' Mama."

"Turn them lights on. I'm about to fill a straight."

"Listen, you sawed-off little pecker shit," Leon would say. "You never seen a straight in your life. Now get out of here 'fore I knock your nose off."

"By God," Ellis would say, and he'd be standing up now in a wobbly crouch. "By God, you better pack a lunch. It ain't going to be no five-minute job."

But Leon would just laugh then, and my dad would say, "Give us another beer, Leon, and we'll go home."

"All right, John. See you tomorrow."

"No doubt."

So they would go home then, west and then south on the highway. Before they got more than a mile down the road Ellis would be asleep, just like Lyman had done those few times, only Ellis was sleeping in the front seat now where, before, Edith had sat beside my dad. The almost-full beer bottle would be standing up between Ellis's legs at his crotch, sloshing beer onto his pants zipper. It didn't wake him. He slept on with his slack stubbled chin rocking on his chest bone.

But my dad wouldn't be asleep. Even after those hard nights at Leon Shields's and all the beer, he wouldn't be able to sleep very long once he was home again and in bed. He was up every morning before daybreak, kicking Ellis awake, frying eggs in the just-rinsed frying pan, ready to begin branding cattle or stacking hay or shoeing horses. Anything as long as it kept him from thinking. He didn't want to think.

Then, towards the end of that three-year period of fierce work and hard drinking, my dad began to get into fights. There wouldn't be any reason for the fights; he would just be at Leon's, drinking and still too sober, and he would start a fight. It wouldn't be about anything. He would hit somebody and wait to get hit back, hardly bothering to fend off whatever blows were thrown at him. He had a bad scar from one of those fights, a white break in the black line of his left eyebrow, which I used to admire when I was still of an age where fist fights seemed to prove something. My dad straightened me out about that too.

"All this does is," he told me, running his thick finger over the wide jagged spot above his eye, "it reminds me how I was a damn fool. It don't mean a thing else. And don't you think it does."

"What was it about, though?" I said. "The fight."

"Nothing. It wasn't about nothing. I hit Frank Lutz because he happened to be there and because I wasn't drunk and because I knew Frank would hit me back. And he did."

"Did you hurt him?"

"Yes. And I went over to apologize to him the next day. I liked Frank. Had nothing against him."

"Did he hurt you?"

"Not much. Not enough."

"Because you were tougher," I said. "Because you beat him."

"No," he said. "And I told you I don't want you thinking like that, Sanders. I said, not enough, because a month later I hit Frank again. For the same no reason. And he hit me again. That's why I got this scar, to remind me to stop being such a damn fool—at least that form of a fool anyway. Now do you understand?"

"No."

"You will."

But I didn't understand, not then, not for a few years more. I only really understood it when later I found out what he hadn't told me about that period of his life—that he and Ellis Burns stopped going out drinking. I was also able to put another set of two and two together and then I understood that instead of drinking beer to keep himself from thinking, my dad married my mother. And I want to think that being married to Leona Turner Newcomb was at least somewhat better than being hit in the face by Frank Lutz. I want to believe that much about it if for no other reason than the fact that pretty soon I came along, I came out of that marriage, and that's what I meant a while ago when I said I was forgetting myself, take it for a joke.

WELL, I was a surprise to them. Not a shotgun surprise, but a surprise just the same, because Leona Turner Newcomb wasn't supposed to be able to have babies. She had been married for ten years—from 1910 until 1920—to Jason Newcomb, who worked in the Holt Bank, with red garters on his sleeves and who sported a clean little moustache under his fine nose. Together they hadn't had any children in a decade. But I don't know that children would have made any difference to them. Children would just have made things stickier, I suppose, because one morning in August of 1920 Jason Newcomb put on a black bowtie and combed his hair wet and then went down to the cellar and hanged himself with a cotton rope. My mother thought he had gone to work, and the bank thought he was taking a sick day. So he wasn't discovered until late that afternoon when my mother went down to the cellar to get some potatoes to peel for supper. I guess by then that his face had stopped being blue but that he had begun to be pretty much bothered by spiders. My mother, Jason Newcomb's wife, didn't like talking about it. She was twenty-seven at the time.

So she was the young Widow Newcomb then, for about five years. She was good-looking enough, too, in a churchy women's society sort of way, with pins tucked neat into her dark blond hair to keep it trim, and she wore high-necked collars with lace and kept her shoes polished. She still keeps herself up, even today out there in that new brick house at the edge of town where she lives with that faint red on her cheeks, which she expects me to kiss, and that blue on her eyes, and maybe that's because she fears that she will outlive Wilbur Cox too and will need to be ready to do it all over again, even in her eighties. I don't know why she bothers; she's in two or three different wills by now, but I know she didn't have Mr. Cox then and she didn't have my father yet either. During those five years that she was still the Widow Newcomb (and he apparently didn't leave her anything but a little gimcrack house in town), my mother kept her nose clean, brushed her blond hair the required one hundred strokes, applied cream to her face, went to the Methodist Episcopal Church, smiled, and during working hours she sold hats to the Holt ladies in Mrs. Kerst's Millinery Shop on Main Street, next door to the Gem Theater, opposite Doc Packer's storefront office. She was probably good at that too—selling hats, I mean. She certainly knew how to say what she thought you wanted to hear. She could even make it sound like something you yourself had thought of. My mother, at that time, must have been one of those women that other women call poor brave dears and then sigh and say My goodness.

Well, she should have been a gambler. She had the nerves for it and the face too. My mother should have been a poker player—or a politician. She might have done even better for herself at the card tables in Las Vegas or in the smoke-filled parlors of Denver. A town the size of Holt, with no more than a mere thousand rural types living here in 1925, had to be a waste of her particular talents, because my mother also knew how to get what she wanted. Behind that polished, perfumed surface, she was all ice and frozen stuff, which she would allow to melt a little bit if and when she saw something she wanted. That was true even if it meant she had to allow someone like my dad, John Roscoe, with his recent reputation for drinking and fighting and his thick rancher's hands, to muss her trim hair and to lift her widow's skirts. She knew he had all those cattle and she suspected that he was not the sort of man to hang himself with any cotton rope in any cellar that had spiders. So I don't believe she even cried afterwards or whimpered anything about respect. No, she would have just allowed the ice to melt in her a little bit, enough so that she could at least pretend that it was wonderful and then make him promise there would be a fall wedding—with the implication of course that there would be a lot more of the same where that came from. My mother was not stupid.

About my dad I can only guess—and he was not stupid either; you can't achieve what he did and then hold on to it too, even during the depression, when just about everything else around him was turning to dust and foreclosed mortgages, you can't do that and not have something more than just gas and sawdust separating your ears—I guess my dad must have been at the point where melted ice seemed preferable to warm beer and a fist in the face. Anyway, they got married in the fall of 1925, which would make Widow Newcomb thirty-two and my dad thirty-five, and then three years later, on March 9, 1928, I came along.

And like I say, I was a surprise to them. So it must have been Jason Newcomb who couldn't have babies that other time. Or at least together with my mother, he hadn't been able to make any. And I don't believe that was the reason why he hanged himself, either. Knowing my mother, I believe there must have been a few other reasons.

So ALMOST twenty years passed.

Prohibition came and went. The Great Depression came—and then lasted so long that people began to think of it as a normal condition. There was a civil war in Spain, a Roosevelt in the White House, a madman loose in Germany, and nothing happened to the Goodnoughs down the road from us. It was all the same slow gray there. Edith and Lyman went on doing all they had to do, and Roy continued waving his grim stumps.

My dad and Edith didn't see each other very much during those years, though I believe they still thought about one another a great deal. My dad had stopped helping with the harvest; Roy wouldn't have him on the place; Roy had begun to trade Lyman's sweat for someone else's help when it came time to cut wheat. So, whenever it happened that both my dad and Edith were in town and then by chance ran into one another on Main Street—and that was rare—they would stop and talk for a minute about nothing important. Only once or twice my dad asked her, "Are you all right?"

And she said, "Yes. Are you?"

And my dad said yes, he guessed he was.

Or—and this happened more often—if he was working within sight of the road and heard a car coming, he would straighten up, and if it was the Goodnoughs he would watch the car pass and notice Edith looking out the window, before the car and the three people in it got shut off from view by the boiling dust. Then my dad would go back to work and not say anything, but you could see that he had his mouth set hard like a horse will do with a curb bit.

Of course my mother didn't notice the Goodnoughs at all. She never visited them nor encouraged them to visit us. My mother had her own car and she always had the Methodist Church. So I was the only one of us who saw very much of the Goodnoughs then. When I was six or seven I started walking that half mile down to the Goodnoughs' house about once a week. I would help Edith hoe the garden or gather eggs or wipe dishes—things I hated to do at home and fought my mother about and wouldn't do until my dad made it plain to me on the seat of my pants. But Edith and I would talk a little bit.

"How's your mother, Sandy?" Edith would say.

"She's buying another dress."

"Your mother looks lovely in dresses."

"But she makes me go to church with her."

"Don't you like church?"

"No."

"Why not?"

"They make you put your gum in a napkin."

84

"Well," Edith would say, "you can chew gum here. We're not in church now."

"But I don't have any gum."

"Don't you, Sandy?"

"I chewed it all already. That's why."

"Well, I guess we'll have to see about that."

So the next time I would walk down to see Edith, she would have a pack of chewing gum in her apron pocket, and she would offer me a stick and take one herself. While we gathered eggs in the chicken coop, with the fierce-looking red chickens jerking their heads about and pecking another smaller chicken behind its head until there was a bare raw spot and all of them squirting that shiny green chicken squirt neat in a dollop onto the dirt, Edith and I would both chew our gum and see if we could make bubbles. Edith would be gathering eggs and I would try to help her, but I couldn't trust some of those red chickens until I had their heads pinned against the back of the roost box with a corncob. Most of the time, I would just hold the bucket for Edith.

"But look at this big brown egg," she would say.

"Is it heavy?"

"Yes, but notice these dark specks along here. They're almost the color of lavender."

"They look like a face," I'd say.

"Yes. And you're a funny old Sanders Roscoe. Aren't you?"

A little later, while we were in the kitchen, cleaning the bits of straw and the chicken squirt off the eggs, I'd say, "There. I did it."

"Did what?"

"Blew a bubble. Look." And I'd have a gum bubble about the size of a withered pea, perched on my mouth.

"Good for you," Edith would say then. "How's your daddy?"

So I saw quite a lot of Edith Goodnough during that time, and she always treated me in a way that made me want to keep going back there. My mother didn't think much of it, though. My mother wanted to know what I did down there all that time, what we talked about. She said they weren't our kind of people. But my dad told her that as long as I did my chores at home to let me be. He said I might learn something at the Goodnoughs'.

So about once a week I walked over to see Edith. I didn't see Lyman very often, though. He was always out in the field, disking or stacking hay. And I tried to avoid seeing Roy at all. I had his hands in some of my dreams during those years, and I would wake up in the dark in my room with those raw stumps still there, just behind my eyes. I could see them whenever I closed my eyes, so sometimes I didn't go back to sleep right away. His hands were all mixed up in that time for me. I didn't enjoy the sight of them.

But outside events finally caught up with the Goodnoughs too. By the close of the 1930s the madman loose in Germany had infected enough millions of other people with his madness that things over there had gone absolutely flat insane. When the butchery and betrayal carried over into the start of the 1940s people here in this country began to wonder what their part in it was going to have to be. There got to be a lot of talk about going to war, talk about taking action, and I suppose all that talk about doing something is what made it possible for Lyman.

The barn door that Lyman was waiting all that time to have left open for him, so he could squeeze through and take off running and never look back, did open then—not much; it was just a crack at first, but enough just the same for him to drive into town by himself one Saturday night, late in the summer of 1940, to drink beer in the Holt Tavern. He had his black suit on and a white shirt. He had a yellow tie knotted under his just-shaved chin. He opened the heavy door and stood there looking at all the people enjoying themselves in the smoky near-darkness.

"It was like he'd took the wrong turn somewheres," Wenzel Gerdts said. "Like he'd come up unexpected inside the women's outhouse. I mean he looked scared and interested at the same time."

Wenzel Gerdts was telling this story to my dad the following Saturday afternoon. I was there too with my dad, standing on Main Street in front of Wandorf's Hardware Store while my mother went across the street to shop for a hat. There were other groups of men standing all along the four blocks of stores on either side of the street. The men stood with one foot cocked up behind them against the brick storefronts or sat on the fenders of the cars parked at the curb, all of them talking in groups of three or four about the weather and corn and Roosevelt and war. Their wives were inside the stores, buying bits of elastic and brown cloth and a week's worth of groceries. They were talking too, of course, above the canned beans and the macaroni, beside the yard goods and the cash register, while here and there a little girl tugged at a skirt and a little boy peeked out like a shy country rabbit. The women went on talking in the stores and they were not in any hurry, because they were in town now and it was a Saturday afternoon in Holt in 1940.

But my dad and I were outside on the sidewalk listening to Wenzel Gerdts talk about Lyman Goodnough. Wenzel was a tall, stringy farmer dressed for the trip to town in clean overalls and he had a fresh cheekful of Red Man chewing tobacco at work in his jaw. As a kid of twelve I was almost as fascinated with the way Wenzel worked tobacco as I was with what he was saying about Lyman.

It was an art the way Wenzel could shoot that long brown spurt of his from where he stood leaning up against Wandorf's storefront, shoot it clean too, over across the sidewalk down tidy into the gutter, and shoot it every time into the same brown puddle, like he was not just showing off (like if I was doing it, like even if I could do it) but was actually trying to be kind to the folks who might have reason to step there. He would chew awhile and talk and then quick, shoot a neat brown spurt into the gutter, and afterwards lick a drop off his bottom lip, and then go on talking and chewing and not miss a beat.

And Wenzel was saying, "Why sure, the poor dumb geezer looked scared and interested at the same time. And don't you know I felt kind of sorry for him? Here's Lyman Goodnough that's been out there on that farm all them years with the hot sweat running down into his pants, and now he's somehow turned up inside the Holt Tavern on a Saturday night and he don't know what to do with hisself."

So Wenzel said he waved Lyman over to the booth where he was sitting with Harry Barnes and a couple of other men, playing poker and drinking tap beer from a pitcher. They poured Lyman a beer and he tasted it, but he apparently didn't like the taste of it much, because he set the glass down and looked around at the faces watching him as if he was a kid at school and they were waiting to see whether he could detect the dog manure they had put in his buttermilk.

"He probably hadn't never tasted beer before," my dad said.

"Most likely," Wenzel said. "It ain't like drinking orange soda pop."

But Lyman drank his glass of beer finally, without tasting it any more than necessary, just throwing it down quick like he was taking cod liver oil or prune juice. Wenzel

Gerdts poured him another glassful, and Lyman drank it the same way, with both hands on the glass.

"But he ain't no kid," Wenzel said. "And I ain't no nursemaid, neither."

So Wenzel poured him one more. He threw that one down too, with his Adam's apple snapping hard above the yellow tie. So by this time Lyman had drunk three of their beers, and about all the profit they had to show for it was that Lyman's eyes had begun to look like they were glass marbles.

But glass marbles must have been enough for Harry Barnes, a bald-headed man of fifty-some and the best poker player in Holt County. Harry studied Lyman's eyes for a minute, and then said, "Boys, I believe Lyman's ready. Deal him in."

"But he didn't know how to play poker, did he?" my dad said.

"No," Wenzel said. "I had to show him."

"Then he got a good taste of that too," my dad said. "How much money did you and Harry Barnes take off him?"

"Now wait a minute," Wenzel said. He shot that quick neat spurt of his over into the gutter and licked the drop off. "It wasn't like that," he said. "Sure we was playing for money—a nickel ante with a dime bump—because Harry Barnes ain't going to play for matchsticks, is he?"

"Not unless they're gold matchsticks," my dad said.

"Sure," Wenzel said. "But it wasn't like you think it was. I tried to explain it to him—what a ace is and about pairs and full houses and straight flushes. But goddamn it, he just don't get it."

"So what you're saying is," my dad said, and I could see he was smiling in his eyes. "You're saying you ain't going to tell us how much money you took off him."

"Now, damn it," Wenzel said. "That ain't either what

I'm saying. I'm saying I tried to explain it to him but he just don't get it. He keeps asking me things like how come a flush'll take a straight, or how come three deuces is better than four cards even when them four cards is two aces and two kings. What in hell was I supposed to tell him then? If I started talking percentages, we was going to be there all night and never get no cards played. Let alone get any money to change hands."

"Okay," my dad said. "So what'd you do? Because you already said how he played poker."

"That's right," Wenzel said. "Lyman played poker. He played poker all right. And that's just the damn hell of it. Call it just a middle-aged farm boy's dumb luck that never had time to play cards before, or say it's because Harry Barnes finally wrote it down for him on one of them barroom napkins. Because that's what Harry done: he wrote it all down for him, all that poker knowledge down there in black ink on a paper napkin. Why hell, even somebody that never played poker before in his life, let alone a hand of whist or old maids, even somebody as green as Lyman is is bound to win if he can just manage to get Harry Barnes to write it all down for him on a Holt Tavern napkin. And the only thing that seemed to bother him was he hadn't drawed no royal flush yet."

"You mean he won some money then," my dad said.

"Won hell," Wenzel said. "Won hell—he won the first five hands he played and he was still drinking our beer."

"Well sir," my dad said. "I guess old Roy Goodnough did you and Harry Barnes a favor keeping Lyman buried out there all these years. You might have to stay home at nights."

"It might be less taxing," Wenzel said. "It surely might." Then he laughed and spat into the gutter again but didn't snap it off clean enough, so that a brown spit string hung from his bottom lip. He wiped it off with his hand and smeared it onto his pants cuff.

"But how long'd Lyman stay there?" my dad said. "How long did you and Harry Barnes let him pocket your nickles?"

"About five dollars' worth," Wenzel said. "And that wasn't near long enough."

Because, according to Wenzel, after Lyman had won the first five hands of poker he played, it began to appear that he was getting bored. It was as if he was saying to himself, So this here is the game of poker that I been hearing so much about all these years. Well, shoot now, it ain't so much. It ain't a tall what it's cracked up to be. So I reckon I'll just see what else there is to do on a Saturday night. And what Lyman did was, he stood up in the middle of a hand that had already been dealt and he went over to one of the waitresses. It didn't seem to make any difference to him that the men in the booth were trying to play cards and that Harry Barnes had finally managed to deal himself three aces and a king of spades. Because when Harry called him back, asked him where in the hell he thought he was going, all Lyman said was, "Oh. You want your money back. Here, you can have it. I don't want it none."

"So he give it all back," my dad said.

"Every dime," Wenzel said. "Dumped it all out on the table."

"Well, it ain't like planting corn or stacking hay," my dad said. "He hadn't sweat enough for it."

"Sure," Wenzel said. "Only you ain't played poker with Harry Barnes."

"Just once," my dad said. "I could see it wasn't gambling. But then you was saying how Lyman went over to some waitress."

"Agnes Wilson," Wenzel said. "He went over to Agnes Wilson, that big hefty gal with pink hair and them big legs that some boys claim is soft as pillows. Anyway, she ain't been working at the tavern long—come over here from Norka when her husband run off to Denver with some telephone operator. She's got that kid that got hisself kicked out of school for playing with ladies' corsets."

Then for the first time that afternoon I said something. I had been listening to them talk and watching Wenzel spit tobacco, but now they were talking about something I knew about. I said, "No, Mr. Gerdts, I believe it was garter belts."

Wenzel Gerdts looked at me as if he was shocked, as if someone had come up behind him and buzzed him with a cow prodder. He seemed to have forgotten that all that time I had been standing there with them in front of Wandorf's Hardware Store. It was as if I was a stray calf that had suddenly decided to speak, even if all I had to say was: "Garter belts."

"Was it?" Wenzel said, looking at me. "I heard it was corsets."

"No, I believe it was garter belts all right," I said. "He was making slingshots with them and selling them to kids for a nickel, three for a dime."

"Did you buy one?" my dad said.

"No, sir," I said. "The elastic was all pooped out. It was too stretched."

My dad started laughing then, and Wenzel Gerdts choked a little on his Red Man chewing tobacco. I didn't know what I had said that was funny, but I grinned and felt pleased that I had been able to make my dad laugh. He didn't laugh much, not openly or loudly. The amusement would show in his eyes, but I don't remember him laughing very often. He laughed that time, though, and maybe because I was the cause of it is the reason why I remember that afternoon so well.

Anyway, when Wenzel stopped choking, he took a silver half-dollar out of his overall pocket and gave it to me. My dad said I could keep it, and Wenzel said, "Now you can buy you a slingshot that ain't already had the stretch pooped out of it."

"Yes, sir," I said. "But not right now. I want to stay here."

"That's right, son," my dad said. "I believe Wenzel's about done storytelling anyway."

"Sure," Wenzel said. "There ain't much more to tell."

But before Wenzel Gerdts went on, he stood there and chewed a while. All along Main Street men were still talking in groups, and here and there a woman was carrying a box of groceries out to a car parked diagonally at the curb. While we waited for Wenzel to continue, a yellow dog came sniffing along the cars, wetting hubcaps and tires, until a man in a straw hat yelled at it, then the dog looked up and trotted across the street and began to work its way back up the block towards the railroad tracks, wetting wheels as it went.

Anyway, after a minute or two Wenzel seemed to have worked his wad to the right pitch and he went on. He told us that when Lyman stood up from the booth where he had been drinking their beer and taking their money, he walked over and stood directly in front of Agnes Wilson. He didn't say anything to her, though. He just stood there hang faced and bashful. Of course he still had that yellow tie on and that black Sunday suit, so the only change in him from when he first put foot inside the tavern door was that his eyes had turned to glass marbles, or more like bloody egg yolks now, because by this time he had drunk more than just three beers. But again, it was as if he was starting over; he didn't know what to do with himself after he had somehow made the first effort. But that didn't seem to matter this time either: Agnes Wilson figured it out for both of them. She said something to him and he nodded, then she set her bar tray down and took his hands and showed him where to put them, one on her soft waist and the other in her white hand, and they began to dance.

"That is," Wenzel said, "if you can call what Lyman was doing with her dancing."

"Why?" my dad said. "Couldn't Harry Barnes write that down for him too? How to dance, I mean."

"I suppose Harry could," Wenzel said. "But Harry didn't need to. Agnes was doing everything anybody needed to do. She had him sucked up against her like he was a fifty-dollar bill."

So Lyman must have felt that he had arrived in heaven. He was on the dance floor at the Holt Tavern with his face hidden in Agnes Wilson's pink hair. Her full, ripe body was pressing him all along his own, and he had dispensed with holding her hand. Both of his middle-aged bachelor arms were wrapped around her so that his white Sunday shirt cuffs showed bright against the black of her waitress dress where his hands rode snug above her heavy buttocks. When the dance band started up another song Agnes would shuffle Lyman around a little bit on the dance floor, but between songs they just stood there, waiting, not moving at all, while Lyman maintained the same clenching hold on her, like he didn't dare let go.

"Like they was two dogs that was locked," Wenzel said. "You should of saw it."

"How long did it go on?" my dad said.

"I wasn't counting the dances," Wenzel said. "And I

don't guess Lyman was neither. He was too satisfied to do something like count."

But it must have gone on long enough that an hour or two passed. Agnes Wilson didn't seem to mind it, though. Occasionally she patted him on the head or tickled a finger in his ear, and now and then she winked at the other people in the tavern, who didn't seem to mind it either; they were all going up to the bar to get their own drinks. They were slapping one another on the back and congratulating themselves as if they were all in attendance at some significant event. I suppose it was an event too: Lyman Goodnough was enjoying himself.

"Until, bang," Wenzel said. "All in a sudden, he's gone. He's took off."

"Wait a minute," my dad said. "You mean he got bored with that too? That don't leave him much to graze on. He's already used up beer and poker and women."

"No," Wenzel said. "No, I don't guess you could say bored exactly. He just stopped squeezing Agnes and left."

"How come?"

"That's what we wanted to know," Wenzel said.

So after Lyman took off, Wenzel told us that Harry Barnes called Agnes over to their booth where, between poker hands, they had been watching it all. Agnes came over and leaned against the table. She held the bar tray behind her and pushed her ample front out towards the men in the booth.

"What become of your boyfriend?" Harry said.

"Ain't he cute?" Agnes said.

"Yeah," Harry said. "He's cute. But what happened to him?"

"Darned if I know," Agnes said. "All I know is, after that last song he asks me what the time is, and I tell him, 'Honey, it's early yet. Only a quarter of eleven.' And then he says to me, 'What time do you lock up?' And I say, 'Not till midnight, honey. We got lots of time left.' And then he says something strange, he says, 'No, we don't. I can't wait no longer.' "

"And that's when he took off?" Harry said.

"That's it," Agnes said. "Right then he left, without so much as good-bye or thank you, kindly."

"Well," Harry said. "I wouldn't take it too personal. You was doing everything you could."

"I know it," Agnes said. "But wasn't he cute?"

Then Wenzel Gerdts stopped talking. He removed the tobacco from his cheek and examined it as if there was something there that might explain Lyman's leaving. The wad of Red Man was white and stringy looking, used up. He tossed it into the gutter, where it sopped up the brown puddle like a sponge. Across the street I could see my mother come out of a store with a hatbox under her arm.

"So you don't know why he left so sudden," my dad said.

"No, sir," Wenzel said. "We never found out. I guess he just had to take himself a pee and he couldn't hold it no longer."

WELL, I don't know that Lyman Goodnough was ever in his life what you might call cute. At least by 1940 he was not. By then, he was a gaunt middle-aged farmer, a little stooped over, and his hair was going. But of course it wasn't his physical appearance that Agnes Wilson was talking about, and as for Wenzel Gerdts's explanation of his sudden exit from the tavern that night, I don't believe either that it was just a matter of Lyman's having to relieve a full bladder. I think it was more that Lyman knew—and was able to remember despite the beer (he had certainly lived enough years in that house with his father to know very well and to remember too)—that when he got home there was going to be hell to pay, and the longer he stayed out the more of it there was going to be.

So he must have paid for it. Maybe not that night when he drove their old car into the yard and parked it in front of the picket fence, but at least the next morning during breakfast, since even Roy must have felt differently about waiting for a forty-one-year-old boy to come home from the tavern than he did about waiting for a twenty-five-year-old girl to return from a night at the movies. It wasn't quite so urgent; he could wait till morning to give Lyman hell. But in the morning, then, Lyman must have had to sit there with his head pounding and his mouth tasting something that resembled pig slop, while the old man, his father, drank and in between drinks said something mean and crazy like, "So you ain't learned yet."

"Learned what?"

"That if you're ever going to mount to a goddamn, you can't stay out all Saturday night diddling."

· 6 ·

But at least Lyman had accomplished that first trial run. He had sampled beer and women and he had had his first real taste of escape. It must have been heady stuff to him. In the tavern that night he had actually done those things himself that before he had only heard about other men doing. Even his father's ridiculous breakfast sermon the next morning must have been satisfying to him: it tied the knot; it closed the circle; it made everything seem bigger and better. To have to endure a lecture about diddling away a Saturday night at a time when his head was still pounding from the beer he had drunk the night before and while the fried eggs he had just managed to get down were threatening to come back up again—it made it all worth it; it was how you paid for having a good time. At forty-one Lyman was like a middle-aged teenager savoring his first hangover. But he didn't make another attempt to escape right away. Instead he went for more than a year on the memory of that first time. He went on working.

Then in the following year on a Sunday morning in December another outside event occurred that made it possible for Lyman to take off and not come back at all. Thousands of miles away something happened that was so explosive that it not only sank ships and killed men in the Pacific, it blew the door off the hinges of the Goodnough barn in Holt County, Colorado. I'm talking of course about Pearl Harbor.

Pearl Harbor was hell and tragedy for most Americans, but it was what Lyman Goodnough was waiting for. Now I don't mean that he would ever have hoped for something that murderous—he was desperate, damned desperate, but he wasn't bloodthirsty—and I'm not saying that he had any idea in the world that the thing he was waiting for, the thing he hoped would happen, would ever take the form it did, because he sure as hell wasn't any prophet either. Still it is true that he seemed to recognize almost immediately that Pearl Harbor was his ticket out, his open barn door. It was like the explosion in the waters of Hawaii was the pop of a starter's gun in a track meet. Lyman heard it, he was ready, and he took off running. He began a race that he wouldn't stop running until almost twenty years had passed and until he had seen half the cities in this country. My dad helped him.

In the middle of the night my dad put him on a train that was headed west. But that was later. That December Sunday in 1941, after morning chores, my dad and I sat at this same kitchen table and listened to the radio. It was exciting and it was awful. My dad said it was hell. But my mother went to church as usual. She put on a navy-blue dress and drove off in her new car to sing hymns and Christmas carols and to put her folded offering into the felt-muted plate that a gray usher passed among the pews. She prayed and afterwards she returned home to cook us a Sunday dinner of fried chicken and mashed potatoes as if nothing was wrong. I believe she spent the afternoon reading in the living room in a stuffed chair.

All the time, though, my dad and I listened to the radio. Between news bulletins we got out the world atlas and discovered the dots in the Pacific Ocean that meant Hawaii and with a ruler tried to figure the miles between Honolulu and Tokyo and between Tokyo and California. The news kept coming in on the radio, and it seemed to me that it was all happening right then, since I was only just hearing about it. I couldn't understand why anyone would want to bomb such a small speck on the ocean in our atlas—before that Sunday Pearl Harbor and naval installations hadn't existed for me: there weren't a lot of sailors in Holt County—but I could tell from my dad's face that something important was happening and what was happening was bad. My dad's face, more than the pitch of the broadcaster's voice, made it seem so. His face was hard set all day. It looked even worse than it did those times when he looked up and watched the Goodnoughs' car pass our house, passing on down the road into dust. He said that what we were hearing on the radio was the start of a war, a world war that now we in this country were going to have to be a part of. He hated it all. He only hoped that it would be over before I was old enough to be called to it.

Of course people in town were talking about it, too. All along Main Street in the poolhalls and the grocery stores they were talking about it, and much of the talk was crazy, wild, frantic nonsense, and it wasn't long before anything seemed possible to believe. The men in the bank and the beer drinkers in the tavern were even speculating that Hirohito would somehow drop down into Los Angeles and start marching up Sunset Boulevard to conquer Betty Grable: there was that kind of fear and excitement loose everywhere. So, with all that going on, I don't remember that we were very much surprised a couple nights later when long after we had gone up to bed and were sound asleep Lyman came and started knocking the holy bejesus out of our front door. My dad just got up and put his pants on and went downstairs to let Lyman in before he broke the door down.

I got up too and stood in the dim light at the top of the stairs to watch. I could see Lyman below in the front hallway; he had his heavy overcoat on and he was wearing his winter cap with the corduroy earflaps. Beside him on the floor was a metal suitcase with a belt strapped around it. My dad and he were talking, and though I couldn't hear what they were saying, I could tell that Lyman was more than a little excited. He began to tie and untie the strings on the earflaps of his cap, and he was shifting from one foot to the other like he had to use the toilet. In my goofy sleepiness I wondered whether that was the reason why he had come over—to piss in our pot—except that wouldn't have explained why he had brought a suitcase. Then my mother was there, too, beside me at the top of the stairs.

"Sanders," she said. "Go back to bed."

"It's Lyman Goodnough."

"I don't care who it is. I want you to get dressed or to go back to bed."

My mother had a maroon robe on with matching open-toed slippers. Her blond hair, treated so that it stayed blond, looked freshly combed.

"Lyman's seen striped pajamas before," I said.

"That is not the point."

"Here comes dad."

My dad came up the stairs and met us at the top landing. His face and neck and hands were dark tanned to the shirt line; against the rest of him they looked purple in the dim light. He had black hair on his bare chest and he was smiling.

"So the vigilantes are up too," he said.

"This is not the time for your jokes," my mother said. "What does that man want?"

"You mean Lyman Goodnough."

"I know who it is. What's wrong with him?"

"Nothing particular. He's just discovered he has something like a backbone."

"And what's that supposed to mean?"

"He wants a lift into town."

My mother looked at my dad as if he was talking utter nonsense, as if she still thought he was trying to be funny. "Now?" she said. "At this hour? Whatever for?"

"He wants to catch the train. He's leaving."

"But that's ridiculous. He can't do anything. Where can he go?"

"He can go west, I suppose," my dad said. "That's the direction the train is headed in."

"West," she said. It sounded foolish and obscene in her mouth. "Well, I hope you had the sense to tell him no."

"No, I told him I would. I come upstairs to get my shirt and boots on."

"Are you insane?"

"Probably," my dad said. "And I'm getting cold standing here talking about it." He turned to go back to their bedroom.

"Dad," I said. "I want to go."

"Get dressed then."

"He's not going. You're not going," my mother said.

But she wasn't even looking at me. She followed my dad into the bedroom, and I followed her down the hallway and stood in the door. My dad went over to the closet and took a flannel shirt off a hanger. She watched him as if it was a conspiracy against her, as if he and Lyman Goodnough had decided to get up a plot. With one hand fisted at the neck of her maroon robe, she watched him unbutton his pants and begin to tuck his shirt in.

"Will you tell me," she said, "why that man can't at least drive himself to town?"

"Yes, but you aren't going to like it."

"Of course not. I don't like any of this. But I assume you mean it's something more than just the fact that he can't get his own car started."

"He never tried it," my dad said. "He's afraid if he starts the car it'll wake the old man."

"Oh," she said. "Well, that does make sense, doesn't it. He can't wake his own father but it's perfectly all right to wake us."

"I said you weren't going to like it."

"Yes, you did say so and you are right about that. But what about her? What about his sister? I suppose she's afraid to disturb the poor old man too."

My dad stopped dressing then and looked at my mother. He wasn't happy. "Leave her out of this," he said.

"Or hasn't she learned how to drive a car at night yet? I've never seen her driving a car at night."

"Keep your mouth off her," he said. "You don't know what you're talking about."

"Yes, I do," she said. "I know more than you think I do."

"No, you don't," he said. "You don't know the half of it."

"All right," my mother said, looking at me in the doorway. "I've had enough for one night. I'm going to bed."

"That's right," my dad said. "I think that's a good idea."

"And you are too," she said to me.

"No, I'm not," I said. "I'm going along. Dad, you said—"

"I told you to get dressed," he said.

"No. That's definitely out. He's not going."

"It won't hurt him."

"He's not going," she said. "He has school tomorrow. He's no Edison, or haven't you noticed?"

"It won't hurt him. And he can still make school."

"I don't want him to go with you. I forbid him to go."

"I believe he's going, though."

"All right," she said. "All right, go then."

But she wasn't looking at me. She was watching my dad. It didn't have anything to do with me anymore—if it ever did.

"Go," she said. "You may as well get yourself involved in this too. You're just like him. You don't care what I think. Why do you bother to ask?"

But she didn't go back to bed yet and she wasn't finished talking. She had more to say to my dad. From their bedroom down the hall I could hear her talking to him while I got out of my pajamas. Her voice was going on and on with steel in it, like she was some lawyer summing up the defense in a bad case, and even though by 1941 it must have been an old defense and an old case, she did not sound tired of it. There was all that steel and ice mixed up in it. But my dad wasn't saying anything. I could hear just the sound of him sitting down on the edge of the bed to put his boots on and the noise on the wood floor as he stamped into them. Then I was dressed and out in the hallway again ready to go downstairs, and I heard him say something to her. It sounded like two words, and they must have been enough, or too much maybe, because after he said them it was only silence coming out of their bedroom. I went downstairs.

Lyman was still standing in the front hallway. The strings of his earflaps were tied tight in a double knot under his chin pulling the bill of his cap down low on his forehead like he was expecting heavy weather, and he was standing there holding his suitcase.

"You coming along too?" he said. "For the send-off?"

"Yes, sir."

I put my coat and stocking cap on, and we stood facing

one another, waiting for my dad. We examined the rug and each other's feet.

"At least," Lyman said after a while, "at least it don't look like it wants to snow."

"No, sir."

"I hope it don't," he said. "Not anyhow."

The rug was an oval braided one made of bright rags, and Lyman's shoes were his best, those black polished shoes he must have worn to the Holt Tavern a year earlier. They had sand on them now from his walking the half mile to our house. The sand was getting on my mother's rug.

"Well," Lyman said. "How's the sixth grade?"

"What?"

"The sixth grade. At your school in town."

"I'm in the eighth grade," I said.

"Eighth," he said. "Well, don't never quit."

"No, sir."

"Take me," he said. "You never know when you might need all your education."

"Yes, sir."

"That's right," he said. Then like he'd been pondering this question for a good long time, he said, "What's the capital of California?"

"San Francisco."

"That's right," he said. "You see?—that's what I'm talking about."

My dad came down the stairs then and put his coat on, and we went outside to the pickup. It was cloudy and just flat dark, but it wasn't going to snow; it was too cold to snow, and there wasn't that heaviness in the air that comes before snowfall. I sat between my dad and Lyman in the pickup with the gearshift between my knees and the light from the speedometer showing yellow on my dad's face.

Nobody said anything for a while. The gravel on the dirt road kicked up underneath the fenders, and then we were on the highway, where there was the sound of the snow tires on the blacktop. Outside the window the headlights picked up the brush and tumbleweeds caught along the fence line beside the highway, and beyond the fence line the country was all dark, with the few trees standing up leafless and showing even darker against Owens's white house on the right when we passed it and again two miles later against Wheelers's yellow house on the left as we passed it too, driving north towards town. There were no yard lights on anywhere in the country.

Then, before we made town, my dad said to Lyman, "I don't suppose you thought to tell Edith you're leaving."

"Why sure," Lyman said. "She knows." He patted his coat pocket. "She packed me some sandwiches. I got them right here with me."

"What does she say about it?"

"Well, I'll tell you," Lyman said. He leaned forward to look past me at my dad. "She says for at least one of us to get away. That's what she told me last night."

"Jesus Christ," my dad said. "When's she going to quit?"

"And I'm going to write her about it," Lyman said. "Edith says for me to see all the sights I can and taste pleasure."

"Well, see that you do it."

"I will. You can bet on that."

"I'm talking about writing her," my dad said.

"Oh," he said, and sat back again to look ahead down the road. He brought one of his big red winter-chafed hands up to play with the belt strapped around the metal suitcase on his lap.

When we drove into Holt all the houses were dark and the big globes suspended above the corners on Main Street were off. I didn't see anything moving. No one was at the depot either; Lyman was going to have to buy his ticket once he got on the train. My dad stopped the pickup beside the cobblestone platform, and though we were almost an hour early, Lyman got out with his suitcase under his arm and stood to face east up the tracks. My dad and I stayed in the pickup with the motor and heater running and watched him wait. Once while we watched him, my dad said, "Well, this is a piece of history that won't appear in no history books." But he was talking more to himself than he was to me.

Finally when the train got there, waving its beam light back and forth above the tracks and making the ground vibrate, we got out to say good-bye. In the light of the conductor's lantern I could see that Lyman's eyes were bleary from the cold and that there was a drip of watery mucus at the tip of his nose. Lyman looked cold and scared. My dad shook his hand, and Lyman patted me on the shoulder, and then in his long overcoat and his best shoes and with his corduroy earflaps tied tight under his chin, he mounted the steps to the train, and that was the last we saw of him. That was the last anyone in Holt County saw of him for almost twenty years. Including Edith.

LYMAN WAS forty-two when he left on that west-bound train, and as I recall his plan involved joining the U.S. Army. The train stopped in Denver, but he didn't get off there and he didn't get off in Cheyenne either, nor in Salt Lake, nor in any other place, until the train had finally stopped for good in Los Angeles to turn around and come back east. I suppose he wanted to be sure there were enough mountain ranges and enough Mormons and mesquite between him and that old stump-armed man to prevent himself from being dragged back and put to work again. Because once he had actually managed to escape he sure as hell wasn't going to take any chances; he wasn't ever going to sweat his overalls plowing sand again, not if he could help it, not if it was just a matter of putting enough miles between himself and that sand. And in the confusion of December 1941, he had that ready excuse: he was going to join the army to fight the Nips and the Huns—never mind that he had never fought a thing before in his life.

I gather, though, that it didn't take him long to discover that, as much as everybody was watching the sky for Hirohito to come drifting down out of some imperial orange-and-red cloud, still, the army recruiters were not about ready to sign on any middle-aged farm boy from Holt, Colorado, even if he was as eager as a mongrel bitch in heat. The army recruiters weren't that desperate yet. So I guess he tried the navy next, and being a little smarter now he no doubt lied about his age, but he wasn't the fuzzy-cheeked piece of dough the navy was looking for, either; not that he wasn't used to being treated like a dog, you understand, they just couldn't be sure he could learn their new tricks. So after the navy I don't guess he even tried the marines, because I know for certain that he hired on instead to work in a Los Angeles airplane factory. And he stayed there in the factory until the war was over, working his daily shift, pulling levers or grinding gears or running rivets and not talking to anybody much but just doing the work they gave him to do. During lunch break he sat off at the edges of the mechanics and welders where he could watch them and listen to their talk, but he never complained, like they did, because he figured he knew of at least one thing that was worse than this. All the time, anyway, he was saving his money so that when MacArthur returned to take that cob pipe out of his mouth and to sign those surrender papers on board that boat in the Pacific,

Lyman already had more than enough money saved up to buy his first new Pontiac automobile.

Then he took off again. His new Pontiac had a full tank of gas; he had seen to the air in the spare tire, and he spent the next sixteen years doing what he said his sister had told him to do: he saw the sights and tasted pleasure. For a half a year to as much as a year and a half he stayed in one city after another. He paid his rent on time for a succession of cheap rooms upstairs over some pawnshop or dentist's office. He worked at a minimum wage pushing cement up construction ramps or pumped gas or shoveled ballast under railroad ties. Afterwards in the evenings he drank beer in dark bars that had booths along one wall and ranks of bottles in front of chipped mirrors on the other. And about twice a month he would follow the big hips of an aging barmaid up the stairs to his own rented room, where he would release her from her girdle and then sweat on her while she watched past his moving shoulder to see how soon the cracked plaster on the ceiling was going to fall and smother them. Meanwhile, of course, he bought more Pontiacs and he kept moving. Whenever the color of his last car didn't just suit him anymore, he would buy another new one, and whenever it seemed that he had seen what there was of Boise or Omaha worth seeing, he would take off and drive to Dubuque or Oklahoma City or Memphis. But he never came home again.

Nobody out here, not even Edith, saw him all that time. I know that for a fact. But I also know, since I've seen every damned one of them, that he did send Edith at least one picture postcard each year with a color likeness on it of the biggest skyscraper there was in whatever city he happened to be stopped in right then. I also know, because I've seen them too—good Christ, yes—that every year come Christmas he sent her a package of twenty-dollar bills tied up with a red bow. But, like I say, he never sent himself home.

He didn't even come home when Roy finally died and stopped fouling good air in 1952. Maybe Lyman didn't know the old man was dead, not in time anyway to come back for the funeral, even assuming he had wanted to. He wouldn't have been easy to locate. Edith would have had to send word to the last address scribbled on the last picture postcard and hope he was still there, since apparently he never left any forwarding address when he moved on, and besides, the only return address he ever used at any time was just general delivery, and that without bothering to pick up his mail very often, because why should he?

Or consider this: maybe Lyman was afraid to come back even then. Maybe he thought until the old man was a good nine years dead with the ground heavy sunk and filled over him and the grass growing thick on it, that it still wasn't safe, that somehow the old bastard's ghost or spirit or voice, whatever, might still be active enough to call him back, lecture him about Saturday-night diddling, and then make him stay there to rake hay and plow sand. And if that was the reason, then you could say Lyman was right to stay away even then, because you couldn't be real sure the old son of a bitch was dead even when you were actually standing there in front of his coffin and saw him lying there like a slab of mean yellow granite. With his head on a satin pillow he still didn't look any thinner or stiffer or any less like a ramrod than he did when he was supposed to be alive. His eyes were closed; that was all. That and the fact that those red stumps of his sticking out beneath his white shirt cuffs had finally quit twitching and waving.

Anyway, whatever the reason, Lyman stayed away for nine years more after the old man was dead and buried deep inside that little cemetery, making it two Goodnough headstones so far there beside Otis Murray's cornfield two miles east of Holt, and then he did come back. He was a little bit tired; his eyes were a little dazed from the sights he had seen, and I suppose there were other parts of him that were a little jaded too from the pleasure he had tasted, but he was still all right, more or less. He was still of some use to his sister. For a while.

ONLY, MEANWHILE, there were those twenty years for her to wait through and to endure. And how did she manage that? What was she doing all that time Lyman stayed away and bought Pontiacs and sent her picture postcards? Nothing.

Well, no, not nothing exactly. She didn't just do nothing all that time. But she sure God didn't go traveling off across the North American continent, either. She didn't even go those seven miles into Holt very often. She stayed home. Jesus, that's about all you can say: Edith Goodnough stayed home. And if you figure it up, if you do your arithmetic from those chiseled dates in the cemetery, then you know Edith was seventeen when her mother died in 1914; she was fifty-five when the old man died in 1952; and she was sixty-four when Lyman finally returned in 1961. It amounts to a lifetime of staying home.

When Lyman left for L.A. and for what he thought was going to be at least a good hitch in the army, it got worse almost immediately. Edith was still doing all the work at home she always did: she was still milking cows, separating milk, cooking meals, washing dishes, and—every day, don't forget—still cutting Roy's meat into bites and filling the buttonholes of his shirt with buttons once he had pushed his stumps through the sleeves. But in the following spring, at a time when Lyman was already beginning to save that airplane-factory money of his and to contemplate Pontiacs, Edith got more to do.

My dad and I first saw it one morning from the gravel road beside the Goodnough cornfield on our way to check cattle. I was driving, I remember, and feeling full of myself because I was actually behind the wheel and out on the road itself, not just turning circles in the barnyard or cutting eights in the horse pasture. So I suppose I had already ground through first and second gear and was abusing high—yes, I was flat pounding along the country road, imagining myself to be Holt County's special gift to Ford transmissions—when my dad said:

"Goddamn it, slow down. Stop this son of a bitch."

I thought, Now what have I done? Have I busted something? I stopped the pickup but it wasn't me. My dad was looking out the window at the Goodnoughs' cornfield.

"Now what do you call that?" he said. "What in the goddamn hell's he think he's doing?"

Because there was a tractor out there in the field with a one-way disk behind it. The tractor was coming toward us from across the corn stubble, and as it got closer I could see what my dad meant. There were two heads sticking up behind the body of the tractor, one just visible above it and the other quite a lot higher.

"Goddamn him," my dad said. "Now maybe he'll manage to fall off and get more than just his fingers mangled. Which I don't care, but I suppose she still does. Jesus Christ."

The tractor came on toward us, grew larger, louder, and then it was obvious that it was Edith driving it. She had her straw gardening hat on and she was sitting there on the tractor seat behind the exhaust stack looking no bigger than a ten-year-old girl. She had both hands clenched tight on the steering wheel, and the disk furrows behind her were as straight as she could make them. And of course it was the old man standing up beside her. We could see him waving his arms, pointing those damn blunt stumps past her head like he was some kind of live Halloween scarecrow and her straw hat was just some yellow corn shock. It made you sick.

When they closed on the end of the field near us, we could hear him yelling at her too: "Brake it. Brake it. Now turn it. Can't you turn this thing?"

My dad opened the pickup door. I thought he was going to get out. "I ought to killed him when I had the chance," he said. "By God, I will yet. The dirty son of a bitch."

But somehow Edith got the tractor turned and got the disk headed back out across the field. As she was making the turn she had looked up once, quick, toward my dad in the pickup, not for help, I don't think, but like she was still saying, *Yes, I know. But it's okay; it's all right*, and then she was past us, going away from us, with the disk rolling up dirt and dust behind her and the noise of the tractor decreasing in the widening distance between her and us.

We watched them out into the middle of the field. Then my dad finally spoke again. "Did you see the belt?" he said.

"What belt?"

"That belt contraption he had buckled across behind him. Between the fenders."

"What for?"

"So he wouldn't fall off. So he could stand there and work his arms. So he could at least protect hisself even if he didn't give a good piss in hell about her."

"I didn't see it," I said.

"Never mind. You saw enough. Start this pickup."

So I jerked the pickup into gear again and drove away toward the cow pasture. My dad wasn't paying any attention to how I was driving anymore; he didn't watch the speedometer. He was watching out the window, and every once in a while I noticed him sort of shake his head as if he was coming out of a hard sleep, as if he was trying to change what he had seen.

But it didn't change. It went on like that all spring. Edith and the old man finished the disking, and then the drilling too. At our place my dad got more and more silent; at the dinner table my mother would tell him what was happening in town, serve him the latest Holt County gossip with our new garden peas, or she would detail for him her complaints about the scandalous manner in which Mrs. Vince Higgims was leading Rebecca Circle at the Methodist Church, but he wouldn't respond. He wouldn't even make his familiar joke about what he called her church gang, her heifer herd for Jesus. I doubt that he was listening to her at all; there was something else, something more important, and it was playing nonstop in his head, and he was concentrated on that.

Then in the long days of July, in that dry heat, he woke up. He discovered that now Roy had begun to have Edith cut hay too. The sun rose at five and set at nine, and most of that time she had been out there under it while he stood over her on the tractor and told her where to turn one minute and when to turn the next and in between times told her how fast. That evening my dad called me over to him, held me hard by the front of my overalls.

"Listen to me," he said. "Are you listening? I want that stopped."

"Yes, sir."

"I want you to go over there in the morning and drive that tractor yourself. Can you do that?"

"Yes, but—"

"Just a minute; I never said it was going to be easy. But you do it. I'd do it myself, only I'd have to kill him first. Understand?"

"All right," I said. "Yes."

His eyes were looking hard at me; I couldn't see anything else. There was something awful in his eyes, hurt and anger, I suppose, but something more too, something further back.

"And, son, if he says one word to you . . . if that miserable cock says just one word—"

"I know," I said.

"Okay," he said. "I'll tell your mom to pack you a good lunch."

He let go of my overalls and I went in to bed.

Early the next morning I was waiting beside the Goodnoughs' tractor when Edith and Roy came out to start work. Edith smiled at me. "Why, here's Sandy," she said.

But the old man wasn't smiling. He was looking at me like I was a form of cutworm or a new strain of corn blight. "What do you want?" he said.

"Nothing. I came over to help out."

"Oh? And who asked you to help out?"

"Nobody."

"That's right: nobody. So you better just hightail it back to home."

"I can drive the tractor," I said.

"You can talk manure too," he said.

"I can, though. I do at home."

"Hah," he said. "Straddled on somebody's pants leg. Or diddling the wheel out in the machine shed."

"No. In the field. By myself."

"Sandy doesn't mean any harm," Edith said. "Leave him alone."

"He's a runt," the old man said. "His ears is still wet."

"At least let him try. He walked all the way over here."

"It would speed things up," I said. "Maybe it would free Edith to do something else. Miss Goodnough."

I gave her a look and she winked at me. "I *am* way behind on the canning," she said.

The old man looked at her and then looked over at the garden behind the wire fence. The beans and peas were beginning to wrinkle on the vines; the radishes had gone to seed, and the whole garden needed hoeing.

"Go ahead, Sandy," Edith said. "Climb up."

"Not so damn fast. I ain't said so yet." He studied me for a minute while he rubbed a stump along the bristle on his jaw. "How do I know you can cut hay?" he said. "I never seen you."

"I cut some of ours last year."

"Don't lie to me."

"I'm not. Ask anybody."

"Hah."

But he studied me some more, examining me now as if I was maybe a little less dangerous than corn blight; more like I was a pissing yellow dog or a talking jackrabbit. He spat between his feet and covered it with one of his shoes. "Drive around this yard once," he said.

I got up on the tractor, an old John Deere, started it, and made a slow circle in the yard in front of the house and then stopped again beside them.

"So," he said, "let's see if you can find reverse."

So I backed up and came forward to the same spot.

"It still don't make enough of a show," he said. "See them cheat weeds over there east of the barn?"

"Yes."

"See can you cut them weeds without chopping no hole in my barn."

So I drove over to the barn, lowered the sickle bar, and mowed the weeds beside the foundation, the section blades cutting them off low to the ground. There was a snarl of

116

rusty fence wire in the weeds, but I managed to see it in time. Then I came back to Edith and Roy.

"Found the wire, did you?"

"Yes, but I missed it," I said.

He looked at the sickle bar for tangled wire or new nicks. "Well, ain't you the big britches," he said.

"Stop it," Edith said. "He's already proved that he can drive a tractor better than I ever will. And probably as good as you could when you were his age."

"I drove horses," Roy said, and made a coughing sound that was his idea of a laugh. "That's what you know about it."

"Still," she said, "you know what I mean. I'm going to start picking peas."

She turned and walked away from him. She could be firm with him, even harsh with him occasionally, when she had to—over the little things. But she wouldn't ever leave him; she just would not allow herself that much freedom. He watched her walk away, a small fine woman in a clean work dress that was still filled out in the right places, even if those places were never going to receive the full attention or the appreciation they deserved. At the picket gate she turned and called to me: "Sandy, you can eat lunch with me."

Then she closed the gate and went up the steps into the house. The old man stood staring at the back door. He didn't seem to be able to grasp that she had gone, disappeared, refused him. The door was shut. Finally, as if he expected some sudden help to descend out of the clear blue, he looked at the sky, then he looked at the tractor where I was, then at his hands, where there sure as hell was not any help. "Women," he said. "That's what I got left to me—a woman and a smart-ass neighbor kid." He spat into the gravel again. "Hot damn."

But the old buzzard had no other recourse. He climbed

onto the tractor with me and I buckled the belt behind him. "Boy," he said, "what the hell you waiting on? Drive me to the field."

We drove out of the yard down the wagon track to the hayfield. The old man stood spread legged and swaying behind me, leaning against the belt when the tractor jolted in the rut. When we came to the gate into the field he said, "Turn in here."

"I know," I said.

"Sure," he said. "Just a goddamn big britches."

That was my name all that day and most of the summer. I began cutting his hay that morning, circling in the field, making my rounds toward the center while the sickle bar rode wet and shining beside the tractor and laid the green grass down in rings. All the time too the old man rode behind me, waving his stumps past my ears to give me directions I didn't want or need and yelling at me above the fire and crash of the tractor engine to turn, Britches, turn, goddamn, even though I was already turning the damn thing. So I must have determined at least a hundred times that if he shoved those raw nubs past my face again or called me Britches just once more I was going to buck the front of the tractor up, so help me Jesus, and pitch the old bastard off, sail him over his lousy belt contraption and, with any luck, if there was any justice under that sun, snap the strings in his scrawny neck. Of course just as often I decided not to. Instead I tried to go blind to his hands and deaf to his fool yelling. But it was a real test, and the only time I recall his being satisfied with anything I did was when the mower chanced to cut through the back of a five-foot rattlesnake. "Sliced him, by damn," he shouted. "Hah."

At noon we rode the tractor back to the house to eat. I didn't know if I could take any more; I was hot, tired, itchy, mad. The old man seemed no different, though. He seemed to have only one gear in his makeup—a kind of full-speed-ahead crazy. When we got up to the house Edith was waiting for us. "Your plate is on the table," she said. "Sandy and I are going to eat in the side yard."

She led me around to the east side of the house. It was shady there under an elm tree in the grass.

"I'll get him started, then I'll bring yours."

"But I brought my own lunch."

"I know that, Sandy," she said.

So I sat down in the elm shade while she returned to the house to start the old man, butter his bread, tuck his napkin in. I leaned back against the trunk of the tree. Now what am I going to do? I thought. I've got to eat two women's lunches and I'm not even hungry. I'm too damn hot to be hungry. The shade freckled across the grass up the side of the house. I took my cap off to let the breeze blow my hair.

Then she came back with a feast on a platter—ice tea, fried chicken, potatoes, peas in butter, fresh bread, home-made ice cream. I wanted to whine and kick my feet, but I ate all she gave me and heard someone with my voice ask for seconds. I suppose it was a cause worth dying of bloat for.

"You don't have to do this," she said, watching me. "Any of this, you know."

"You don't either."

"I want to," she said.

"So do I," I said. I was half in love with her myself.

"I know, but just the same, Sandy. And you thank your daddy for me, too. Will you?"

She knew all right. She knew. I was there driving the tractor so she wouldn't have to and I was stuffing myself stupid while she watched me with those brown grown-up-woman's eyes—because my dad had sent me. I guess it was enough too, because I did all the tractor driving there was to do at the Goodnoughs' that summer, raked hay, cultivated corn, all of it, and ate my mother's lunch on the half-mile walk to and from their house, hiding the bucket in the soapweeds between times, because how was I supposed to tell my mother I didn't want or need her lunch either? She wasn't wild about my being over there in the first place. She had her suspicions.

Anyway, I think I grew three inches that summer and began to get hair in places I didn't have hair before and to gain weight. I was too busy to notice it much, though, and too confused to care.

W HEN THE SUMMER ended I went back to school where things were a lot less complicated. I began high school that year and played a clumsy halfback on the freshman football team and held sweaty hands at a dance or two with a plump little girl named Doris Sweeter. Doris is married and divorced now in Denver, I hear, and the best our football team could manage was a nothing-to-nothing win over Norka, but none of that matters anymore—didn't matter much then either—because at least in school I didn't have to stand still while somebody held me hard by the overalls and asked me to do something he couldn't do himself without first killing someone in order to do it. And nobody was fanning my face with ruined hands or screaming insanity at me, and nobody was watching me eat while she wished maybe I was somebody else or at least her own boy, and if things had been different I might have been, too. No, school seemed like a positive relief after the summer.

But it didn't last long enough. Spring came. So it started

all over again. Only this time my dad wouldn't have it, not any of it; he made it all stop. But at first it was just the same: I was driving the pickup and we were going to check cattle or fix fence, something of the sort, and it was Saturday morning, early, bright, with not enough wind to blow the sand off the tops of the hills, and there, out there in the field, there was that damn John Deere tractor again. Two heads were sticking up beyond the exhaust stack, one somewhat higher than the other, and the tractor was coming toward us from across the corn stubble pulling a disk. My dad didn't have to tell me to stop. I braked the pickup to the side of the road, and this time he not only opened the door, he got out.

"You stay here," he said.

He walked down through the weeds in the ditch, stepped up over the fence, and stood waiting in the stubble on the exact ground the tractor would have to use if it was to make another turn and go back out across the field. But no matter what the tractor did, my dad wasn't going to move; he was planted there. The tractor came on. The two heads above it took shape, became Edith's straw hat and the old man's hard face. There were stump-arms ruining the air above her hat. The tractor still came on. Its discharge and explosion increased steadily as if someone had loaded it with firecrackers, ladyfingers when it was far across the field, and now cherry bombs as it got nearer. My dad stood still, waiting.

Have you ever seen one of those documentary movies, or a TV news clip, say, showing a little white farmhouse with some outbuildings spread around it, and off in the distance but not too far off, not far enough, sure not, there is a tornado coming? It's all darkness and huge, massive, the tornado coming black all the time and the white house standing there waiting for the damage. And you know it's all inevitable; you know it's going to get it: the windows are going to burst, fly out in space, scatter like thrown water, and the roof's going to crash, and you wish the damn fool running the projector would have the sense to reverse the goddamn film so that afterwards you wouldn't have to note the straw sticking out of any tree trunk or watch while an old woman lifts the chimney bricks and the two-by-fours and the window shade off the little girl in her pink dress. If you have seen that then you know how my dad looked waiting in front of that tractor. I won't forget it. I won't forget how his back looked.

But the tractor came on and I thought: *Jesus, at least her feet can reach the brake pedals. At least she will remember to kill the throttle. At least by now she knows how to turn the goddamn steering wheel. Doesn't she?*

Because my dad wasn't going to move. And he didn't move. He didn't have to. Edith got the tractor stopped a foot in front of him; it stayed there racing in idle like a leashed dog growling, wanting to gobble his pants zipper. The old man was wild.

"Stand back, Roscoe," he yelled. "Get away. I ain't got time for no jaw."

My dad didn't say anything.

"Well, by God," the old man screamed. "Run him down then. If he don't move, run him over."

But of course Edith wouldn't do that, didn't do it. Besides, now my dad was doing all that needed to be done. He stepped up to the tractor and jerked the magneto wire out, ripped it off and threw it away from him into the weeds of the barrow ditch. The tractor coughed and died.

So then I thought the old man had finally gone completely crazy. I had never seen anyone go full-out wacko before, flat rage and spit, scream murder, but he was doing all of that. And all the time too he was hitting at something with his arms, flailing them windmill fashion, hitting again and again, hard, until the blood showed red on his wrists and bad stubs. Watching him from the pickup I thought at first he was trying to hit Edith, punish her, but that he was so mad, so far gone, that he couldn't even do that, because in fact he wasn't hitting her. Then I saw that it was the belt he was hitting, that leather contraption buckled behind him between the tractor fenders, which kept him in place, and he was trying to break it with his stumps and wrists because he had no fingers left to work the buckle. He was furious. He kept hitting at it; Christ, then he was kicking at it. It was raging lunacy.

But I don't suppose it lasted all that long, not as long anyway as it takes me now to tell it, because when she understood what he was doing and actually managed to believe it, Edith ducked her head, reached past him, and unbuckled the damn thing. He stumbled off the tractor, fell to his knees, stood up, and came running around the tractor to my dad.

My dad stood waiting for him like a bulldog might stand and wait to see what injury a gopher with rabies might do him. The old man hit him in the throat. My dad stepped back. Blood from Goodnough's stump was smeared across his neck. The old man swung again and missed.

"Daddy," Edith yelled. "You old fool."

He hit my dad again, in the face this time, under the eye, leaving some more of his own blood. My dad caught him by the front of the shirt, held him eye level, then flung him hard onto the ground. The old man faltered, seemed to catch his breath; he pushed himself up from the plowed sand with his red stumps and came again, flailing his arms. My dad blocked most of that wildness but caught one in the ear. So he had the old man's blood all over his face, and that was enough. He hit the old man with all his weight on the point of the chin, rocking his head back. The old man went down. I thought he was dead. My dad must have thought so too; he knelt beside him and lifted his eyelids. Edith scrambled off the tractor. Together they carried him over to the pickup, let down the tailgate, and laid him flat in the back. He was one hell of a mess: his hands were caked with sand; there was a raw blue swelling beginning to show on his chin; he had sandburs stuck all over his clothes. He wasn't dead, though. He was still alive and mean in his eyes.

They stayed in the back with him while I drove the pickup over to the Goodnough house. At the house my dad carried him like he was folded clothes up the steps and on up to the bedroom, where he laid the old man down on a bed.

"Wash his face off and get some ice. He'll live."

Edith went back downstairs. The old man stared at my dad out of yellow watery eyes. He didn't move any but just lay there, making a bad mess of the bed and watching my dad. Then his eyes filled and ran down his cheeks. I suppose I felt sorry for him then, too, the old bastard. He wasn't any good; he was less than no good. His face was all pinched up, and there was that water grizzling down his cheeks into his shirt collar. But for the first time I did feel sorry for him.

Edith came back with a wet cloth and a bowl of ice cubes. She cleaned his face and hands and applied the ice to his chin, picked the sandburs from his clothes. The old man paid no attention. She took his shoes off.

"I want him out of my house."

"Be quiet," Edith said. "Haven't you done enough?"

"This is my house."

"It doesn't matter whose house it is. Be quiet."

"I want him out."

"Forget it," my dad said. "I'm going." He leaned over the old man. "But don't you ever put her on that tractor again. You hear me?"

124

"Get him out of here."

"Next time I'll kill you."

"Get out."

"I mean that. I'll kill you first."

The old man's eyes were full of water again and he began to shiver in his bed like he was cold. We left then. At the bedroom door I looked back, and Edith was covering him with a blanket. She was crying now too.

We went downstairs and outside to the horse tank. My dad washed the blood and grit off his face, then we walked over to the pickup. My dad got in behind the wheel. He drove us in to town, to Holt, to the Payday Liquor Store, where he bought a fifth of whiskey and some beer. He brought it out in a paper sack. Then he drove us back out here to the country and stopped the pickup on top of a sand hill in a cow pasture.

"Son, you ever drank beer before?" he said.

"No, sir."

"It's time you started."

So in the middle of a Saturday morning in 1943 I sipped the beer my dad bought me until I was drunk, while he drank whiskey and talked. He talked for hours, talked, said more to me that morning than he had in all the previous fifteen years we had lived together. He told me about his mother, his father too, what little he could remember of him, told me about the Goodnoughs, how it started with Ada and the two water buckets, how it was when Roy lost his hands, told me how he and Edith and Lyman had driven to the movies together in town for six weeks one summer. And once he had started telling it he couldn't seem to stop; he couldn't seem to explain things enough. There was too much of it.

I didn't interrupt him. I sipped my beer, took a piss now and then in the sagebrush and soapweeds, and listened to him as well as I could. But towards the end of it

I remember saying something innocent and foolish like, "But it's not fair."

And he said, " 'Course it's not fair. There ain't none of it that's fair. Life ain't. And all our thinking it should be don't seem to make one single damn. You might as well know that now as later."

· 7 ·

Only in fact my dad couldn't accept his own advice. Against the odds and against all kinds of craziness he kept trying to change things, to ease them, even if he couldn't finally make them fair. I suppose some of that has rubbed off on me. It's the reason I'm telling you this. It's why I can't accept the idea of anybody wanting to put a woman like Edith Goodnough on trial for a thing in the world, let alone murder.

But at any rate that Saturday morning was the last time she had to drive a tractor. That same week my dad arranged it so that Charlie Best, who neighbored us to the south, would work the old man's ground on shares. I don't know the details, but I remember that Charlie had a hired man, a gap-toothed old plodder named Ralph Johnson, and it was Ralph Johnson who did the farming and all the tractor driving at the Goodnough place for the next nine years or so—until the old man died, that is, because after her father was dead Edith leased the ground to me. But while he still lived, breathed air and drank black coffee, nobody named Roscoe touched his land. It would have been too much. It would have been like kicking a man when he was down, like rubbing his nose in his own shit. My dad understood that; he accepted at least that part of it. So, without allowing the old man to see his hand in it, my dad arranged for Charlie Best to lease the land and then helped Charlie keep things up at the Best place.

After that we all settled into our ruts again. And sometimes, looking at this story, it seems to me like that's about all it is: a series of independent ruts. Some of them lasted for four or five years and some lasted for twenty, but they were ruts just the same, a bunch of worn-out cow paths winding down occasionally to water and a bit of rest and maybe a good blow for a while over a block of salt, but then back again once more into all this Holt County sand. Hell, you can see it any time in any cow pasture.

But at least Edith Goodnough's particular rut was slightly changed now. She didn't have to disk stubble or cut hay while the old man rode insane behind her. No, all she had left to do now was take care of him, keep up the house and the garden, and still milk cows; and then the cows gradually took care of themselves: they died. One by one they got too old to milk; they were trucked to Brush to the slaughterhouse and were not replaced.

And as for the old man, he was changed some, too, now. For one thing he stopped talking. After he ordered my dad out of the house that morning, the old bastard wouldn't say a piddling word, not a damn thing. And in some ways that was all right too; at least he wasn't wasting air damning you anymore. But in other ways it made it harder. Now Edith had to try and guess what in the hell it was he wanted, and if she didn't always guess right then he would stump-shove his bowl of mush off the kitchen table or he would piss his pants while she watched him— all out of meanness and that bitter old man's silence that he refused to break. So most of the time from first spring until late fall she fed him quick and then took him outside to sit in the car alone where he could watch while Ralph Johnson made slow progress steadily in the Goodnough corn- and hayfields. In the winter months she sat him on a straight chair in front of a south window.

Also, she went on collecting Lyman's postcards—he was in Mobile now, now in Montgomery, then in Baltimore—and she continued to collect the bow-tied twenty-dollar bills he sent her at Christmas. The cards and money were kept in separate boxes in a dresser drawer in her bedroom. Later she would pin the postcards, picture-side out, on the walls of the living room, but she didn't start that until the old man had died. The old man didn't seem to remember who the blazes Lyman was when she showed him a picture of a glass building or some photograph of Robert E. Lee waving a saber from atop a marble horse. He seemed to confuse Lee with Lyman. Or, occasionally, if he did seem to recall just who Lyman was, then it only made him madder. He would spit on the floor or wet the front seat of the car. So Edith stopped showing him the postcards and kept them to herself. She was saving them.

OVER HERE we had our ruts too. My dad and mother went on tolerating one another for the duration. The separate and independent lives they lived didn't change much even though they still ate at the same table and slept in the same bed. My mother had her church work, her circle, and she was on the school board for a term or two. But the war years were hard on her: she couldn't keep fashionable. The shelves and racks in the Holt dress shop were empty almost always, and you couldn't purchase a bolt of cloth to make something yourself. The army got all the good cotton and wool for uniforms.

"They take everything," my mother said. "And all that material is just going to get soiled. Or perforated."

So, once during those years, she and Mrs. Schmidt,

who was the wife of Holt's one doctor after Marcellus Packer died of a stroke in the tavern, drove in my mother's car to shop in the big stores in Denver, and they managed to find a pair of stockings apiece and a few dresses. But the trip to Denver turned out to be a one-time affair, a single charge. When Doc Schmidt found out where his gas coupons had gone he was not exactly ecstatic. If nothing else he stopped leaving his coupons out in the open on his dresser top. So what I remember of the hurried-up victory celebration on the football field in 1945—the band played marches, I remember; the mayor spoke and there were preachers on the wood platform—all that is mixed up with the memory of my mother's anticipation of stocked shelves again, dresses and hats. "Thank God," she said, when we heard about the armistice on the radio. And I don't guess the only thing she had in mind was the end of killing. But then I don't suppose she was the only one who felt that way, either. Maybe she was a little more honest, that's all. Because to do her justice, it was what she had to live on.

In different ways my dad suffered over the war, too. There was that bad business with Edith and the tractor because of the war—I mean Lyman would never have managed to jump up and run off if there hadn't been a war—but there was also the fact that my dad had spent enough nights drinking and fighting to have a pretty good idea of what men could do to one another for no reason; and now with the war they had a reason, and they were actually being trained and encouraged to do more than just hit one another in the face. So, while I can't say much of that touched me hard, I believe it made my dad sick. He hated it. And sometime back I think I said he wasn't a man who laughed a lot—well, now he didn't seem to laugh at all. On the other hand, to do him justice too, he must have made some money during those years. The cattle market stayed steady with the increased need for meat, and he went on castrating calves and experimenting with seed bulls and hauling fat cattle to the sale barn. I suppose he learned to live with the connection between his raising beef and all that blood being spilled in Europe.

THAT LEAVES ME. And like it or not I can see you're going to have to hear some more about Sanders Roscoe. It's the price you pay for asking questions about Edith Goodnough.

So. I told you I was in high school. Well, I finished high school. I graduated from Holt County High in 1946—hell, I even went to college. But during this period I've been talking about I was still in high school, still trying to play some kind of halfback while beside me there was this big fullback who was so good that he was going to make unanimous all-conference and second team all-state. That was Bud Sealy, of course, and he was all right then. He hadn't begun to show any signs of becoming a sheriff or a son of a bitch yet. No, he was just a big tough kid with a fast car. Only, looking back on it now, I suppose it might have been then that he began to develop a habit for being hard in the middle of things, develop a knack for taking advantage of any opening, never mind whether that opening was on the football field or between the legs of some girl, or, like later, right on the front page of some damn big city newspaper. But I might be pushing things by saying that. That's just hindsight. I might be trying to force square pegs into round holes, because if what I've just suggested is true, none of us saw it. I sure as hell didn't see it. At the time I was a lot more interested in trying to get Doris Sweeter to allow me to see more of her, to let me hold something more of hers than just her sweaty hand.

Then, like Lyman, I left. I went to college at A.&M. in Fort Collins for a while. It was my mother's idea as much as anything, though I wasn't opposed. She wanted a son with a college diploma, and what I wanted was to get away from home. My dad agreed to it too; he thought I might be capable of learning something. Well, I don't know that I learned a damn thing that matters, at least not of the sort he had in mind—though I can't be sure of that now either. He probably knew all along.

Anyway, Fort Collins was a hell of nice little town then; it's developed middle-age spread since—like the rest of us, it has some heart trouble. But in the four years I was there it was still the sort of town that even a green kid from Holt County could survive in. I mean it provided me with the kind of trouble that, once I got out of it, left me only a little bruised and scratched up but not a lot smarter than I was when I first got there. It wasn't the kind of trouble or sidewalk show, say, that any seven-year-old kid from any slum sees every day and survives if he's lucky but ends up changed forever afterwards even if he does. No, I just had some sore places to show for my trouble. It didn't change the way I see things. It took Holt County to accomplish that.

But at least I got away from home. For a while I managed to get shut of Holt County. It didn't mean anything, though; none of it did. It was just college. I didn't even graduate. There was this little matter of chemistry: they required people studying animal husbandry to pass chemistry, and I never did. I tried it twice too. But somehow the theory of chemical formulas, even the logic of chemical elements, escaped me. How could anybody be so damn sure that if you added two parts of hydrogen to one part of oxygen it always came out water? The combination of things never seemed that certain to me; things weren't that simple, not even with elements as basic as water. So I

132

never passed chemistry, and after four years I still failed to do the one thing that might have satisfied at least my mother. Her son didn't receive a college diploma.

You understand, though, that I was still about half willing to return for a fifth year and a third try at chemistry; I hadn't quite finished playing the jackass in Fort Collins; and then while I was making my mind up to it the bottom fell out. Matters caught up with me in the summer of 1950. I began to learn those things that my years of college couldn't teach me, hadn't in fact even touched. I was home again.

I got my first solid lesson on June eleventh, I remember exactly. My dad and I were on horseback in native sandhill grass, driving cattle—maybe you noticed the tops of the hills in that pasture southeast when you drove in here. At any rate it's a big pasture, an entire section, all grass and sagebrush and soapweed with two windmills pumping cold water into fifty-foot stock tanks. That section's never been worked or turned under by any plow. It was part of the land my dad accumulated during those three years he was drinking hard and working harder in the middle 1920s, after Edith Goodnough decided she couldn't leave home, that she wasn't free enough to move even a half mile west. You ought to ride out into that grass before you leave; it might give you some idea of what this country looked like before it was chopped up and fenced into titled lots. On the other hand you may feel the way Edith's mother felt about it. I think I told you Ada died without ever appreciating it. She didn't like it; she still wanted Iowa. Well, she didn't understand what she saw out here.

Because it's damned fine if you know how to look at it. And no more so than in June after a wet spring. The spring of 1950 was wet, too. The grass my dad and I were riding through that day was thick, green, tall, spotted with wildflowers, rich. The cattle were starting to slick up with it, to smooth and fill out again after the winter months and after dropping their calves in March, and the calves, those damn little white-faced ballies, kicking and galloping along beside their mamas, their tails riding straight up into the air like white flags, were full of frisk, for all the world innocent yet of what was waiting for them. We were driving them down to a holding pen and a work corral beside one of the water tanks. There was a good squeeze chute at one end of the corral, and we were going to run them into the chute, squeeze them immobile, and then vaccinate and brand each one and castrate the bull calves.

So I was riding one part of the pasture and Dad was riding another, both of us driving cows and calves, and the range bulls mixed in with them, the bulls tailing the cows slow and hardheaded the way they do, thick necked, their balls swinging, down toward the holding pen. It felt good to be in the sun, to sweat in the open on horseback after nine months of school, and Hammer was working the cattle all right now. He hadn't believed at first that it was his day to work, until I had to boot him around some, ride the morning's green out of him to set his mind right. So it was all going smooth enough, and I was trailing cattle, pushing them down easy toward the corrals, turning the calves back when they tried to run off, popping the butts of the bulls with the knot at the end of my rope. At the water tank I got them shut up behind a back gate where they would stay milling in the heavy dust, bawling and plopping shit, until we were ready to work them. But Dad wasn't in yet, so I rode back out to help him.

My dad was beyond help.

I found his horse out there in the pasture stamping flies away and chewing bluestem grass. He trotted off when I rode up to him. Dad was fifty feet away. He was lying on his face in the sand beside a clump of soapweed. I got down and turned him over and saw his face. It wasn't a pretty thing to see. It was all bluish, mad, shocked, his eyes were wide open. I didn't know what to do. He was already dead, though, and I could see it hadn't been easy. His hands were gnarled hard at his chest; clutching at his shirt, he had torn some buttons off; and there were deep wet ruts in the sand where it looked as if he had been trying to kick something away from him with his boots, like it was a snake or a rabid dog. One of his legs was still cocked to kick again.

So what was I going to do now? What in hell was I supposed to do? We were out there in that native pasture, and it was all finished by the time I found him. Finally I put his arms down at his sides and straightened his leg and brushed the sand from that white scar that Frank Lutz had given him. There was grit in his eyes too from lying on his face with his eyes open. I wiped the sand out of those brown staring eyes and then closed his eyelids. There wasn't anything to do after that; I wanted there to be something more but there wasn't. So I sat beside the length of his body and just cried. I didn't even know how to cry for him; my chest and throat felt like somebody was kicking me. Then the flies found him under that June sun and I was almost glad they did. It gave me something more to do: I could fan his quiet face with my hat. And I did that for a long time, sat there and fanned him, waiting for the moment when I knew I would have enough force to move again, to gather him up and ride him home. I suppose it took a couple of hours before I felt ready.

When I got him home Doc Schmidt confirmed for me what I knew I had seen when I turned him over. My dad died of a heart attack.

It also turned out that I was right to have delayed taking him home, because in the next forty-eight hours my mother and I had some bad fights. The fights closed everything down, shut it all off. She was going to bury my dad in the town cemetery.

"No, you're not," I said.

"I've already purchased two plots from the city. You should have told me sooner."

"I'm telling you now. You use them. Dad's not going to."

"He is, though."

"No, he's not. You don't have the right to do that."

"I'm his wife. That gives me the right. I put up with him for twenty-five years, Sanders."

"Shut up," I said. "Can't you shut up about that?"

Her eyes went flat then. Her hands were shaking. "You think that was easy?" she said. "You do, don't you? You think it was all my fault that I wasn't enough for him. Well, you don't have even the first idea what it was like. You've always taken his side against me, even from the very beginning you did. It was always you and your father together, and somewhere—don't ask me how—but somewhere I was supposed to fit in."

"You had your dresses," I said. "Your goddamn church meetings."

"Church?" she said. "My God, you're stupid. You think I would have cared about the church if there was anything else?"

"Well, it's too late now. Dad's staying here."

"We'll see about that."

"No, we won't. It's already decided."

So I played the bastard with her. I admit I was a real son of a bitch about it. But I was not going to let her take him into town to that damned cramped little cemetery so that one of the boys who worked summers for the city could water and mow the grass over him and so they could mount plastic tulips beside his grave on Memorial Day.

And in the end I had my way about it. I told John Baker, the mortician, to prepare my dad for a funeral out here in the country. He could shave him and dress him up in a suit if that would please my mother, but I didn't want any powder or rouge smeared on his face to make him look alive. He was dead. Let him be dead. He wasn't to go out looking like some wax manikin.

The funeral was on June fourteenth, in the heat of a clear morning. The whole country showed up—people like Charlie Best and Frank Lutz and Agnes Wilson and Wenzel Gerdts and Ellis Burns and Leon Shields and even old Ludi Pfeister from Kansas with his canes, who were all my dad's friends, and others too, my mother's friends from church. Edith Goodnough was also there. We walked up to that rise, past the corrals and beyond the horse barn, to the just-dug hole beside the old grave that was sunk past ground level, my grandmother's grave. When we were assembled the minister spoke to us, told us about a man he himself didn't know much about, while my dad's friends who did know him stood unhatted in the sun and wiped away the sweat that trickled down their white foreheads. Up close to the grave we were in the shade of that big cottonwood and it was cooler.

After the service several people shook my hand and one or two tried to tell me that at least he had died doing something he enjoyed. But I didn't listen to that. My dad should have lived for another twenty years. Then my mother took her friends down to the house to drink ice tea and to visit and commiserate while the box was being lowered into the hole, and I told John Baker to go on, that I would fill it in myself. That left only Edith there with me.

It didn't take long to fill in the grave. The sand was loose and moist, making it easy to shovel. When I had finished packing it into a long mound behind the plain stone that reads JOHN ROSCOE FEB. 24, 1890—JUNE 11, 1950, I stood back with Edith to look at it.

Edith had been crying. She was wearing a new dress and she had done something to her hair, but she hadn't been able to do anything about her face. Her face had gone to pieces. I put my arm around her.

"He asked me to marry him," Edith said. "Did you know that?"

"Yes. He told me."

"But I couldn't. You understand, don't you, Sandy?"

There was a little bit of wind in the cottonwood over us. The leaves were turning and washing in the wind. Below us on the road, cars were starting back toward town.

"Yes," I said. "But understanding it and liking it aren't the same things."

"No," she said. "No, they are not the same things."

Then she was crying again, for the last time that I have known her to cry. There wasn't much sound to it. I held her hand and felt like hell.

· 8 ·

So I was home again for good now. At twenty-two I took up the responsibility of managing the ranch my dad had made, the big cattle operation and the quarters of farmland. It was almost entirely clear of any debt when I took it over. There was plenty to do, though, and in short time I began to discover what it meant to be my dad in Holt County, to make decisions which afterwards you had to live with. Meanwhile my mother and I struck an edgy quiet kind of truce. We talked to one another when it was necessary. I took her out to eat about twice a month and sometimes to an acceptable movie in town when there was one, kept her car in tune and changed the snow tires, and on her part she held her tongue when I didn't come home on Saturday nights. We avoided any topic that would take us back to that other June. That lasted about two years.

Then in the spring of 1952 we had another fight. It was one evening during supper, after steak and potatoes but before the dessert, that my mother dropped some news on me, an announcement she wanted to make. She said she preferred that I hear it from her before someone else had the chance to tell me and get it all wrong.

"I'm thinking of marrying again," she said.

I took a drink of coffee and lit a cigarette. "Okay," I said. "Do whatever you want."

"I intend to. But I wanted to discuss it with you first. It will mean some changes in both our lives."

"Not in mine," I said. "I'm not marrying him."

"Now that's precisely what I was afraid of. Must you always be so pigheaded? You make me tired."

"I said for you to do what you wanted. Isn't that enough?"

She got up and cut two wedges of hot apple pie and scooped ice cream onto them and brought them to the table. I started to eat mine.

"You haven't asked me who he is. Don't you care who I marry?"

"I figured you would tell me."

"All right," she said. "It's Wilbur Cox." She was good and angry now, shoving Wilbur's name across the table at me like it was a court summons, a sharp slap in the face.

"Congratulations," I said. "I hope you'll be happy with him."

"As if you cared."

"Sure, I do. But you can't live out here with him. I don't want Wilbur Cox messing about."

"Don't concern yourself. We intend to build a new home in town."

"Your ice cream's melting," I said.

I got up then from the table and put my hat and coat on. The ice cream was melting on her pie, running down the sides and puddling in the dish.

"I'm not finished talking to you," she said.

"I'll be at the tavern."

"But it's not Saturday night."

"No, it's Wednesday. And don't wait up: the tavern doesn't close till midnight."

I suppose I should explain. I don't expect you to like my response to her little news—she certainly didn't like it—but you might try to understand my side of it some.

It was less than two years after my dad had died—that's what bitched it all for me. A month less than two years. Hell, she had waited longer than that after her first husband died, Jason Newcomb, that miserable bank teller who hanged himself in the potato cellar. For me, my dad was still as clear and present everywhere about the place as if he had gone just the day before. He was still there for me wherever I was, whatever I was doing, working cattle or fixing fence, and it seemed to me that he should have been enough man for any woman to last a lifetime.

Now I suppose that's an illogical, an unsound way to think, but that's how I felt about it. And I didn't have the slightest notion that she even knew Wilbur Cox to marry him. Of course I understood that she knew him—everybody knew Wilbur Cox. He sold life insurance. He had that tidy little brick office on Main Street in Holt and drank coffee everyday with the boys in the café. He was tall, stringy as a green bean; he oiled his hair. Maybe you will understand what I mean about him if I tell you that he is one of those guys who likes to shake hands a lot, shaking your hand with both of his. But like I've said before, my mother was not stupid. She no doubt already had Wilbur Cox picked out. She must have seen very clearly in advance that Wilbur was going to be the form of husband she could manipulate, rule and run, make him stay home and attend to business, and she did all that. He fit into her scheme like an obedient poodle. Well, there was always something grasping about her, still is for that matter. She can't let go. She has to go on striving at things, refusing to let them be as they are. She can't abide them until she has changed them to meet her own mold. I don't believe it makes her happy, though.

Anyway, I relented a little in December. When the solid brick house at the edge of town was complete with carpet and paint, I stood up for her at the wedding. I gave her away. I even agreed to sell a dryland quarter to pay for the house.

THERE WAS at least one other thing to happen in 1952 that has some bearing on this story. It must have been October, but you can check his gravestone if it makes a lot of difference to you: old Roy Goodnough died down the road from us. He went in his sleep. Edith went in to his bedroom that morning to dress him for the day in his overalls, and she found that she wasn't ever going to have to do that again. He was as rigid as stone; his mouth was locked open, like a piece of box iron. So she drew the sheet up over his face and went downstairs to call me.

"It's over," she said.

"I don't know what you mean."

"He died last night. Will you help me make the arrangements?"

I wasn't surprised she called me. Since the death of my own dad I had been checking on her once a week, stopping by the Goodnough house in the early evening before I went home to supper. The old man would already be fed and put to sleep, and Edith and I would sit in the porch swing, visiting, passing that best hour of any day together while the barn swallows hunted bugs and the locusts sang from the elm trees. She began to keep beer on hand in the refrigerator, too, because she knew I liked it in the evening after work, and I would drink beer while we talked and pushed the swing a little. Occasionally on those evenings she would recall the things she knew about my dad, and it seemed to help us both get over him.

So now the old man was dead. That much was over. He was buried in town, in the plot west of Ada's. It was how Edith wanted it arranged. She said the old man had blocked her mother's view of the east while she lived, he wasn't going to do that in death. There was still the problem of his mouth, though. I don't know how John Baker got the old man's mouth to stay closed for the funeral, but I suppose he had to break the jaws and wire them shut. And that was funny, that the old man died with his mouth locked open after he had spent the last nine years of his life refusing to open it, declining whatever to say yes or no to anything, but just sitting hard in his chair before that south window in the winter or watching from the car during the summer while Ralph Johnson made those slow circles in the field. Well, he sure as hell would not have liked what he saw the next year. It might even have made him mad enough to speak again. Because, like I say, after he died Edith insisted that I begin to lease the land myself, and I did that. I've been leasing it ever since.

THERE FOLLOWED about a ten-year period in my life that I am not particularly proud of. For most of that time I was drifting, falling headlong and heedless as in one of those old grade-school fire escapes that were constructed like covered slides in which you entered at the top and shot down through several loops and twists and then scooted out at the bottom into a mudhole. It was a long wild ride I was on, and for quite a while it seemed like the thing to do.

Clevis Stouffer was a good part of that heedless drifting, though he was not the cause of it. I had my own motivation, my own inspiration. Clevis was merely ready on hand and more than willing to drift with me, content to ride along and to contribute his share. I had taken him on as hired man to help me work the Goodnough place, after leasing it from Edith, because he was a good hand, a good farmer. He knew then, and I believe he still knows, as much about Case tractors and Gleaner combines as any two men in the country, with the kind of curiosity about machines that can't rest until it understands fully just why that loaded spring and that set of cogwheels have to interlock the way they do in order for the thing to work and propel weight.

He was a hell of a guy, Clevis was—big, sloppy, about six feet three and a good 230 pounds, with a heavy stomach above his belt that kept his shirttails free and flapping, and he was smart. There were people who thought he was stupid because he talked slow, but they didn't know him. They hadn't seen him tune a car or heard him recite an hour's worth of dirty limericks in the Holt Tavern. I had known him since high school; he was usually on the outside fringe of things in school because he was so big and so slow and also because he had to work all the time, but sometime during our freshman year he decided that I was one of his friends, and that was all right with me. As for his family, Old Man Stouffer was a gandy dancer for the railroad. That is, on those days toward the end of the week when the old man was sober enough to work anywhere, and his mother, a fat little German immigrant, did wash for people in town and bore a string of babies. Clevis was the oldest of eleven kids. They all came to school in a flatbed truck.

When Clevis started to work for me I moved him into the house in much the same way that my dad had done with his crony Ellis Burns in the 1920s. We had the place to ourselves: my mother by that time had already spread herself into that new brick home in town with the rose carpets and the flowered coach. After a two-weeks' honeymoon at the Brown Palace Hotel in Denver she had come back to Holt and had begun her continuing tenure as Mrs. Cox, allowing Wilbur to go on shaking hands with folks at his life-insurance office and to drink coffee with the boys when he felt thirsty, but he damn well better be home by six o'clock every evening and squire her to church every Sunday. That apparently was satisfactory with Wilbur, and things were not unsatisfactory for Clevis and me. We worked pretty steady at keeping the ranch going and at making a profit for Edith. By the end of the first year, though, we had something of a problem: the house looked and smelled like a buffalo wallow, and there were enough empty beer cans accumulated at the back door to tin at least three sides of a big barn.

"By God," Clevis said one morning. He was standing in the kitchen doorway holding his boots in one hand, looking like a great big sleepy kid who had just wakened from a dream that made him mad. "Listen," he said. "Now this here is getting serious."

"What is?" I said.

"This." He held his boots up. "I can't even find my goddamn dirty socks that I took off last night. Are you wearing them?"

"Hell, no. They wouldn't fit me."

"Well, by God, something's got to be done about this. I can't work without no socks."

"Got any ideas?"

"Yeah," he said. "One."

Clevis's one idea was Twyla Thompson. Twyla was a local girl with a happy red face. She worked seasons at the grain elevator beside the railroad tracks, and the men driving trucks loaded with wheat or corn took their time when they arrived at the elevator to dump the trucks, because Twyla had full breasts and skin like cream and she was always cheerful. She was built to last too, being as broad and muscular across the hips and shoulders as Clevis himself was, though she stood a good head shorter. The idea for Twyla was for her to move in with us, and I don't know how Clevis did it, but somehow by striking the right chords or by pulling the proper strings he managed to persuade her to do that, to come out here and be a live-in maid, and it was like her that when she saw the advanced state of things in the house she gave us only a medium lecture and called us big filthy pigs. The maggots in the kitchen sink and the sour piles of clothes in the corners didn't seem to phase her. In two days' time she had the place in order again: there were white sheets on the beds, green vegetables on the table for the first time in nine months, and the beer cans were smashed flat and hauled to the dump. She was not a girl who was afraid of work. Between the two of us we took turns paying her monthly salary. She slept in the guest room with Clevis, though, so he was the only one who was exercising that other kind of option that went with her living here singly with two men. Not that I would have minded it myself, you understand—but Clevis had made the arrangement, and for a long time I tried to respect that.

Then I stopped respecting it. We had gone along well enough for four or five years. There were a few rocky spots, of course, but for the most part we had settled into an ordinary routine of working hard all week and then partying all night on the weekend, the three of us always together in the house and about the place and then still together those Saturday nights, with often another girl along to drink with us and to keep it balanced and occasionally to come home with me and not to go back until Sunday afternoon. But at first the work had been the primary thing. We managed in the beginning to maintain the level my dad had achieved. That's true—we worked the ranch and the quarters of wheat and also the extras at Edith's, all of that—but gradually it got to be more important and damn sure more fun to stay out at night, not just on Saturdays when everyone drank and danced and played cards and shot pool, but during the week too, even if we had to go out of town to locate people to party with, and then we weren't getting up in the morning at five o'clock anymore, nor at six or seven either, and things were not getting done. It was all sliding; we were drifting. Instead of making four or five passes with the disk over the fallow ground, the summer fallow, now maybe two passes were enough and pretty soon one seemed like a good plenty. Sure, and it got so it was a good idea to buy a new red pickup so we could tour Denver on Tuesday. That's right, and it became the thing to do to buy a bar-room full of people all the drinks they wanted, never mind if you never saw them before and would never see them again. We were all friends, weren't we? Of course, and mainly—why what harm could there be?—it got so it was perfectly all right to go to bed with Twyla. Both of us, I mean. Like we were still just taking turns paying her salary.

Only she wasn't any whore. Far from it. She was Twyla Thompson, born and raised in Holt, Colorado. She was one of us, don't you see?—a local girl with a fine red face who before she was persuaded to come out here to this ranch had worked cheerfully at the grain elevator amongst the clouds of wheat and corn dust. She was not the sort of woman to somehow shut off her emotions, her warm full feelings, while still leaving her legs open. So it began to take a toll on her. Christ yes, it had to do some harm. I remember that she learned finally to keep her own large supply of gin in the kitchen cupboard, that toward the end she was always at least half drunk by suppertime. We would sit down at the table to eat, the three of us, and her eyes would be too bright, like glass. Then she might spill some coffee, knock over the salt shaker. Once I re-member she slopped some hot soup onto Clevis's hand and she took his red hand up and kissed it and held it with tears in her eyes.

And that was the worst goddamn hell of it: all that time she was in love with him. Do you understand what I'm saying? I knew she loved him. She was good to him, good for him, that big sloppy open-faced Clevis Stouffer, with his flour-bag stomach and his flapping shirttails and his dirty socks. He was what she wanted, needed. They made a pair, the two of them together, like a couple of plain solid blocks of mineral salt. And on his part, though he never said so or even showed it much, I believe he was at least half in love with her. He certainly deserved something good in his life, and Twyla was that all right; she was good.

Only here I was—that's what I mean—I was here, too. Things might have been all right if it had been only two of us, or if Clevis and Twyla had lived in town, or even if they had rented some nearby vacant farmhouse or just bought a trailer and put in electricity. But none of that happened; that wasn't the way it was. It was always three of us, here, in this house. We had our routine, our little family arrangement, and what made it possible, the thing that allowed it to continue, to go on and on regardless, was that in some ways they were both dependent on me: I owned the ranch, didn't I? I was the hotshot, the rotten dowel pin. The bank account was in my name. And I played on all of that to prevent things from changing. I knew we were on a dangerous ride, but I still didn't want to end it even if I had known how. It was too much of a good thing, a heedless, continuous, romping jig and party— when I could keep from thinking. Not thinking, refusing to think, got to be a steady habit for me.

I remember sending Clevis out for the afternoon to swathe hay, for example, or to buy baler parts in Sterling sixty miles northwest of Holt, while I stayed home. And he'd stare at me and say, "What are you going to do while I'm gone?"

"Oh, I've got those heifers to move."

"Yeah," he'd say. "Why course you do."

So he understood it all right; he recognized the drift, but he would go on anyway, and then after he was out of the way I'd spend an hour sipping iced gin from a shared glass with Twyla in the middle of the afternoon, and in time I'd be breathing the good perfume of her thick orange hair and tasting the salt of her round white shoulders. Because after the first time with Twyla in my room in the afternoon while the sun speckled on the bed and the curtains billowed in the open window, the second time was easier. There was a lot less fumbling afterwards and somewhat less the need to avoid the look in anyone's eyes, of playing it secret, of pretending there was nothing there between us to pretend about. Then after the third time it was easier yet. I stopped trying to justify anything but just accepted it as you might accept the shipping fever that came with a truckload of delivered sale-barn calves: there was always going to be some bad mixed up with the good. That's how I was thinking—or not thinking. Matters would take their own irresistible course, I thought, and meanwhile more than anything it felt just fine to be in bed with Twyla. She had all that rich creamy skin, those large ready breasts like fresh bread, and she was soft all over with so much warm woman's flesh to feel against your own. There was nothing professional about her, though. She wasn't practiced or schooled at bed. No, it was more that lying with her—while you smoothed her stomach or stroked her rich thighs—for an hour there were little jokes between you and easy laughter, as if you and she were just two kids in clover, say, and that what you were doing in bed on clean sheets was not a thing that was dangerous or harmful to anyone but merely the simple play of children. Besides, being the warm-cheeked girl she was, she wasn't used to refusing the feelings of anyone.

It went on that way for a year. Maybe more, I don't know. But I remember how it ended. The consequences I can recall in detail. We were driving home one night, the three of us as usual, drunk in the cab of the red pickup after closing the Holt Tavern on a Wednesday. The radio was blaring Hank Williams above the rattle of wind coming through the rolled-down windows, and we were singing with the music and shouting jokes at one another as we watched ahead down the road through the windshield smattered red and yellow with dead grasshopper bodies, squiggling legs and veined wings. Then we were home again, here in this house, this kitchen. We each had another drink, and Twyla said she knew of one more joke she could tell us.

"You got our entire attention," I said.

"Not mine," Clevis said. "I got to bleed my lizard." He stood up and went to the bathroom. Then he came back and opened another beer. "So what's your joke?" he said.

"Promise you'll laugh?"

"Sure," he said.

"Because I think it's funny anyway." She wasn't looking at us; she was watching her finger follow a scratch in the tabletop, as if that interested her. "It's just that one of you gets to be a daddy pretty soon, and I don't know whose name to pick." Then she did look at us. "Don't you think that's funny?"

"Hell," Clevis said. "You never could tell jokes."

"Just a minute," I said. "You're telling us you're pregnant?"

She nodded. Then she kind of laughed, her eyes shining at us with gin and what must have also been fear. "I mean I don't know which one of you got me like this."

"We could always draw straws," Clevis said.

"And I'm sorry," she said. "I'm sorry. I'm sorry." She was still smiling at us, but there were tears flowing down her cheeks now into her mouth, and she couldn't wipe them away fast enough to keep up with them.

"What are you crying about?" Clevis said. "Hell, girl, you just bought the farm."

"Don't."

"Why not? I can't afford no kid. You and him hash it out."

"But you promised me."

"I never promised you nothing."

Her mouth was still open in that awful smile. "You promised me you would laugh."

"Oh," he said. "Well: ha ha."

"Leave her alone," I said.

"How's that?"

"I said leave her alone."

"Now that's funny—coming from you. That's real funny."

"You know what I mean."

"Sure. You send me over to Sterling or some goddamn place else so you and her can jump in bed as soon as I'm gone, and now you tell me to leave her alone."

"It wasn't like that."

"Wasn't it? Well, don't tell me about it. I couldn't stand no more jokes tonight. I'm wore out."

He got up then and started to walk back to the bedroom.

"Cleve," Twyla said. "Honey, wait."

"What for?"

"Don't you want me to come with you?"

"Nah," he said. "You can sleep with lover boy tonight. That shouldn't be no surprise to anybody."

Then he left the kitchen. We could hear him in the back bedroom stomping on the floor and after that the rattle of the bed when he lay down heavy to sleep. I sat with Twyla for a while, not talking; it was too late for talk; I wouldn't have known the right words anyway. Finally I went to bed myself, leaving her sitting there with her red cheeks, like those of a healthy child, shining wet under the light. She had been an unselfish, uncomplicated girl, but now, six or seven years later, with my interference she had become something different. It was not only that she was pregnant without knowing for sure whose baby it was or that she didn't know how to ask one of us to claim it—it was more that she had become a woman staring unfocused at a grease spot above a kitchen sink out here in the country in the small hours of a Wednesday night.

She was still here the next morning when I got up. She was asleep with her head twisted uncomfortably on the kitchen table, her shoulders slumped forward. I started some black coffee on the stove and went outside to see how the day looked. Clean, with high clouds gathering in the west, the day appeared acceptable. But the pickup was gone. I went back into the house. Twyla was awake. She looked as if during the night she had been disassembled and put back together with flour glue. Her face was all pasty.

"Did Clevis take the pickup?" I said.

"What?"

"Where did Clevis go?"

"Portland, Oregon."

"What do you mean Portland, Oregon? Here, drink some coffee." I poured coffee into a cup for her. "Drink it hot," I said.

"He said because it was a long ways off," Twyla said. "He said he wanted to see the water."

"Water? Jesus Christ. What else did he say?"

"Nothing. Only for me to say he would send back money for the pickup when he found a machine job."

"But I don't care about the pickup. He can have the goddamn pickup. I want to know why you didn't go with him."

"Because," she said. "He never asked me." She was

talking very woodenly; she might as well have been repeating a ten-year-old market report or reciting Dick and Jane, something as indifferent as that. "I was waiting for him to," she said, "but he never said so."

"Listen to me," I said. "I don't know what you think of me. Maybe you still like me some—I don't know; we've had some good times—but whatever it is, you love him, don't you? You want this baby you're having to be his, isn't that right?"

"I don't want no baby. Not no more."

"Yes, you do. You will. Here, listen now: I want you to go to Denver for a week or two. I want you to take yourself a motel room. Rest up, see some movies, buy some clothes, whatever you're going to need. Then I'll come there and see you have enough money so you can go to Oregon. Will you do that?"

"It won't make no difference."

"Yes, it will. It's the only way, Twyla."

"I'm just sorry," she said.

But later that day Twyla allowed me to take her to Denver and to install her in a Holiday Inn near the Stapleton Airport. Then I came home and went about selling the remaining quarters of farmland my dad had accumulated. I take no pride in that. I had to sell some land anyway to pay off the bad debts I had run up through constant partying and buying red pickups and by acting as if I was so rich and so smart that any form of steady discipline could go to hell. Anyway, in part because of my debts, I decided to make a clean sweep of it, so I sold those last quarters and kept only the pastureland, the native grass and the hayfields, so I could still run cattle, and then I returned to Denver and put Twyla Thompson on the plane with fifteen thousand dollars in her purse.

All of that took longer than I expected. It was more like a month than two weeks. But by the time I checked her out of the motel Twyla looked quite a lot better. She seemed almost cheerful again, like a big wonderful farm girl, and her stomach was starting to show. "Sandy," she said.

"I know," I said. "Take care of yourself. And tell Clevis . . . Just tell him hello for me."

Then Twyla, in a good blue dress with white trim, walked up the ramp onto the plane. About a year later I got a postcard from her saying the baby was a boy. She didn't say what he looked like. But she did sign the card Twyla T. Stouffer, so I had to assume she found Clevis and that they were together again the way they belonged. She failed to include a return address though, and I've never seen nor heard from either one of them since. Still, I permit myself to believe they remain together, growing fat in the same house somewhere in Portland, Oregon, where they raise a big brood of fat red-cheeked babies. They would have good babies.

DURING all that period of brainless pell-mell drift, the only solid base I had was Edith Goodnough. She was still there in that house down the road. Despite everything—and she could see what was happening all right, don't think she couldn't; there was never any lacy veil or donkey's blind covering her brown eyes—she was nevertheless willing to talk and visit with me in the evening, though what we talked about now while rocking in the porch swing was nothing, not even recollections of my dad. I just stopped by to be there for an hour, and that happened usually whenever for some reason I had not been able to stop thinking, whenever even for a minute I had recognized the true crux of the matter here at home. Then sometime soon afterwards, that same evening or the next day, I

would drive down to see Edith. I wouldn't tell her anything about it. I didn't have to. She seemed to know. She
would link our arms and for a while we would rock and
listen to the locusts in the trees in the nearby dark. But if
I at least had her, she had nothing for herself. At that time
she was trying to live solely on Lyman's postcards and his
packages of twenty-dollar bills mailed each Christmas in
brown wrapping paper and a clumsy red bow.

She was completely alone. My dad had died; her father
was finally dead, and Lyman was still back east somewhere, seeing cities. So it was not just for an afternoon
or a month that she was alone, but for one year after
another, on and on, with no particular reason for believing
it would ever be one jot different. If you have had that
happen to you, then you know that living like that—alone,
making yourself cook three meals every day for one person,
playing the radio all the time so there will be some human
noise in the house even if it's just the tinny counterfeit
sound of some actor wetting his pants over Pepto-Bismol,
because if it's not that then it's getting up to silence and
going to bed in silence, since chicken cackle and bird twit-
ter will go only so far—that can do something to you:
make you brittle or dull, cause you to go slightly touched,
drive you slowly a little crazy. You forget how to string
words together. You can't recall the true weight of words.
It's as if they all come out in a gush, like a cow pissing,
or they don't come out at all. Well, something along those
lines happened to Edith Goodnough.

For one thing, there got to be stories about her. People
in town and high school kids began to edify one another
with tales of Edith: how she was turning crazy all alone
for nothing; how she was starving to death on tea and
toast; how it was skunk cabbage and water she was starving
on; how she slept in the barn. She was partial to Elvis

Presley, they said, and likely to disappear. The only story, though, that might have any truth to it was the one Bill Kwasik told me one night in the tavern.

It was in that last year that Clevis and Twyla were still here. They were dancing to jukebox music, and I was drinking beer at the bar, watching them in the mirror. Then Bill Kwasik, who lives with his wife and kids four miles east of the Goodnough place, came up to me and said:

"Well, I see our neighbor is taken with the stars now."

"Which neighbor is that?" I said.

"That Goodnough woman. What's her name—Edith."

"Oh? What makes you say that?"

" 'Cause," he said. "I come home the other night from Lions and I top that rise west of our place, and there she stands in my headlights. I damn near hit her."

"What was she doing?"

"Nothing. Stargazing. Hell, I thought she was hurt. So I back up beside her and ask her if she's all right. 'Yes, I'm all right,' she says. 'Well, can I give you a lift home?' 'No,' she says, 'thank you.' 'But Miss Goodnough,' I say, 'I mean, what in hell are you doing out here? It's way past midnight.' And she says: 'Never mind, Billy. You can just tell people I was taking a walk. A walk,' she says. 'Never mind,' she says. She don't even have a coat on."

"Let her be," I said. "Forget it."

"Sure," Bill Kwasik said. "I wasn't going to do nothing to her. I thought she was hurt."

"I know. But just leave her alone."

"Well, she's going to get herself run over if she don't watch out."

But no one ran Edith over, and she went on walking out at night alone along the road. She also busied herself with those damn picture postcards. She had them straight-pinned in rows on the walls of the living room so that if you cared to—and I didn't—you could trace Lyman's progress yearly for almost twenty years across the country, starting in the West, then the Middle West and the Deep South, and finally the East, like he had some feeble notion of reversing the tide of pioneer migration so as to end up at the beginning, where, for him, the first wrong step had been taken, where his old man's old man had been carried in his great-great-grandmother's arms down the plank off some boat in shit-filled diapers. The pictures on the cards, arranged like that, displayed in neat long rows like bathroom tiles, were bright circusy things: glass skyscrapers, blue fountains, statues, city parks with pruned trees and green park benches. They made you think of cheap carnival notices, of circus posters cut up in pieces. And always, on the backs of the cards, was that brief, childish, infuriating scribble of his, which told you next to nothing.

> Dear Sis,
>   How are you? I am in Cleveland. Boy, it's hot.
>   Love, your brother,
>   Lyman

That's the sort of nonsense he wrote to her, and how she managed to live on just that much, I have no idea. If it had been me I'd have torn the damn things up and thrown them out with the chicken scraps and the hog slop—and then goddamned him again for not coming home yet, the slow son of a bitch. But Edith didn't feel that way at all. I think she was convinced that he at least was having himself a good time seeing this country's sights, traveling, broadening himself, so that when he eventually did come home—and she never doubted that he would return finally—things would be better again for her too, that some of his recent experience of the world would rub off on her and add something bright to her life. It was all a vague dream to her. I don't understand it completely, but I suppose her loneliness fed it, made dreaming possible while the years passed and she went on adding to her postcard collection and taking walks at night under these high white stars.

Of course the rest of us thought he would never come back. He'd been gone so long what difference would it make anyway? Besides, what we remembered of him hadn't been something you would pin much hope on—a tall, lank bachelor with thinning hair and loose red hands that played vacantly with jackknives and straps on metal suitcases. No, I figured the only way he'd ever return would be in a wood box shoved in amongst piles of crated fruit on a railroad refrigerator car. Someday, I figured, the manager of some cheap boardinghouse in Buffalo, New York, or Trenton, New Jersey, would happen to remember that he hadn't seen Lyman lately, that the rent was overdue, or that there seemed to be some rank, foul stench oozing out of that room upstairs; so he would mount those dark stairs, knock, get no answer, then try his master key and discover Lyman dead as fish on the sagging bed, and then after looking in his wallet and removing rent money and a little extra for the trouble, he would ship his cold stiff body home to a rural address in Holt County, Colorado. But Edith knew better than the rest of us.

She was certain that he would come back. I remember spending a long evening sitting next to her on the couch, with the postcards pinned neat on the walls around us, during that first winter after Clevis and Twyla had gone. It must have been soon after Christmas because she had a new package of twenty-dollar bills.

"Did I tell you Lyman's in Pittsburgh?"

"Is he?" I said.

"Yes. He sent me another card and this packet of money."

She handed me the money to admire. I turned it over a couple of times and gave it back. "What's he doing in Pittsburgh?"

"I believe he's doing very well."

Then she stood up from the couch and brought a shoe box from the bureau and set it on my lap. "Open it," she said.

"Now, Edith," I said.

"It's all right. There's no secret between us, Sandy."

So I opened it. Not that it was any surprise to me; I knew what I'd find inside—all those packets of unused, unspent dollar bills, all of them twenties, all still wrapped like a seven-year-old kid might wrap them in red bows. It was obvious which packets had been sent first, too. The bows tied around the earliest bills looked frayed and ragged, as if they had been handled too often in the long silence of evening, as if they had been fussed over—not for themselves, though, because I don't think for a minute that the actual fact or worth of the money meant a piddling thing to her. I doubt that she even counted it. It wasn't money she needed; she had all the farm profits. Instead, those damn bungled packets of green stuff seemed to represent something else to her, something more, and just because they had been tied, stamped, and mailed by Lyman's hand. I suppose she thought they were proof of something.

"But why don't you spend some of this?" I said. "Buy something. You could take a trip yourself. Get away for a while."

"Oh, I will," she said. "When he comes back."

"But that might not happen, Edith."

"Of course it will." She looked at me like I was a little slower than usual. "Of course he'll come back."

"Okay," I said. "He will then."

She took the shoe box from me and put the lid on it. "There wouldn't be any point if he doesn't," she said. "Would there?"

So it was then that I put my arm around her. I felt so damn sorry for her. It seemed to me she had lost so much of her life to waiting, and she was still waiting even now. And for what? For nothing, I thought. For a wandering bum, a damn mush-minded permanent escapee, her brother. So I pulled her close; she rested her head against my shoulder. She was thin and small. Under the cotton of her dress I could feel the points of her shoulders and the clean edges of her shoulder blades. Her hair had grown a little gray at the temples but it was still curly and still primarily dark, and her eyes were still clear brown, though behind them there was a kind of pained, distant look. The skin of her cheeks, with threading wrinkles beside her eyes, was smooth. So we sat together for a moment on the couch, and I ran my hand over her hair, cupping her head, and out of affectionate concern for her I kissed the top of her head, and then—smelling her hair—I began to kiss the side of her face, her smooth soft cheek, and then it was not just concern that I was feeling, and suddenly I was pressing against her mouth and she was not resisting or stopping me but allowing it to continue and maybe even returning some of it. I slipped my hand into the back of her dress and felt the silk there, the points of bone along her spine and her bra strap, and then it stopped. I stood up.

I walked over to the doorway and stood with my back to her. "I didn't intend for this—"

"Sandy," she said. "Look at me."

I turned to face her. She was still seated on the couch with the shoe box of Lyman's money beside her. Her dress was low on one shoulder.

"You didn't mean any harm," she said.

"Maybe not," I said. "But I'd better go."

"Yes, but only if you promise you'll come back. We've been more than friends for a long time; I couldn't stand it if that ended too."

"I'll stop by tomorrow. Or the next day."

"Don't make it too long," she said.

Then I left and went outside and damned myself for a fool, while the stars winked overhead like so many clowns' eyes. What in Christ's name did I think I was doing? Sure she was good-looking. Of course she was a fine woman, a person you just naturally felt good being near and wanted to help if you could. But what help was any of what I'd been doing on the couch? That was a lot of help, wasn't it? She was thirty-one years older than I was, after all, and more to the point, she might have been closer to me than just a good neighbor woman down the road if in 1922 my dad had been able to persuade her to give up her iron sense of duty. Sometimes, hell, it seems to me that I'll always have more of balls than I ever will of brains. Sometimes I'm flat a goddamn fool.

Anyway, after that night I didn't go back the next day, or the next. It was almost two weeks before I returned to see Edith, and then when I entered that postcard living room again I made a point of sitting on a straight chair. I stayed away from the couch. Edith, though, was no different than she had been before. She was still pleasant, a little vacant maybe, like she was still caught inside that fog dream of hers, but pleasant nonetheless, as if nothing new had happened between us. So it was comfortable with her again, and I went on stopping by the house in the evening to see her, to visit and pass the time between old friends. I did that at least once a week as the winter turned spring and the pattern returned.

THEN TOWARD the end of July—this would still be 1961—she called me one evening early. "Good, you're home," she said.

"I just came in."

"I have a surprise for you. Will you come for supper?"

So I cleaned up, combed my hair and shaved, and drove down to the Goodnough place. And there, parked in front of the house at the picket gate, was a new green Pontiac with out-of-state plates, and inside the house, sitting with his elbows on the kitchen table and that foolish lap-dog's grin on his face, was Lyman Goodnough.

"Well," I said. "I'll be go to hell."

He stood up to shake my hand. "Long time no see."

He sat down again and grinned some more, as if he expected me to make some appropriate formal remarks upon his safe return to the house. Edith stood beside him with a hand on his shoulder. She was beaming; her face shone like a fresh pink poppy. I admit they made a picture, the two of them smiling at me from across the kitchen table, but I wasn't up to it. I wasn't so forgiving as Edith was.

In the almost twenty years that he had been gone, renting rooms in this country's cities and sending penny postcards home to prove he had, Lyman had gone bald, turned shiny as glass on top; he was still tall and spare as a rail, only now instead of wearing farm-boy overalls and sand-caked shoes he was draped fancy in a new houndstooth suit that was too hot and too heavy for July; on his feet he sported black-and-white wing tips that any Las Vegas gambler or East Colfax pimp in Denver would have thought twice about wearing in public. He was a sight.

Edith herself was dressed as for a party. She had gotten out a silky summer dress that must have been fashionable in the 1920s and had combed her hair back from her face in a way I'd never seen before. It was obvious that she was pink with pleasure at having him home. During dinner, I remember, there didn't seem to be enough that she could do for him; she kept popping up and down like a girl who was having a boyfriend over for dinner and family approval. She was positively solicitous and festive at the same time, worrying cheerfully whether Lyman had enough roast beef and sweet potatoes to eat and concerning herself happily as to the hotness of his coffee. Meanwhile, Lyman masticated and talked with his mouth full; he sat there picking his teeth like a landlord and regaled us with news of his wide travels. Los Angeles, California, was bigger than we could believe. Mobile, Alabama, on the other hand, wasn't so big, but it was hot. Over dessert, he allowed that we could keep New York City. He'd had all he wanted of New York City, New York.

That's the way dinner went that evening: Lyman gave us travelogue while Edith fed us roast beef and cherry pie. Afterwards, after we had finished eating and Lyman had talked himself full circle home again, Edith put on an apron and began to sing to herself over the dishes in the sink. Then her brother coaxed me outside to get the benefit of his Pontiac. It stood purple-green under the yard light, one of those long heavy boats they made in the early sixties, with chrome. He opened the driver's door. "Try her out," he said.

"I don't think so," I said.

"Just sit in her then."

"No thanks."

"Well, she drives like a wet dream. Already put eleven thousand miles on her."

"Sure," I said. "All right. But what in goddamn hell took you so long? It's been almost twenty years. Didn't you know she was waiting all this time?"

"Who?"

"Edith. For christsake. Your sister."

"Oh. Well," he said. He shut the car door. "There is a lot of cities, Sandy. You just don't have a idea till you start looking."

"And you had to see every damn one of them, is that it?"

"No, sir," he said. "Nope, I skipped a few. I found out they was much alike."

So that was Lyman Goodnough. What in hell were you going to do with him? Well, of course Edith knew very well what to do with him. She took him in and fed him supper—because after all, despite everything, despite almost two decades of waiting, he was home again now like only she knew he would be. And she was glad that he was.

Outside under the yard light Lyman stood in front of his car flicking dead grasshoppers and dead millers off the chrome of the grill. "You suppose she has some more cherry pie?" he said. "That's one thing I missed."

"Don't tell me," I said. "Tell her."

.9.

Now I don't pretend to think that a mere stretch of six years is anywhere near enough time. But I suppose if that's all you're given and no more, then six years will have to do. In the end that's what Edith Goodnough had: she had six years of what you may call fun. Or good times. Or better, just the day-in, day-out mean rich goodness of being alive, when at night you lie down in the warm dark pleased with your corner of the world, and then you wake the next morning still pleased with it, and you know that, too, while you lie there for a time listening in peace to the mourning doves calling from the elm trees and telephone lines, until finally the thought of black coffee moves you up out of bed and down the stairs to the kitchen stove, so that once again you can begin it all afresh, with pleasure, with eagerness even. Because yes, Edith had that for a while. During that period it was written all over her face. Her brown eyes shone and snapped for six years.

Of course you might always wish that it had been longer, or that it had come earlier, when she was still young, when she still might have borne children, when my dad was still alive, but wishing for such things is a waste of time; it doesn't make them happen. My dad taught me that, told me as much that day in 1943 when he knocked sense or at least fear into Old Man Goodnough and then afterwards talked to me while I drank beer for the first time and got drunk. So I try to remember it, and even today, knowing what I do about the end, I still take satisfaction in remembering that though Edith was sixty-four when her brother finally returned in his wool suit and Pontiac, and despite the fact that Lyman himself was sixty-two, still, together, almost as if they were honeymooners, they had those six good years from 1961 until 1967 before things suddenly went bad again. It doesn't change those years to know that after 1967 things turned so much worse finally that something desperate had to be done to end them. Regardless, they were still good years, good times. I believe that.

THE GOOD TIMES began that same evening, the night Lyman was home again for supper and I was asked over to enjoy the surprise of him. I told you that after we'd eaten he wanted me to see his car and that I refused to sit in it. At the time I was still disgusted. Here he was back in the house again after all that lapsed time; he was eating his sister's cherry pie and sporting those damn two-tone wing-tip shoes under her kitchen table—without one word of apology or real explanation for having taken so long. But I got over it; I decided that if it made Edith happy—and I could see that it did—then it wasn't my business to be disgusted or angry or any more asinine than I'd already been. So I tried to partake of their enjoyment. I helped Lyman carry his miserable beat-up metal-and-cardboard suitcases into the house.

He spread them out on the living-room floor. It was like he was Saint Nick in July. Like he was some far-flung sailor returned home safe from the seven seas. Hell, I don't know—it was like he imagined himself to be some modern form of Marco Polo come back from the farthest reaches of Outer Mongolia with spoils to prove it. He had treasure for us, for the farm-stuck cocklebur home folks. His suit-cases were loaded with the stuff. He spread it around. He gave each of us something. Edith prized what he gave her about fifty-seven times more than it was worth, as if what he'd given her actually amounted to something. She danced back and forth to the mirror to wonder at the latest doo-dad he hung on her. But, in truth, it was all just junk, an old bachelor's collection of tourist trinkets. You can buy better things on Sidewalk Sale Day in front of Duckwall's in downtown Holt. But that didn't matter to Edith: it was from her brother. He gave her a scarf from Boise, Idaho; a heavy bracelet from the Omaha stockyards; a silver neck-lace affair that dangled a thin pendant in the shape of a Georgia peach. And me, why me he gave a shoehorn from Pittsburgh, Pennsylvania. It had the name of some shoe-store scratched on the tin handle. I took it and didn't laugh. But what the hell did I need with a shoehorn, even if it was from Pittsburgh? I wear boots.

Anyway, I said, "Thank you, Lyman. I appreciate this."

He went on dispensing and displaying his junk, his proof of travel. By the time he had finished Edith looked like a circus gypsy. She was weighted with cheap neck-laces, purple scarves, earrings and dangling bracelets—all with city names on them. She gave him in return a hug and a kiss; they were having a fine time of it. Then she took him by the hand and led him around the walls of the living room to examine and explain each postcard he had sent her, and each one reminded him of something, re-called for him in droning detail the days and months he'd spent in each place. Edith was as attentive as a lover. She kept saying things like, "And this one you sent from Cleve-land, didn't you? What happend there?" And he would tell her of course; Lyman didn't require much prompting. He was full of stories. I watched them from the rocking chair, feeling as out of place as an old maid aunt chaperoning at a kids' party—they were having such a time.

When they had made the complete circuit of the postcards, Edith sat him down again on the couch behind his opened, emptied suitcases. "Now there's something more I want to show you," she said.

"Can't we have some more pie first?"

"No, you can't. Not yet. I've got a surprise for you."

She went over to the bureau and brought back that shoe box of hers, the one with those damned unspent, unused, never-even-counted twenty-dollar bills wrapped in bows.

"What's this?" he said.

"Yours. Ours now."

"How come . . ."

He looked up at her from the couch, and she was staring down at him out of all those years. He didn't know what to say. He rifled through the fussed-over bills, stacked them in piles, counted them out on the couch.

"That makes twenty-seven hundred dollars," he said. "How come you never used it?"

"Because."

"You never spent a one?"

"No."

"Look here, Sandy," he said. "She never spent my money."

"I know it," I said. "I've seen that box before."

I stood up to leave then. Edith tried to keep me there for more dessert, but I was full. I was too full, for the moment, of everything.

They walked with me to the back porch door. From my pickup I looked back at them; they stood waving at me from the lighted doorway—a tall gaunt bald-headed man in a winter suit beside a trim little lady with shining brown eyes—two kids in their sixties with arms linked.

I went home. In the kitchen I poured myself a long shot

of Jack Daniel's without water or ice, threw it down, poured another and seated myself in the easy chair in front of the television to watch the ten-o'clock news and weather. Lyman was home and Edith was pleased. Bleary eyed, I watched Rusty Thompson, the Denver weather man, predict sun for tomorrow.

So Edith and Lyman Goodnough got to be kids for a while. It was like they were just-bloomed teenagers, full of overdue sap and pent-up vinegar. The time was ripe for it, too. The country, remember, and even Holt County, was up for grabs during that period. I'm talking here about the 1960s, when kids everywhere were growing hair and wearing costumes, showing their breasts and generally refusing to do whatever it was their folks knew damn well they should do, had by God better do if they knew what was good for them, until some of them began to get permanent greetings and immediate marching orders from a Texas president, and then it turned out that it wasn't so good for them after all, because so many never came back alive. It was a stupid war. We lost two boys from Holt County to it. They were our insane ante in that murderous poker game. But I'm not going to talk about that: too much has already been said about it and none of it helps. No, I'm talking about my neighbors, the Goodnoughs, who were also kids in the sixties.

I suppose you could say that what happened to them was like they were having a second childhood—only that wouldn't be accurate. You can't have seconds of something until after you've had firsts of the thing. And of course they never had firsts. Ada Twamley, their mother, had been too weak chinned, too consumed with dreaming backwards, to see to it that Edith and Lyman were allowed to be kids while she herself still lived; then she died and left them alone in total charge and control of the old man. And that old son of a bitch didn't believe in any such luxuries; kids were laborers to him, custom-made, self-sired farmhands to be ordered around however, whenever, he deemed fit. Besides, there were always those stumps of his and that routine meanness, as if he figured it was not only his God-given right but his particular duty too to be forever mean and harsh. But I already told you some of that, told you too that he released them finally by dying in that upstairs bedroom with his mouth locked open. Of course it took Lyman nine years to realize it. But, anyway, now he had; he was home again. For the first time in their lives, Edith and her brother were absolutely alone on that farm in that house down the road from me.

They didn't quite know what to make of it at first. What in the world were they going to do with all that vacation time, that freedom from duty and direction? Well, they didn't do anything rash, exactly. On her part Edith learned to sip gimlets from a barroom goblet, to go a little giggly and pink cheeked in a nice sort of girlish way. And as for Lyman, once he was home and realized there wasn't anyone there to tell him what to do, Lyman refused to change clothes. What I mean is, he wouldn't wear work shoes or overalls again. He went on dressing up every day like he believed he was a banker, a retired mortician. Every day he put on his wing tips, his dress pants, shirt, and tie. He was definitely finished with farming; he wasn't going to plow sand anymore. As far as he was concerned, I could go on farming their place just as I had done for the past ten years. They got their share of the profits regularly; they had that twenty-seven hundred dollars Edith had saved; it was fine with Lyman. So now they had both money and freedom, and a new green Pontiac waiting outside at the picket gate.

They put miles on it. If the slightest urge took them—
and it took them about three times a week—they went to
town. To see a show, watch a softball game, buy some
blue grapes, get a sack of Bing cherries, whatever. Why
hell, they even started to drive out Saturday night to dance
at the Holt Legion. There they'd be, Edith sipping gimlets
and Lyman nursing Coors beer in a corner booth, until
Shorty Stovall and the boys struck up their rendition of
the "Tennessee Waltz," and then they would rise and slide
slow around the floor in a kind of funeral two-step, her
hand on the padded shoulder of his houndstooth suit coat.
Also they drove to Denver, went to Elitch's Amusement
Park, viewed the summer show at Central City, toured
Estes Park, ate the trout dinner at the Broadmoor Hotel
in Colorado Springs, watched the buffalo herds trot across
the highway in the Black Hills. By God, where didn't they
go? It got so they were a regular traveling concern.

And you understand, before this time Edith had never
once seen a thing of life beyond the Holt County border?
Not a thing, not once. Now the whole of this Rocky
Mountain region was hers. She only had to mention an
interest, hint that she wanted to see something—"Lyman,
how far down do you suppose it is from the Royal Gorge
Bridge?"—and they would take off to find out. Lyman
himself was ready to go; in the previous twenty years he
had grown used to traveling on any impulse. Gasoline was
cheap, his Pontiac was new. On an urge, then, usually
Edith's, they would shut the back porch door and leave,
see themselves some new sight, and then come back tired
but satisfied, and the next day Lyman would hand wax
his green car while Edith finished unpacking and fed the
chickens and began to listen for the next urge to take her,
tell her what it wanted her to see. During that six-year
period they must have passed this house at least a thousand

times—going places. I'd see them at any time of the day or night, driving, the windows rolled down, the dust rolling up behind them. Lyman would always be at the wheel in his dress shirt and tie, as solemn as if he was going to trial. Beside him would be his sister, Edith Goodnough in a pale lavender or blue dress, waving at me like a girl as she passed my house on the way out.

But I don't suppose they were off traveling all that time, because they also began to fix up that old frame house, which their father had constructed by himself with wagon-hauled lumber from town before either one of them was born. He had kept the house up all along but had never seen any reason to do much extra; it was tight and kept out the wind, which was what he required. To do more would have been too much. So sometime in there Edith and Lyman painted it a bright canary yellow and had the Wilky brothers from west of town give it a new shingle roof. Inside, they bought some new carpet for the down-stairs living-room and parlor floors. They had me over to see the carpet.

I admired it, then Lyman brought me back to the kitchen. "Look there," he said. "What do you make of that thing?"

"Looks like a Kelvinator dishwasher to me," I said. "But what do I know? Maybe it's a new form of TV."

"Watch this."

"Oh, now, Lyman," Edith said. "Sandy doesn't have time for this too." She swatted at him.

"Course he does," Lyman said.

"Course I do," I said.

And I did. We sat down at the kitchen table and drank soda pop while their new dishwasher worked through the entire soap and rinse cycles.

"There. That click means it's done," Lyman said. "Now won't she get lazy with that thing in the house?"

"Lazy as a hog," I said.

172

"Never you mind," Edith said. "Either one of you. Who knows—I might take a notion to get fat too. Then what will you say?"

"Nothing. Good," I said.

Together they were having such a hell of a fine time of it. It was fun to watch them.

So in the summer of 1963 I got married. Or, to be more accurate, I should say Mavis Pickett decided she was not going to wait any longer.

"Aren't we ever going to be married?" she said.

"Sure," I said. "I was just waiting for you to pop the question."

"That's not funny."

"Isn't it?"

"No, it is not."

It was about two o'clock in the morning and we were driving north out of town towards her folks' place after the annual Fireman's Ball at the Holt Legion. I was about half drunk, feeling pretty good, but Mavis Pickett wasn't either of those things. She was stone-cold serious. We had been going out together for at least two years, off and on, and in her view of things our going out to dances and to movies and local parties had not led us anywhere. She was twenty-nine years old. She wanted to be married.

Which is all right, of course. Only I'm still not sure why it was me she chose to be the beneficiary of that. It's enough to give me pause even now. I wasn't what you might call a great catch. I was thirty-five. This gut you see here was already beginning to polish my belt buckle. I had knocked around, drunk too much, worked too little, developed bachelor habits. I was never going to be one of your sandhill millionaire successes: I didn't have the ambition for it. No, if I was ever going to amount to a decent hill of beans or just a load of dung out of the ordinary, then I should have begun to show some sign of it by then. And I hadn't. So I don't know what she saw in me. Maybe it was the challenge. At the time Mavis was working as an L.P.N. at the hospital, and she was used to dealing with cold feet and lost causes. On the other hand, I had good reason to believe she loved me. I'm pretty sure she still does. Probably that clouded her view.

But when a woman like Mavis Pickett loves you, says in so many words that you're her form of It, who are you to argue? You're a damn fool if you do. I wasn't that much of a fool. She was level-headed and good-looking at the same time. That's an unusual combination. She had thick blond hair and green eyes, and when she was crossed she could run the strong stuff out of your backbone like it was so much water; she didn't appreciate nonsense. We've had plenty of good times in thirteen years together. We've managed to survive the bad times. If she wasn't in town right now waiting for me to come in a couple of hours to pick her up so we can visit the hospital again, she would no doubt tell you that I'm too bullheaded, that sometimes I lock gates that should be left open. I don't think logically, she would say. On my side, I might wish occasionally that she had a sense of humor—but it's worked out. For both of us.

At any rate, Mavis got us married toward the end of July 1963. I didn't put up much opposition. I didn't even argue a lot when she insisted that I had to do the proper thing, that I come to Sunday dinner and ask her father, old Raymond Pickett, whether he had objections. All I said was:

"How about if I wrote him a postcard?"

"You're coming to dinner," she said.

"What if I called him on the phone?"

"No. You will be there at one o'clock. After we get home from church."

"I'm not going to church. I don't believe in it."

"All right. But you will be there for dinner. And you will ask him face-to-face like you're supposed to."

"What if he wants to know what my intentions are?"

"Make something up. You're good at that."

"Well, Jesus," I said. "You're a hard woman."

"Yes, and you can stop cussing. It'll be all right. It'll be just fine."

"Like hell," I said.

"You'll see," she said.

Mavis was a little old-fashioned that way. She still is. She has a firm idea of how things are meant to be and she usually sees to it that they turn out the way they're meant to. They certainly did that Sunday afternoon, cooked chicken and all. I put on a white shirt at twelve o'clock and knotted a tie under my chin, then I drove north through Holt's church traffic and on another eight miles to the Pickett place, where at a heavy oak table supported by a massive pedestal I ate fried chicken and refrained from sucking the grease off my fingers. It was one of those long quiet awkward dinners. Mavis and her mother talked above the platters of food and fine china while her father and I allowed that it was about normal weather for the time of year. Afterwards, according to plan, the womenfolks cleared the table and Raymond Pickett and I removed ourselves to the parlor. We sat down opposite one another.

After a time I said to him, "I suppose you know what I'm doing here."

"I see you got your tie on," he said. "I figured there was some reason for it."

"There is."

"More than just to eat Mavis's chicken dinner, you mean."

You understand the old son of a gun, that old wheat farmer, wasn't going to help me any. He was enjoying himself; it was better than a Sunday afternoon nap. Usually he was the sober type, steady and humorless as a corner fence post, but now with a straight face he was playing me like a calf.

"That," I said. "And also to see what you thought of Mavis and me getting married."

"Tell the truth," he said, "I haven't given it much thought."

"Mavis has," I said.

"Has she now?"

"Yes. Considerable."

"And what does she think about it?"

"She's in favor of it."

"But you ain't said nothing about yourself yet. Most times I believe it takes two to get married."

"Oh, I don't mind," I said.

"Well, now," he said, looking at me. "Well, now. She's in favor and you say you don't mind. I guess that'll have to do, won't it?"

He kept looking at me. He had the usual white forehead and burnt cheeks and neck that all farmers have, but I could see where Mavis got her eyes. Finally he bent down over his knees and began to untie the laces in his town shoes.

"I don't like these tie-up shoes," he said. "Always make my feet hurt. The missus says that's so I'll keep awake in church. Most times she's right too."

He didn't take his shoes off—I was still company as yet—but merely loosened the laces good, then he sat up straight again and in his own time blew his nose thoroughly, one nostril then the other, loud, and put the handkerchief back in his hip pocket.

"I don't know whether you know it, Sanders," he said,

176

"but I was well acquainted with your father. I used to see him at farm sales. He was a good man, your father was. I don't know your mother."

"No," I said. "She doesn't go to farm sales."

"I suppose not," he said. "Well, now. About this marriage business—it sounds like Mavis has her mind all made up."

I nodded.

"She's like that. So I don't see where it would do me much good to object even if I wanted to. Can you?"

"No."

"I thought as much. Well, it's nice having girls in the house. I believe I'll miss that."

That was all he said. We talked about wheat prices and farm futures afterwards. Then the women came into the parlor with us, and after a while Mavis and I excused ourselves and went outside to walk along the windbreak planted westerly towards a slight hill.

"Well?" she said.

"Well what?" I said.

"What'd he say?"

"Weren't you listening from the kitchen?"

"Yes, but I want you to tell me."

"Well. He said I was a damn fool to want to marry any daughter of his. You're too hardhearted, he said. Then he asked me if I had any intentions to speak of."

"He did not."

"Sure he did. 'What are your intentions?' he said. Go and ask him."

"All right then, what did you say?"

"Nothing. I didn't say a word. I told him I didn't have any intentions. Other than throwing you down in bed every chance I get."

"You've already done that."

"I plan to do it again. Right now."

"Don't be silly. They can still see us from the house."

"Hell," I said. "We're as good as married already, aren't we?"

"No," she said. "But we will be. Now stop that and tell me what he said."

THE ONLY interesting particular I recall now about the wedding was the thing that happened just afterwards. The wedding was over; we had promised our mutual I do's; Mavis and I were coming down the church steps to get inside my paint-smeared car and away from all the thrown rice. People were gathered in two rows along the steps and sidewalk—her folks; my mother and her last husband, Wilbur Cox; Edith and Lyman Goodnough; a crowd of others, friends. We had just about reached the safety of my car when Vince Higgims, Junior, one of my drinking partners from the Holt Tavern, grabbed Mavis up in his arms and started to run with her. She still had that white dress on and that collection of stiff petticoats, all of which swooped up so high in his arms that you could see her garters and clear to Denver if you wanted to. Vince Jr. was about smothered. I believe his idea was to kidnap her, spirit her away so that I would have to come look for her. Which might have been funny, only Vince didn't know Mavis enough. In no time Mavis worked one arm free and jammed Vince so hard in the Adam's apple with her elbow that he dropped down cold like he'd been shot with both barrels. Her white dress and stockinged legs were all over him, the two of them sprawled out on the church curb, so that after they were eventually untangled somebody had to take old Vince over to Doc Schmidt to determine how much damage he had suffered to his throat. It turned out he was lucky; he just had to stay off solids for a week.

Vince said it was enough to scare him off weddings altogether.

When I was sure he was going to at least be able to drink again, Mavis and I got in the car and drove off for the honeymoon. We went across the Continental Divide to Glenwood Springs on the Western Slope and stayed a few days in the great old Hotel Colorado, where Teddy Roosevelt had once spent some time, and we swam with the tourists and arthritic patients in the block-long hot pool that smelled of sulphur. Later we drove up the valley to Aspen and spent an afternoon and an evening amongst the wealthy summer crowd. Then we came home again to this house. Mavis was still working as a nurse at the hospital, but when she wasn't changing bedpans or taking blood pressures she was remaking our house to please her, and I went back to farming and ranching, cultivating corn, baling hay, and cutting calves. It was nice coming in for supper and finding her still there every evening waiting for me. She looked good and cool and fresh after I'd been outside in the sun away from her all day. After supper we often had the Goodnoughs over to play Rook or went to their place, and about twice a month the four of us went to the Legion dances on Saturday night. Mavis and Edith got to be good friends. She could tell you some things about Edith that I can't.

Then it was August 1967, and Mavis wasn't working at the hospital anymore because she was eight months pregnant. Her stomach was swollen and hard, blue veined, tight. I could feel with my hand how the little beggar kicked and swam, did his half gainers and watery flips, like he was showing off for us inside his warm sac, like he believed he was nothing so much as a green frog cavorting for all the world in a horse tank. But I was a little concerned about it too. I knew at thirty-three that it was somewhat late for Mavis to be carrying her first baby, but she wouldn't hear of it. She refused to let me worry. She had helped any number of babies get born at the hospital, and now she had all the confidence and all the equipment she needed to bear this one. I could stop worrying. So I did and we were both pleased about the prospect of having a little boy in the house. It would be a boy, we knew that. We were looking forward to it.

Bᴜᴛ Aᴜɢᴜꜱᴛ is also traditional Holt County Fair time, and 1967 was no different. It's considered a big deal around here; everyone and his horse attends, able or not, one hoof in the grave or not. It gives us the opportunity—and the excuse too, I suppose—to visit with folks we haven't seen for a year.

In the week before the fair is to begin the Lions Club rakes up the accumulated twelve months of trash at the fairgrounds; they burn the trash and the blown-in tumbleweeds behind the buildings, then they loiter in groups, eating Rocky Mountain oysters and potato salad and drinking beer from kegs. Meanwhile the 4-H kids in the county have begun to fit their steers for the judging by clipping the heads and ears of the animals and by ratting the tails into balls; the kids' mothers and aunts and grandmothers choose their best bread-and-butter pickles for display; somebody begins to work up the racetrack with a disk for the horse races, and somebody else helps the stock contractor unload his bulls and bucking horses at the chutes across the arena from the grandstand. On the afternoon before it is all to begin the carnival people finally pull into town in their battered trucks. They're usually a bad crew of greasy characters, appearing dog tired, looking as bored with it all as if they have seen it all, and maybe they have. Sweating and cursing, they establish the booths and rides in the fresh-mowed cheat weeds. So then it's time. Opening day begins with a parade.

It's not much of a parade. Just a hometown affair so as not to worry Macy's, but we went to it that year anyway. This was despite Mavis's eight-month condition. I told her we ought to skip it.

"We can go this afternoon," I said. "We can walk around the booths and then you can watch the rodeo from the grandstand."

"You're not listening to me," she said. "I have to get out of this house. I'm sick of this house."

"All right. I can see that."

"And you know I won't be any more uncomfortable in town than I am here. Don't you know that? But I'll tell you what it is."

"What?"

"It's because you're embarrassed to be seen with me. I'm getting too big."

"That's crazy," I said. "Vince, Junior, told me the other day when he saw us together—he told me you make me look skinny. Hell, he thought I must be losing some weight, and I told him to keep thinking like that."

"So what are you talking about?"

"It's just that I'm afraid you'll get tired. That's all. Then I'll probably have to carry you around on my back and come damn near ruining myself."

"I won't get that tired," she said.

"You're sure?"

"Yes. Now do we go to the parade together or don't we?"

"All I know is," I said. "You're getting flat unruly. That's a fact."

So we went to the parade all right. We did the entire opening-day program. Only we didn't go alone. We drove in to town with the Goodnoughs in Lyman's Pontiac. The

181

day before he had waxed it fresh for the occasion, and I figured the big back seat of that boat of his would be good for my wife. When we got to town that morning he parked the car on a side street away from traffic, then the four of us walked over to Main Street and found a place out of the sun in front of the Coast to Coast store on the east side of the street. There were already hundreds of people lining both sides. Some of the old-timers had arrived early enough to unfold lawn chairs along the curb, and there were kids everywhere, teenagers in shorts and little kids with balloons and cones of ice, and all the townspeople and area farmers. A little after ten o'clock the parade started.

The color guard came first. They came marching north up Main Street from the high school toward us, and everybody stood still while they passed, four middle-aged veterans stuffed into wool uniforms and sweating plenty. They were followed by some guys on horseback; then the school band was there playing some march or other while the band director hotfooted it along beside them; some more horses then; then the Holt County Fair queen and her two attendants rode up, each of them in new felt hats and bright cowgirl outfits and looking straight ahead without a smile when one of the girls' horses raised its tail to drop road apples along the pavement in front of everybody; then some kids on decorated bikes; then a half-dozen boosters in convertibles and some more horses; then a float or two, the Future Farmers of America float with some high school boys dressed like Arabs smoking cigarettes in long holders; and the local implement company's float consisting of an old manure spreader with a painted sign taped to it that said: WE STAND BEHIND WHAT WE SELL; then the candidates for county clerk waving and smiling from convertibles, acknowledging the folks of voting age and throwing candy to the kids, the kids all scrambling for it and their mothers checking to see that it was wrapped in wax paper; then some old tractors and antique cars and still more horses. The city street cleaner with its spray of water and rotating brushes ended the parade. It was finished by eleven o'clock.

"Well," I said. "That appears to wrap up any parade for the year. Now what?"

"I say we eat," Lyman said. "Sis here got me up before breakfast."

We all looked at Edith. "Oh, I don't listen to him anymore," she said. "Next thing you know he'll want a tray in bed."

"That's the idea," he said.

"No," I said. "You want to be careful. One summer she brought me a tray of food out to the side yard every day and I just about died of bloat and discomfort."

"Do you remember that?" Edith said.

"Sure. Every mouthful."

"That was a long time ago. You were a nice little boy then."

"I still am."

"Of course you are," she said. She patted my cheek.

"Sometimes he is," Mavis said. "But I agree with Lyman. I'm starving."

The cafés in town were all crowded with people waiting to find places to sit down, so we drove out to the fairgrounds. Inside the gate a deputy sheriff waved us over toward the parking lots; Lyman parked his Pontiac at a chalked line and we locked the doors to his satisfaction, then we ate lunch behind the grandstand in one of the booths that had a lean-to roof built out over one side with wire screening nailed onto two-by-fours to keep the flies out. There were always a lot of flies during the fair. It tended to discourage some people's appetite to see flies swimming in the mustard and pickle relish, so a couple of years previous the fair board had ordered screens put up. We each had a hamburger and something to drink; Mavis ordered another sandwich and we kidded her about it. Afterwards we decided to see the exhibits and some of the livestock judging before the rodeo started.

When we got to the hog barn they were judging the January boar-pig contest. We sat down to watch the fun from the second row of the bleachers. In front of us was a good-sized enclosure of heavy fence panels with sawdust spread deep on the dirt floor. The 4-H kids had already run the pigs into the pen and were trying now to move the pigs back and forth in front of the judge so he could see the muscling. It was hard work. The pigs were tall, long, tough hided, independent. It was hot in there under the tin roof. The pigs were hot; a pig doesn't have a very good cooling system, you know. They kept moiling, trotting off to look for mud. Their round eyes looked mean, heavy lashed; their big ears flopped the flies away while their squirreled tails twisted and switched as they moved, and they were all grunting and squealing up one hell of a pig racket. If anything, the kids looked hotter, more miserable than the pigs. The kids were red-faced from the strain, and nervous, dressed right for the show in new blue jeans and white shirts and wielding hog canes and racehorse bats in the attempt to keep those damn big pigs circling to the best advantage in front of the judge. It required considerable whacking and wielding of canes to do that.

Meanwhile the judge stood ankle deep in the sawdust and pig squirt in the center of the pen. He had his arms folded and he did not look happy. He was hired as pig judge; he took himself serious as Sunday. I believe a cold beer in a cool bar would have saved him. And all the time the 4-H kids were having a hell of a time of it: the pigs wouldn't cooperate. They were either trying to dig out from under the fence panels with their tough snouts and so get shut of that miserable hot business, or they were fighting, a bad racket then, a higher pitched squeal than before, if that was possible; it made your hat jump—the two pigs squealing, chewing at one another's ears and jowls while the kids whacked at them, beat with canes and bats and called for the board—"Board! Board!"—until one of the men standing on the outside stepped over the fence and shoved a heavy sheet of plywood down hard between the screaming pigs and stopped the fight. Separated, the pigs would look sort of dumbfounded, like where did that other son of a bitch go, I ain't finished chewing on him yet, and so it would all go on again as before.

Only towards the end there was a slight hitch in the routine, I remember: one of the pigs pissed all over the judge's alligator boots. The kid who owned that pig was in trouble and he knew it. He began to kick sawdust onto the mess but it didn't help a lot. The damage was done. Finally in pure hope he looked up into the judge's face for mercy, for a sign of humor. But the judge apparently didn't have any, or not enough anyway, because when it came time for ribbons the pig with the empty bladder didn't win a thing. In the bleachers we were offended. The pig was our popular favorite. Edith and Mavis booed the judge for an idiot.

"Men," Mavis said.

"Now you can't blame that on us," Lyman said.

"I do," she said.

After the hog judging we walked past the sheep in the wood pens panting in the heat, and saw the quarter horses, their round-muscled butts shining smooth under the lights in the horse barn. Working our way down the alleys between the 4-H kids sitting on tack boxes in the cow barn we saw the show steers and fat heifers lying half asleep on clean straw. The cattle were all trim and neat; some of them still had their ratted, puffed-up tails protected by plastic bags to be clean for the beef-feeding contests when the time came. The cattle were hot.

Outside again, we walked over to the exhibits in the home-ec. building. The county women had their quilts on display, and their artwork, flower arrangements, and pickles. When we got to the bread-and-butter-pickle department we found that Marvella Packwood had won it again. The out-of-town judge had hung a blue ribbon on her pickle jar, which amused Lyman and me a good deal. Everybody in the county knew that Marvella Packwood had just delivered her third kid without benefit of a single marriage certificate. There were folks who found that not only scandalous but excessive. It was the times, they said.

Mavis said, "Don't you say a word, you two."

"But that there was a woman judge," Lyman said. "You ain't going to complain about that?"

"She thinks like a man," Mavis said.

"Looks like a good jar of pickles to me," I said. "Look at that color. I probably ought to 've married her. I always did fancy bread-and-butter pickles with my dinner steak. Didn't you, Lyman?"

"I couldn't get any," he said. "Not where I been. New York never heard of them."

"See there?" I said. "Marvella's doing Lyman and all of us a service. They ought to give her another ribbon."

"Don't be funny," Mavis said.

"They could stick it to her belly."

"Yes. And you've already got one girl eight months pregnant with child. Isn't that enough?"

"I don't know. I can't tell yet."

"Come on," Edith said. She took Mavis's arm and they started to walk away. "These men," she said, "have been out in the heat so long they're getting plain mushy. They're not as strong as we are."

To cool off after the pickle exhibits we went back to the food concessions and had cold drinks. Lyman and I each drank a beer. While the others stayed there in the screened-in shade, I went over to the ticket booths to buy reserved seats in the grandstand for the rodeo. People were starting to file in; there was going to be a good crowd. I stood in line to buy the tickets, watching the people dressed up western for the day in new boots and straw hats. Then Doub Ragsdale, a farmer I knew south of town who had irrigated circles of corn and was doing all right with them, came up behind me. "Hot, isn't she?" he said.

"Ought to make the corn grow," I said. "You can't fault it."

"Yeah, but it wants to rain."

We moved forward a step.

"The wife and kids with you?"

"Over there." He pointed towards the gate. Louise, his wife, was standing with their two boys in the sun in orange stretch pants and a flouncy blouse. She waved at me when she saw I was looking at her.

"Your oldest boy going out for football this year?"

"Maybe," he said. "He's still awful scrawny."

"He'll be all right. Just keep feeding him."

"Yeah, he eats. That's one thing he knows how to do. But he's soft like his mother. Look at them orange pants. It's not like when you and me was little shits."

"No," I said. "Some ways it's worse."

"I don't know," he said. "I don't like it."

That was always Doub. He had that big house and all that irrigated corn, but he complained worse than any wheat farmer will. A wheat farmer will tell you how he's lost his crop five times to dust, flood, drought, hail, and rust before he finally admits that he's harvested it. But I have never understood what Doub had lost. Maybe his perspective.

Anyway, I bought the rodeo tickets and went back to collect the others to go up into the grandstand. The seats were in the center section high up under the roof. We climbed up the aisle steps past all the people we knew, stopping to talk and joke some as we worked our way towards the seats. Edith, I recall, was especially lively that afternoon. It made her feel good to be among all the people, and everyone felt it, enjoyed seeing her, was glad she was happy; it was like she left a wide ripple of pleasure behind her. The women along the aisle took her hand, and the men slapped Lyman neighborly on the back.

When we reached the seats I settled Mavis and the Goodnoughs in their places with cushions to sit on, then I went back down to help with the calf roping. I had agreed to run the roping barrier, but that was all. I wasn't going to rodeo anymore myself; at thirty-nine I was at least four years of marriage past the time when I still had thoughts of being a cowboy. Besides, I didn't want to break my neck bucking off some horse or bull and leave Mavis to bury me. I had doubts about how much spadework a pregnant woman would do. The way I figured it, she would probably only plant me a foot under, then the dogs would dig me up and chew my toes and chase one another for my arm bones. The thought didn't appeal to me. I was satisfied to watch somebody else break his neck while the people in the stands applauded.

The rodeo started as usual with the grand entry. A bunch of guys and girls galloped their horses in figure eights in the arena, then there were some introductions so the rodeo marshals and the fair queens and all the notables could spur their horses forward and lift their hats to the crowd. Afterwards, the national anthem was blared over the loudspeakers; the cowboys held their hats, and the people in the stands rose up and sang; then the invocation was given by the Baptist preacher, who found enough cause to praise God for twenty minutes. When that business was finished, they all stampeded out of the arena and it was time for the first event, the bareback riding.

The rodeo went about as usual that afternoon. There were five or six pretty good young cowboys from different parts of the country, but only about two or three first-class horses. It was getting harder every year for a stock contractor to find good bucking horses; the horses weren't as big—they didn't have much of that raw plow-horse build anymore—so they weren't as rank as they had been twenty and thirty years ago, which meant the scores weren't as high, and I seem to recall only once when they had to open the gates and bring the ambulance into the arena. That was when this long-necked goosey kid from Valentine, Nebraska, stayed on his saddle bronc the full eight seconds. He was still on after the buzzer rang, riding with both hands now and hollering and still trying to hook his horse for some reason, while the pickup men kicked up beside him to take him off, but he didn't seem to know how to grab onto one of them and get off. Then the trouble was they all got to racing too fast, and when they came helling up to the end of the arena the pickup horses knew enough to stop but the saddle bronc didn't. He jumped the fence. I mean he tried to. I suppose he might have made it too, only there was a three-quarter-inch strand of cable strung along the top of the fence posts to discourage any steeplechasing or impromptu fence jumping; so at the last second the horse decided to stick his big raw-boned head under the cable like he thought maybe he could snake through that half foot of empty space between the cable and the top fence rail, like maybe he thought he was some form of circus lion doing the hoops in the center ring. He didn't make it; he slammed to a loud, solid stop. Meanwhile, the kid from Valentine sailed headfirst over the horse's neck and ran his face up against the steel cable.

The cable didn't give a lot, but his face did. They called the ambulance in and rode him off to the hospital to rebuild his nose and sew up his cheek. Afterwards some of the cowboys were riding the pickup men pretty hard about losing a horse race that it appeared they were going to win. Until it came down to the wire, that is. The pickup men felt kind of foolish about it.

"Hell," one of them said. "The knothead wasn't even trying to turn his horse. He acted like he never saw fences in Nebraska."

"Well, you introduced him," somebody said.

"That's a fact," he said. "I doubt he forgets it."

I stayed down there in the arena for the duration of the rodeo, drinking warm beer behind the chutes with the boys and running the barrier for the calf roping when it was time for that event. It wasn't anything onerous. I had to string the rope barrier across the open-ended stall when the roper had his horse backed up inside it, then check to see that the horse didn't break the barrier before the calf was released from the near chute. If the barrier was broken I was supposed to wave a red flag at the judge. I did that twice when a couple of boys got antsy and couldn't hold their horses back. The judge looked over at me from the center of the arena where he was watching the dallying and saw the flag, so the two boys got ten seconds added on to their times. The times weren't anything to blow about anyway. Booger Brannon, a big heavy-set cowboy from south Oklahoma, won the calf roping with a nineteen-seven. Ordinarily he wouldn't have placed.

It was late afternoon by the time the bull riding, the last event, was finished and the final quarter-horse race was contested and won. There would still be a good three hours of sunlight because of daylight savings, but I felt as tired as if I had worked. I suppose all that warm beer contributed to the feeling. At any rate, I was ready to go home. I still had evening chores to do and I wanted to see Mavis seated in a easy chair with her feet up. I believed she must be tired.

The crowd was coming down out of the grandstand, so I waited beside the gate for my wife and the Goodnoughs. I didn't see them. I saw Doub Ragsdale and Louise come by with their two boys, all of them looking miserable and hot, like they weren't satisfied, and then Pace Givens stopped to talk a minute. Pace was a dirt-poor farmer who was trying to hang on to a couple of dryland quarters east of town. His teeth were all rotten and gone to hell.

"By God," he said. "Sanders, by God."

"Yeah," I said.

He was slapping me on the back. I could smell the whiskey on him. "You're all right," he said. "Didn't I ever tell you that?"

"Once or twice," I said.

"Well, don't never weaken."

"That's right."

"Don't never weaken, Sanders."

"Take care of yourself now," I said.

"Hell, I'm all right," he said. "You know why?"

"Because you never weaken."

"I never weaken. That's why."

He was talking at me from about six inches distance from my face; he smelled strong of cheap whiskey, and there were people watching us and smiling as if it was a joke, but I liked Pace Givens nonetheless. He was going to lose those dryland quarters too. They just weren't enough anymore for him to survive on. He slapped me again on the back and walked out the gate in his droop-seated, rag-cuffed overalls.

My wife hadn't come down from the grandstand with Edith and Lyman. I climbed up into the stands; there was no one there except a young woman trying to get a little boy to wake up enough so he would walk and not have to be carried. I began to feel a little worried. I knew this entire opening-day program would be too much. I went back through the gate, looked around, didn't see them, and walked out to Lyman's car. It was still there, green and dust coated now with the afternoon traffic. So I returned to the buildings, walked through the exhibits and the show barns, and finally found the three of them drinking pop in the concession area. They didn't appear concerned. Mavis and Edith were laughing at Lyman. They were giving him some kind of silly shit about something, and Lyman wasn't altogether pleased.

"What's the joke?" I said.

"You don't want to know," Lyman said. "Just buy me a beer. These damn women won't allow nothing but soda pop."

"Don't you dare," Mavis said.

"That's right," Edith said. "He has to admit it was a good system first."

"What was?"

"The system we had for the races."

"Don't listen to them," Lyman said. "Just buy me a beer, will you?"

"Of course. But what happened to your money?"

"I don't have any money. Would I be drinking this damn stuff if I had any money?"

"What happened to it?"

"He lost it."

"The hell I did."

"But we know where it is. Don't we, Edith."

"It's right here," Edith said.

"Listen. If you ain't going to buy me a beer, at least loan me a goddamn dollar. Is that asking too much?"

"You have to admit it was a good system first."

"Damn your damn system."

"I think he's getting mad now."

"All right, here." Lyman stood up and drew a checkbook from the pocket of his dress pants and sat down to write in it. "Here," he said, "I'll sign you a check if you don't think you can even trust me for a goddamn dollar."

"Just a minute," I said. "I trust you. But what the hell are you talking about?"

"I'm talking about that goddamn fool up at the counter that won't take my check. They got him in on this, too."

"Who?"

"These women. Look at 'em, laughing like two cats."

I looked at them again. Mavis was smiling; her hands were folded comfortably on her swollen stomach, and Edith's eyes were snapping bright brown. They were delighted. So I made them a little speech.

"I don't understand any of this," I said. "But I believe Lyman here is in need of a drink. So I'm going to buy him one, system or no system, whatever the hell it is. And I'm going to drink one myself. Now do either of you ladies object to that?"

"I believe Sandy is getting mad too," Edith said.

"No, he's not. He never gets mad. Do you, sweetheart?"

"Of course not," I said. "I just get thirsty."

"But I guess we've had our fun," Mavis said. "What do you think, Edith?"

"I think so," she said. "And let us pay for it. We've got all the money there is."

That set them off again. They were giggling like teenagers and digging in their purses to stuff my hands with bills. I took the money and bought Lyman the beer he wanted, the beer he in fact needed bad now, the beer he was even beginning to get a little mad about not having sooner. I brought it back from the counter in paper cups. I still didn't understand it, but it seems they had made side bets with one another during the quarter-horse races.

Edith and my wife bet each of the six races against Lyman, betting their system against what he knew was good sense. I don't claim to understand that either—perhaps no man could—but their system had something to do with how the color the jockey was wearing complemented the name of the horse the jockey was riding. They gave this as an example: a horse named Cajun Scoot was ridden by a jockey wearing chocolate and peach. That made it a sure winner. It was like ice cream. I didn't see it. But anyway, five of the six horses the women bet on came in ahead of Lyman's horses, and as a result they had won all the pocket money Lyman was carrying. To clinch the matter, they resolved to spend all their winnings—all of Lyman's money—spend it all right there under his nose before they went home that evening. They started by buying that paper cup of beer Lyman wanted but which they weren't going to allow until he agreed it was a good system. You can't tell me women don't have a complicated sense of fair play.

Their resolution to spend all his money, though, meant we weren't going home yet. I would have to do chores in full dark, and Mavis wouldn't have much opportunity to put her feet up. Before we could drive home, we had to do the carnival: throw darts for stuffed monkeys, lick the cotton candy off our fingers, play bingo, toss nickels, drink more beer, ride the Ferris wheel. They got a lot of mileage out of his money. I remember the Ferris wheel best.

Now I'm not big on Ferris wheels. I suppose I feel a little funny riding up and around in a continuous circle with my gut squeezed tight against the locked bar so I won't fall out, while below me on the ground a crowd of kids are waiting in line for me to get off and give them a chance. The kids can't see why I'm doing it and I can't either. But it wasn't too bad that evening. Mavis and I were holding hands over the little boy in her stomach, and we rode up together in the rocking seat in the near dark. The colored lights were on all over the carnival, outlining the booths and the rides; over the loudspeakers they were playing some scratchy rock-and-roll music. From the top we could see far out over the fairgrounds, the grandstand and buildings and across the arena to the bucking chutes where the bucking horses were grazing in the paddocks, and to the south the town, the streetlights on at the corners and the mass of dark trees and rooftops. Edith and Lyman were in a seat in front of us. That's what I mean when I say I remember the Ferris wheel best. It's the picture I hold in mind when I think of that period in their lives.

If Lyman had every really been mad about the beer, he was over it now; he had his arm around his sister. They weren't talking much but just enjoying the late evening. As we came down on the back side of the wheel we could see them below us, rocking a little in the flicker of the colored lights, the music playing, his hand tapping time on her bare arm and her head relaxed a little toward his shoulder. If you didn't know them, you might have believed they were an old couple who still had reason to ride a Ferris wheel together. I hold that picture in mind. We went home afterwards.

On the highway south of Holt is a short wooden bridge called the Five Mile Bridge. No creek or river runs under it, just a weed-choked wash that fills for a day or two in the late spring, when we get most of our annual rainfall. The bridge is not much to speak of, but in this country where there's not much call for bridges of any kind it serves as a landmark. People use it when giving directions to outsiders. Also, it's been the site of two accidents.

One of them involved Buster and Barry Wellright, two

brothers who live ten miles farther south of me in the sandhills. There is a story that goes with it. The Wellrights are middle-aged boys and poor, almost as poor as Pace Givens but with less reason for it, except that they have a habit of drinking too much; they stay too long at the tavern. Consequently they don't always get themselves organized very early the next morning when they get up. The proof of their nightly habits is their big beer bellies and Buster is missing an ear where a corn picker chewed it off. But that's another story. There are a lot of stories about Buster and Barry. They provide a good deal of entertainment for the entire county.

Anyway, this particular story goes that they were driving south on the highway one Saturday night after Tom Bowland finally quit trying to coax them out of the tavern and just turned the lights off. So it was about three o'clock. They were driving in their pickup and they had just about reached that Five Mile Bridge when Buster happened to look up from his drunken slouch and noticed that they were off the road. The pickup was bouncing along in the barrow ditch with the summer weeds flying up over the hood like cornstalks. He punched his brother. "Barry," he said. "Barry, get this son of a bitch back where it belongs."

Barry kind of lifted his head and looked around him. "Nah," he said. "You do it, Buster. You're driving."

It's never been fully established who was driving—the Wellrights dispute it themselves—but whichever brother it was didn't make it. The pickup smashed into the end of the bridge. When they were satisfied that they couldn't back up or for that matter move at all, since the bumper was wrapped hard around a steel post, one of them turned the engine off so they wouldn't be blown to bits and they both settled down in the cab for a nap. The next morning people going to church found them sound asleep with horseflies buzzing in their open odoriferous mouths. The people thought they were dead, until they stuck their heads in the window and smelled. Buster and Barry weren't dead; they just didn't want to bother anybody for help at that time of night and they were too contented for the moment to walk home. It would have been a good twelve miles, and walking that far they might have had to go to bed sober. They didn't want that.

None of us wanted what happened to us, either. Edith, in particular, hated it. I think she blamed herself. But it wasn't her fault: Lyman was driving. Still, there's no point in fixing blame. It happened and it's over. Come August it'll be ten years.

Only I think I mentioned earlier how I thought the big back seat of Lyman's Pontiac would be good for my wife. It shows how much I know, because it was and it wasn't. My wife didn't die. Coming home from the fairgrounds, after the nickel toss and the beer and the Ferris wheel, she was asleep in the back seat with me. Up front Edith was dozing in the passenger seat beside Lyman. I wasn't paying a lot of attention; I was half asleep myself, watching the month-old wheat stubble and the dark shining corn flow by beyond the fence line.

I came to when we bounced off the near side of the iron bridge rail. We were shooting across to the other side then where we caught the far end of the bridge; the car spun, crossed back to the right side of the highway, cleared the bridge, and then dove nose first off the road-edge; it slammed into the bank of the barrow ditch and rocked back with a leaded jolt onto its top. We were thrown upside down scrambling on top of one another with sharp cutting edges of glass everywhere. There was the bad smell of gasoline, the sound of something dripping. Lyman was out cold; Edith was moaning in shock about her arm. Mavis and I were shoved together, her face twisted away from me against the dome light and her knees drawn up against her stomach. She was crying.

"The baby."

"Are you all right?"

"But the baby."

"We've got to get out of here. It'll catch fire."

I started kicking with my boots at the door, but it was jammed hard against the ditch bank, and the other door was sprung so it wouldn't open. The back window was smashed free of glass except for jagged pieces around the edges, so I kicked those off and crawled out into the ditch. I began to pull Mavis out after me.

"Please don't," she said. "Please don't move me."

"I have to. I can't leave you in there."

I pulled her by the arms as carefully as I could, trying to cradle her head and to support her back, and she was still crying in a soft whisper. I got her out and laid her down in the weeds away from the car. She was lying there in the dark with her knees up. Over her legs her dress was wet and sticky, but I didn't tell her that. I went back and pulled Edith; she cried out when I tugged one arm so I shifted to the other, and then Lyman after her, out the back window into the ditch. Then a car was there; against the headlights I could see figures sliding down toward us from the lip of the road.

It was Ed Taylor and his wife. They helped me carry Mavis and Lyman to their car; Edith, though she was still in shock, was able to be led up the steep bank. Ed drove us all to town to the hospital.

But it wasn't enough. The baby came that night anyway after a bad time with the forceps and quite severe hemorrhaging. He was born dead. It was a boy too, like we agreed it would be. He had a shock of black hair and on his face a blank pinched look like an old man; there were bruises on the sides of his head from the forceps, and one of his ears was torn. The nurses showed him to me so I could attest to his death. Later, when Mavis came out of the anesthetic she wanted to see him. I told her no, she didn't; I felt bad enough myself and I didn't think seeing a dead baby would make her feel any better either. But she said, "I want to see him."

So I took the dead little boy in to her, and she had him then, lying flat on her back, with one arm around him on her chest. Mavis was just pale and quiet with tears shining in her eyes; for a while then she was gone from me, gone from all the world and all of us still in it, retreated into someplace where none of us could reach her or interest her in county fairs or jokes about pickle exhibits and betting systems. None of that mattered now. And I began to think it was going to be bad trying to get the baby from her, that I was going to have to talk hard to get him released from those quiet, pale arms; but she wasn't crazy; Mavis wasn't mad. She was just deep hurt and saying good-bye to him, and finally she told me his name was John for my father; and then she held him up to me and I took him back to the nurses, while she fell off into a sad sleep.

So for a day or two I had three people to visit in the Holt hospital. Lyman wasn't a lot to talk to, though; he was groggy with pain-killer and as distant as last Thursday. They had him in traction with a broken neck. And down the hall Mavis stayed quiet for a while, sleeping when she could, and when she couldn't sleep staring in pain towards the far corner of the room. So it was Edith I talked to during that brief period after the car wreck. They had her arm in a cast, and she kept saying how sorry she was, like she had assumed all responsibility for the wreck, as if she had been driving the car herself.

"I'm so sorry," she said.

"I know," I said. "But it wasn't anybody's fault. It happened; that's all. And anyway, he's out of it now. Maybe that's something."

"Don't say that," she said. "I was looking forward to him, Sandy. I wanted him to come down the road to see me. Like you used to, all these years ago."

"Yes," I said. "He would have liked that."

"I think he would have," Edith said. "I wanted him to."

So I went from one room to another, did chores at home and returned, and then several days later, when both Mavis and Edith were strong enough to be released, we had a private funeral for him up on that rise above the barn. Lyman was still in traction in the hospital, so it was just the three of us—Mavis, still pale and quiet and in pain, and Edith with her arm in a white cast, and me with some stitches where the glass had cut my face. We buried the box, which seemed only half as big as a peach crate—it weighed nothing—buried it beside the little boy's grandfather and great-grandmother. None of us said anything when the damp sand was packed firm on top of it. We couldn't think of words that would make any difference.

Then it was finished. There was just the feeling afterwards of being empty. My wife couldn't accustom herself to there being nothing inside her, nothing kicking and stretching anymore to plan for. She spent a lot of time in the room she had prepared for the baby. It had a crib in one corner with a new sheet stretched tight on the mattress; the store tag was still on the sheet; over the window there were fresh curtains. I found her up there one afternoon in front of the window staring towards the Goodnoughs' house.

"I didn't want to spoil their fun," she said. "They were having such a good time."

"Yes. You did the right thing."

"I don't regret that part of it. Do you?"

"No. I don't regret that part of it. Will you come down-stairs with me now?"

"In a minute," she said. "I'm all right. I was thinking about Edith."

A half mile east of us Edith had pain and Lyman to contend with. Lyman was becoming a child.

· 10 ·

It DIDN'T HAPPEN right away. It took almost ten years more for it to get so bad that there seemed to be only one option. But long before the end of 1976 there were already beginning to be too many signs to ignore—which looking at it now, while telling you about it this long quiet Sunday afternoon in April, reminds me—signs that pointed even then to his steady slide and eventual total collapse into an old man's awful form of childhood. He became as cranky and unpredictable as a two-year-old. For one thing his car was gone.

They totaled his Pontiac. He never had another one. At about the same time we were burying that little box of ours on the hill above the barn, Bernie's Wrecking Service winched Lyman's last green Pontiac up out of the ditch weeds and towed it to town without salvaging even the tires. It's still there in the junkyard west of the city water-treatment ponds. You might want to take a look at that too before you leave this area; the car stands in the middle of the weedy lot with the hood propped open by some high school kids who scrounged for cheap engine parts but gave up and left without thinking to close the hood. It's getting pretty rusty. The windows are all smashed out, and the blood inside on the upholstery looks as if it was just coffee stains. In fact you would probably take it for that, believe it was just coffee stains, unless you happened to wonder why there was so much of it upside down staining the roof material around the dome light like it had puddled there.

Lyman stayed in the hospital for almost three months after the wreck. It was close to Halloween before Doc Schmidt released him. I drove Edith into town to bring him home, and he looked like maybe the nurses had gotten him up to go trick or treating. Around his neck he was still wearing a padded horse-collar affair, and his face showed green and yellow bruises; on his bald head there were crosshatched welts where they had stitched his scalp. When we walked him out the door and down the hospital steps, he seemed somewhat shrunken—shrunken and old-man brittle and confused. The sun hurt his eyes. On the way home when we passed Five Mile Bridge he stared rigidly ahead without a word.

At the Goodnough place I helped Edith get him out of the car and take him inside to rest. We laid him on the couch in the living room, where the postcards he had sent her during those twenty years of his travel and escape from the old man were still pinned in neat rows on the walls. He closed his eyes and went to sleep with his freckled hands lapsed onto his chest. Edith and I went out to the kitchen.

"Do you have time for coffee?" she said.

"I've got to get back to work. But Mavis and I will be checking every day to see how it's going."

"He'll get better," she said.

"Sure," I said. "But you call us if there's something you need. You don't have to go this alone, you know."

"We'll see," she said. "But thank you, Sandy. And tell Mavis thank you."

"She'll be over this afternoon. Now you get some rest too. You look tired."

"There's too much to do," she said.

Lyman did get better but he never got well. He never fully regained that crotchety spryness and bounce that he had shown for those six years before the accident; now, more and more, he was just crotchety. He was irritated by little things of no importance—his toast was cold; his shoestring was missing its plastic end; his sock had a hole—and he would pout. In the living room you would find him staring vacantly at the postcards on the wall. In time the padded horse collar around his neck came off and the bruises on his face faded; the welts on his scalp became thin white scars, and he still dressed himself every morning in suit pants and dress shirt with a bow tie at the collar. But he didn't appear so trim or city-dapper anymore; his clothes seemed to hang on him like they were at least one size too big, as if someone had bought his shirt and pants thinking he would grow into them. He didn't. He developed an old man's stoop. Towards the end he was using two canes.

But for a while that first winter there was talk of buying another car, of replacing his Pontiac. They certainly had more than enough money to do that. Hell, they could have paid cash for three Cadillacs if they had wanted to; it had been that kind of year for wheat and they had no debts of any kind. So twice I drove them into town to shop for cars, looking in the show windows at Happenheimer's Pontiac Dealership on the highway and sitting in that smell of new cars on display, trying out the comfort of fresh leather seats and playing the radio, while Hap himself hovered over us and talked heavy-duty shocks and horsepower but avoided mention of any trade-in. Like everybody else in Holt, Hap was aware of the wreck; he knew why the Goodnoughs were in the market for a new car and had the good sense not to say so. On the second trip to town Lyman decided to try one out.

It was kind of a silver-gray, two-door Bonneville, a nice

car. One of the mechanics backed it quick out of the show-room and left it running. We got in, Lyman behind the wheel, and I thought at first it was going to be all right. I thought he could manage driving again. He seemed competent enough, able. But it was the hour for kids to be walking home in the afternoon from grade school, bundled up in the dry cold in stocking caps and mackinaws, throw-ing snowballs and kicking ice clods in the gutters, and at an intersection Lyman damn near ran over two girls and a boy who were crossing in front of us. I don't know—maybe the low winter sun slanting from the west blinded him.

"Lyman," Edith said. "For goodness sake, stop!"

He hit the power brakes too hard and threw us forward against the dash. In front of the car the kids' faces looked shocked, white, big eyed. They stood there staring at us, then the boy—he must have been a fourth- or fifth-grader—gave Lyman the finger, and they scooted up onto the curb, where they regrouped, yelled at him and then ran off laughing like big stuff along the sidewalk. Lyman was sweating.

"Here," he said. "You take it."

"Nobody's hurt," I said.

"Goddamn it, I can't drive anymore. I don't even want to."

"We'd better go home," Edith said.

Lyman and I changed places. I drove back to Happen-heimer's and there was no more talk of buying a car. Edith, I think, was relieved. It was one thing less to contend with, to be responsible for, to manage and determine that it came out right—or at least to prevent its causing harm to anybody else regardless of what it caused her. Never mind me, she would have said if you had asked, and I didn't ask; it was not the sort of thing you asked of a woman like Edith Goodnough, that small trim lady who went on

205

surviving, who continued to endure by plain courage and a clear eye to duty, and no matter how much you might have wished to God that she would just relax that white-knuckled hold of hers for a while, for a week, say, or a day or even an hour, she wouldn't. She would not. I don't believe she would even have known how. It was like she held the reins of the world in her two hands and she had seen enough of old men's fingers, mangled and chaff coated in the stubble behind a wheat header, and enough of dead babies, miscarried in the hospital because of car wrecks, to fear ever letting go, even for a minute. So I believe at the very least that she was relieved when Lyman said he wouldn't drive anymore. It was that much less to worry about. But she herself would not drive either. She had decided not to. I suppose she understood too well how it would be an affront to Lyman for him to have to sit there in his banker's outfit while she drove. It would have been like twisting some kind of bad knife in his guts every time she did it, and you have to remember she loved him—she wasn't going to do that. So Happenheimer lost the sale of a new car that winter. Neither Goodnough ever drove again.

It meant they were dependent on us. For the next ten years if they—except that later it was just Edith—if they needed to get out or had to go somewhere, had to see Doc Schmidt or buy bread and navy beans at the store, Mavis and I took them. Hell, we didn't mind. It was never anything like a chore to either one of us; we were glad to do it, and for a while we tried hard to take them both along whenever it was anything we thought they might like or be able to manage. I recall once—this must have been sometime during the next three years, since Lyman was still willing to leave the house—once, the four of us went out on a Saturday night to dance at the Legion.

Shorty Stovall was being touted to be there again with

his band. The whole town was full of it; there were posters in the store windows and an entire half-page ad in the *Holt Mercury*. Christ, you would have believed it was the Second Coming. Well, it was something to do on a Saturday night. We asked Edith and Lyman to go with us.

Spruced up for the occasion, we drove to town and arrived early enough at the Legion to hold the corner booth, which the Goodnoughs favored. We sat down in the darkened room, which was already layered with smoke, beside the bandstand, where sure as hell—the ads hadn't lied—Shorty and his boys were making warm-up noises. They each had Stetsons stuck down over their bushy heads, Shorty in a red hat, the boys in black, and the whole band had the kind of doodad beads hanging from knots on the leather strings of their vests that little kids will play with. They were drunk or doped to the gills. While they hit their warm-up licks they kept saying stuff to one another and then laughing, like whatever it was the other guy had said flat proved he was witty. It was better not to watch them, to just listen to them play once they got started, because in fact they could play music. It only made you sick if you watched them.

After we had been there for a few minutes Marvella Packwood came over to take our order. When she wasn't canning pickles or populating the town with another baby, Marvella waited bar at the Holt Legion. I suppose that was where she discovered the fathers for her kids, only she seemed lately to have slacked a little in her efforts, because there hadn't been a new kid sired in a couple of years. I wasn't up-to-date on her pickles. Anyway, she stood in front of us now in a purple low-necked shirt and pink jeans so tight the stitches showed; she was carrying a cocktail tray while she popped gum. "What am I going to get you folks?" she said.

"Marvella," I said. "You're looking good."

"You think so? I just bought this blouse this morning. Like it?"

"Why sure. Don't you, Lyman?"

"I don't know," he said.

Marvella leaned over the table, showing a good deal of what she had under the blouse to Lyman as she patted his cheek. "What's the matter, darlin'?" she said. "Don't you feel any good tonight?"

"I feel all right," Lyman said.

"He needs a drink."

"That's what I'm here for. I try to do all I can with what I have." She tossed her head back, the muscles of her neck bulging as she laughed.

We gave her our orders. When she was gone back to the bar to bring the drinks, Mavis poked me sharp in the ribs. "What's that for?" I said.

"Don't ask," she said.

"You mean her? Why hell, I was just trying to buy some insurance."

"You don't need any insurance. I paid it last month."

"I'm talking about Marvella."

"So am I."

"No, I mean if you pay her a little attention she'll bring us our drinks without having to call her."

"You're paying too much attention."

Marvella came back with our drinks on her tray and bent over to set the glasses on napkins on the table.

"Miss Packwood, you do look fine tonight," I said.

She popped her gum, I paid her, and she left. Mavis poked me in the ribs again. I was beginning to believe that I would have to change sides with my wife so she could damage both sides equally, but it didn't come to that, because pretty soon Shorty started playing, and after a few fast numbers to establish the band and to warm up the crowd he began a slow danceable version of "Release Me."

"Come on," I said to Lyman. "Show us country hicks how you learned to do the box step in Rochester."

With enough prodding from Edith and Mavis, Lyman finally agreed to stand up and dance. The floor was crowded with farm couples and town folks, the women in bright dresses and matching heels and the men beginning to sweat a little under the arms as they pumped their ladies' hands in big swings across the floor. Everybody was enjoying himself. Across the room I could see Vince Higgims, Jr., trying to sweet-talk the latest target of his affections, a big solid black-haired girl who didn't appear overly impressed, and at the bar the middle-aged Wellright boys were in earnest conversation with the mayor. The mayor was squeezed onto a stool between them. He was nodding his head, and Buster was saying, "Am I right?"

And Barry was saying, "You damn right he's right."

The mayor kept nodding his head like he knew all too well that Buster was always right.

Things weren't right on the dance floor, though. Shorty had finished "Release Me" to whistles and applause and had started another slow one, but I couldn't see Edith and Lyman. I had been watching out for them too, noticing how they slid slow in their customary two-step around the outside edges of the dancing couples so as to avoid being crowded or bumped by the active younger set, and from what I saw they seemed all right. Lyman had looked a little stiff maybe, but then he always did. He had a way of holding his bald head tilted on his neck above that white shirt and bow tie like he was listening for something, or like he was hard of hearing, and Edith as usual had a light hand on his shoulder, the two of them dancing quiet and slow and very serious, as if it required concentration to get the steps right. But they weren't dancing anymore. They weren't in the corner booth either; our drinks were still there half finished on the table.

"Maybe they went to the restroom," Mavis said.

They hadn't. We checked both restrooms, which were crowded with people who were joking and visiting while they waited their turn at the toilets. We didn't find them so we went outside thinking they might have stepped out to get the air after being downstairs in the heat and thick smoke. Under a streetlight my car was parked in the graveled lot. That's where we found them. Lyman was in the back seat crowded far over into the dark corner. Edith was talking to him but Lyman wasn't talking, at least not while we were there.

"Anything wrong?" I said.

"Lyman wants to go home."

"Is he sick? Lyman, what is it? I thought you were enjoying yourself."

He wouldn't look at me, wouldn't talk. He was in some kind of childish pout.

"He isn't sick," Edith said. "He just wants to go home now."

I looked at Mavis for help. "That's fine with me," Mavis said. "Actually, it sounds like a good idea. This husband of mine's notion about insurance was about to get him in trouble."

"Sure," I said. "It'll save wear and tear on my ribs."

So that was the end of dancing, and the end too of any other late-night forays to town for the Goodnoughs. Edith told us later what had caused it. It didn't amount to much but it didn't have to: Lyman had already begun his approach towards the edge. What happened was they were dancing slow and serious, like I told you, and at the end of Shorty Stovall's version of "Release Me," while deciding whether to dance the next one or to return to the booth, one of Happenheimer's salesmen slapped Lyman on the back. It was Larry Parks, a guy with bangs combed down over his forehead. Parks had apparently drunk enough to believe that it would be a good idea to mix business with Holt Legion, Saturday-night pleasure. Sort of snatch Lyman while he was ripe, you understand, while he was oiled. Only Lyman wasn't oiled.

Parks said something like, "When you coming in to check out our new cars? We got in a good-looking shipment of Pontiacs last week."

And that was all. I suppose it was innocent enough, but it was stupid. Happenheimer knew what the score was with Lyman, because I had emphasized it to him myself, in private, the day we test-drove that two-door Bonneville, so you might have thought he would have leaked it to his salesmen. And maybe he had. Maybe Parks was just trying a little dance-floor free-lance in order to improve his commission. I don't know.

I don't suppose the details matter. It's just that his back-slapping attempt at salesmanship didn't leave the Good-noughs much. They had been finished with driving, and now any thought of night life was out too. About all they had left for themselves was a trip every six months to Doc Schmidt and a weekly drive to the grocery store. But that didn't last long either. About a year later, when old Doc Schmidt retired after more than forty years of service to the community, closed his practice and moved himself and his wife to Tucson, Lyman decided he was through with doctors; he wasn't ever going to another one. That left only the grocery store. You understand what I'm say-ing?—the goddamn grocery store. Here he had traveled all over this country by himself for twenty years; after-wards with Edith he had seen more of this Rocky Mountain region in six years than I'll see in a lifetime; and now, in no time, he was satisfied with a seven-mile excursion into town—after cabbage and macaroni and beans.

Well, it didn't take long for even that to be too much for him. He shuffled a little closer to the edge. That's right, he refused to step outside for any reason. He wouldn't leave the house. He was too busy traveling in the parlor.

About four years after his last Pontiac was wrecked, Lyman began to retrace his transcontinental trip. He sent off to Los Angeles and Boise and Omaha and Mobile and Cleveland for brochures, for chamber of commerce pamphlets, for bus schedules and train routes. Without once leaving the house, he was seeing the country again. He was traveling. He had his own old man's travel bureau established with boxes and maps and a desk in the parlor. He could tell you what train to take from Boston to Chicago, what connections you had to make, what there was to see in the Windy City once you got there, where to stay—do all of that even if he was never going to take that train, make those connections, or see the Sears building himself. He didn't want to. It was out of the question. If you had offered to pay his way and to sink him in luxury on a chartered jet, he would not have gone. He had limited his world to a space twenty feet square at the west end of the house. There he sat every day beside a lamp, poring like a travel clerk over road maps and glossy city flyers. To protect his eyes, Edith finally bought him a green visor, which he wore loose on his bald head, propped on his old man's, hair-filled ears. It still about makes me sick to think about it. Not just for him—for her too, I mean.

I BELIEVE Edith's one compensation during those last awful years was Rena Pickett. Edith loved that little girl, still loves her, and so do we. Why hell, Rena fills us all up, ornery as she is, bullheaded and independent as she is.

She favors my dad. She has his straight black shiny hair, his way of standing with one leg cocked and a hand on one hip, his manner of listening to you while you talk. And when you've finished talking, come finally to the end of your adult speech, when you've run down at last, believing for once that you've persuaded her to see your side of sound reason, she jumps up and goes ahead and does whatever it was she intended to do in the first place, before you started filling the air above her with words, before you ever got it into your head that you might make progress this once towards some form of mutual agreement, or at least obedience, or anyhow the willingness to wait long enough for you to turn your back and get out of the way before she disregards everything you've just said and runs off to do what she was going to do anyway. She's always been like that.

For example, when she was about two, we tried pretty seriously to impress upon her how she had to stay in the yard. We told her that she was not to cross the gravel road in front of the house. But that same afternoon when we missed her and looked up, there she was in the native pasture across the road, high-stepping down the hill. In one hand she was carrying her soggy diaper like it was something of herself that she was not about to leave behind; she had an elm stick in her other hand. She was following her little pot belly through the tall grass and sagebrush. There were cows and calves in the pasture, too, the cows all bunched up on stiff legs, watching her pass. But the dog was with her. She and Jack had been hunting prairie dogs on the hill. It was the reason for her stick.

Or another time: when she was older, about six, I was

trying to make her see the correct side of things, giving her the benefit of considerable wisdom and experience—until she interrupted me.

"Oh, Dad," she said. "Dad, you don't know anything and you know it."

Then, having straightened me out, she flounced off to play dolls or to discover kittens in the hayloft. And how was I supposed to argue with what she said? I was wrong on both accounts.

In that way she favors her mother. While she may have a band of round orange freckles pocked across her nose like I did when I was a kid, she still has her mother's and her Grandpa Pickett's eyes. Those green eyes that look past you or through you like you weren't there, as if you didn't amount to anything more than smoke—a minor obstruction, say, a kind of highway mirage, between her and the thing she intends to see. She will see the thing, take it in, accomplish it, no matter. The girl has backbone, and I'm damn grateful she does.

She was born on August 3, 1969, with no trouble. After burying what should have been her older brother in a box above the barn, Mavis and I saw to that. We took precautions, did nothing rash, curbed any thought of Ferris-wheel rides or drives home afterwards that would have been too late. We believed we were being given another chance and were not about to lose it. Of course it made for a long, slow nine months of housebound waiting, but it was worth it, because if Rena Pickett was compensation to Edith these last seven years, she has been more than that to us. She's our daily satisfaction.

She's also meant a good deal to her grandmother, that eighty-four-year-old woman who still lives in brittle comfort with a retired life-insurance salesman in that brick house at the northeast edge of town. Leona Turner Newcomb Roscoe Cox likes having a granddaughter to buy pink dresses and white kneesocks for; she seems to believe that such things close the gap, that they put all the grasping and all the arguments behind her, that the past is past. Well, the truth is, we've all grown older. She said the other day that she and Wilbur were thinking of taking a boat tour of the Bahamas. I told her I thought that would be a good idea. I said, "As far as I know the boat won't stop at Havana."

But this is not Leona Cox's story. I'm talking about Edith Goodnough.

It was about a year after Lyman began to spread himself in the parlor that Edith decided to vacate the upstairs. Edith was finally getting tired. It began to show even on her. Her brown hair was turning gray fast now, losing its curl. There were purse lines at her mouth. She seemed to have to catch her breath after any kind of movement, whether it was to sweep the floor, feed the chickens, or just to stand up from the kitchen table to crack eggs. Also, every day it was growing more difficult for her to climb the stairs ten times, to be everywhere at once, to do all she'd been doing for seventy-some years and still believed she had to go on doing. She wouldn't let herself do less; it wasn't her way. Well, it was wearing her thin as water.

And meanwhile, Lyman was getting sorrier all the time. His mind was closing down hard. There seemed to be about one thought only in that old head of his under that green visor—parlor travel. He hung on to that daily business like it was a drive chain in a Model T, like it was a cotter pin on a bull wheel, and he demanded Edith's help to make the thing go. Often there were times when he couldn't make his travel connections come out right and she had to leave the dishes to soak or let the peas burn while she helped him. He was as demanding as a child—she had to come now; not a minute later—and the worst hell of it was, he was still strong physically. Sometimes in those last years I caught myself thinking, What if he died? Or, what if a stroke put him away for good in the hospital? Wouldn't that be better after all, some relief for her? But none of that happened. Lyman stayed as tough and stringy as a roping steer, even if he did end up using two canes. He was still capable of leverage. If Edith somehow managed to persuade him to take a nap in the afternoon on the couch, he would spend half the night demanding her help with his travel charts. All the time he was sending himself on imaginary trips to Memphis or Mobile. He was working up little jaunts to Los Angeles for himself. It went on for hours.

When it went on for more than a year, Edith asked me to help her move the furniture. She wanted to know if I didn't think it would be better to move the bedroom furniture downstairs, to set it up in the living room next to the parlor where she could be closer to him when he called in the night. It sounded like a good idea to me. They could shut off the upstairs altogether; there wouldn't be any reason to climb those steps again. So I went over in the afternoon to help her accomplish that. That was when I understood for the first time that there was only one bed in use up there. She wasn't trying to hide it. It was a double bed in the west bedroom, with an old-fashioned quilt spread.

"This what you want moved?" I said.

"Just the dressers out of this room, Sandy," she said.

"What beds do you want?"

"They're out in the garage. In storage."

"Oh?"

"We stored them out there when Lyman came back—to make space for his things."

She was looking at me steadily from where she stood in front of the window, the country open and flat and dry behind her. She looked tired, a thin aging woman with her mouth pursed. She had begun to fashion her gray hair into a kind of knot. We stood there facing one another in the room where she had been born, where Lyman was born two years later, both of them with my grandmother's help, and where Ada had died holding my grandmother's hand, the room where the old man finally died in his time with his mouth locked open like box iron. It was a lot of history to be worrying about a double bed.

"Well," I said, "why don't I start with these dressers?"

I started pulling out the drawers and carrying them downstairs. Then I banged the dressers themselves down the steps and went outside to bring the beds in from the garage. The beds Edith wanted were old cast-iron single beds, stored overhead on the rafters. I dusted them off and set them up like she wanted, one on either side of the living room against the walls. She was making a dayroom out of it. When we were finished it looked all right too. Comfortable and clean, with matching spreads on the two beds, and the dressers set up in the corners with a clothes closet moved into the pantry. Lyman stayed busy in the parlor the whole time. He was studying a road map.

"Where you headed today?" I asked him. "New York City?"

"Salt Lake," he said.

"Hell of a place," I said.

Then I went home to feed corn to castrated bulls and to fork hay to fat cattle. And you can make of the Goodnoughs' bedroom arrangement whatever you want to. Stir it according to your own lights. Myself, I don't make anything of it. If they wanted to sleep in the same bed, warm their feet under the same old-fashioned patchwork quilt like they had when they were kids before this century ever began—well, that was their business, because when you know people all your life you try to understand how it is for them. What you can't understand you just accept. That's how I felt about Edith. At the time I could still remember like it was yesterday how she fed me chewing gum while we cleaned chicken squirt from brown eggs at the kitchen sink and how one summer she brought me ice tea and lemonade when I was driving tractor in a hayfield and an old man was waving stumps past my head and screaming nonsense in my ears. I intended to help her however I could. It was not my business to ask fool questions that didn't concern me. That's where Rena Pickett came in. To help Edith, I mean. Only help isn't the right word.

From the time Rena was born in 1969 Edith enjoyed her. I already told you how she was a compensation, but she was more than that. I suppose it had something to do with having a little kid dancing around in the house where otherwise there were only old folks, something to do with a little girl's noise and giggles breaking up all that daily silence, that ongoing concentrated crotchetiness filling the parlor and the entire downstairs. Why hell, Rena put some fun into that yellow house, and Mavis and I encouraged it. Whenever there was occasion to be out at night or excuse to go to the National Western Stock Show in Denver, Rena went to Edith's. She went there a lot, not just when we were gone but often for a whole day when we were home during the summer and also for an hour or two during the week after school. By the time she was six she was going there by herself. She'd throw a halter on Echo and trot down to the Goodnoughs'. We didn't worry about her when she was there; it was obvious that she and Edith got along together like two beads on the same string. Besides, it was educational. I'll bet Rena is the only seven-year-old kid in all of Holt County who not only knows how to scald a chicken and pluck tail feathers but also how to get from Dallas to St. Paul by train and bus. Because she was a help with Lyman too, you understand. My daughter could bring that old man out. She treated him as an equal. Together they played travel in the parlor for hours.

On a late-winter afternoon if I went in to bring Rena home for supper I'd find her with Lyman, the two of them sitting at that loaded mahogany desk in that west room, the light from the overhead lamp reflecting off his bald visored head and her shiny black hair, her hair fallen forward around her face. The maps would be tacked up on the walls. Around them on the floor the whole room would be full of stuff, cluttered so you couldn't walk, overflowing: all those damn brochures and pamphlets and flyers; schedules for the whole country creased five times and looking used up; all of it spilling out of cardboard boxes; a hell of a mess. If Edith wanted to clean in there she had to dust around them; they knew where they wanted things. They allowed her to store the extra piles of stuff on the steps leading up to the unused bedrooms, but she had to ask first. And that was all right because Rena was keeping Lyman occupied; he was almost happy when she was there. So, while Edith folded clothes or cooked supper, the two travelers were busy, engrossed in serious play, both of them sitting bent over that desk where Rena colored train tickets and Lyman studied the numbers in his train schedule and tried to figure how to get them to Detroit if they boarded in Denver. It was solemn business. And Rena would be saying something like:

"I'm just sick of this orange. I'm going to make them red."

"Red what?" Lyman would say.

"Our train tickets. Don't you know we got to buy train tickets? Did you forget that again?"

"I ain't forgetting nothing. Tickets is your business."

And a little later:

"But look here. We got us that same damn layover in Chicago. Three hours' worth."

"How much minutes is that?"

"I just told you. Ain't you listening?"

"You said hours. And you're not suppose to say 'ain't.' "

"Mind your own business."

"Well, you're not suppose to."

And a little later still:

"There. I'm done with all these tickets. Now hurry up with that schedule thing."

So, in time, they would take up red tickets and board the train and pretend to see all that country between Denver and Detroit, with a three-hour layover in Chicago, where Rena would say she was shopping for presents for her school friends and Lyman would say he was drinking himself a bottle of cold beer.

At Christmas Edith gave my daughter a green visor like the one her traveling partner wore. It was Rena's favorite present. She hung it on a nail beside the maps in the travel bureau.

T HEN, about a year ago in March, the Goodnoughs acquired an old milky-eyed dog by default, and at about the same time we learned that there was reason for us to worry about Rena's going over there by herself to play travel with Lyman. Lyman had finally reached that edge of his. In fact, he seemed at times to have passed it. For days his mind would be about as good as it had been; he might still manage to function in the parlor, more or less, but then for no reason that anybody could detect he'd be gone for half a day, turn blank and vacant, his mind as empty of sense as a dead stick is of sap. He'd go silent in some corner or he'd babble from his bed in the living room about nothing, about railroad ballast, or car keys and fence wire. I remember he spent one entire afternoon talking about nettles. I also remember how Edith reported that he pissed on the clothes in the makeshift closet in the pantry one time; apparently Lyman thought he had discovered the toilet among his sister's dresses. But that was later in the fall. In the meantime he was still trying to travel. And when things didn't connect right he could turn violent. He used those canes of his.

Now whether the dog had anything to do with Lyman's final collapse, I don't know. Probably not. Probably it was just coincidence. If it hadn't been a dog, it would have been something else just as trivial. However you look at it, it doesn't make any sense. Anyway, the dog wandered into the yard one night. Edith found it the next morning when she went out to feed the chickens and to break ice in the water pan.

It was an old black-and-brown dog with mottled white on its belly, a mixture of border collie and spaniel and whatever else had been available and interested at the time. There were clots of matted hair on its back legs, and its eyes were milky with cataracts. It slept a lot and whimpered when it wasn't sleeping. There was a leather collar buckled around its neck when Edith found it, so we figured some town folks had dropped it off—they will do that; ask any farmer who lives within a ten-mile radius of any town what he has discovered in the ditch in front of his house and he'll tell you—just shoved the old dog out onto the road in front of the Goodnoughs' mailbox with the mistaken notion that such a thing would be kinder than a ten-minute trip to the vet and a quick injection. Anyway, being the kind of woman she is, Edith kept the dog. She fed it and brought it into the house.

That's when the trouble started seriously with Lyman.

221

I suppose you'd have to say he was jealous of the damn thing. It was like he felt his sister was spending too much of herself caring for something that wasn't him. Like a kid, he wanted her total concentration and concern to himself. If she wasn't looking, he'd give the dog a boot, hit it with his cane. Things got worse. Then my daughter had to be there when it all went to hell.

It was one of those late-winter, early-spring afternoons in March, that in-between time when a gray sky can't decide what to do, drop snow or spit rain, so it does a little of both. Rena had come home as usual on the bus after school, and I had taken her with me to the Good-noughs' to play in the house while I worked on a tractor I kept stored out of the weather in the machine shed. It was getting along towards five, darkening already, and I had turned on the drop-light over the tractor. Then Edith was calling me from the steps of the back porch.

"What?" I yelled back at her. "I'm out here."

"You better come to the house."

"I'll be there in a minute."

"What?"

"In a minute."

"You better come now."

She turned and went back in. What in the hell? I thought. I walked across the wet graveled yard and inside the house, in the kitchen, I found Rena on Edith's lap. Rena was crying, her face close against Edith's shoulder. Rena didn't cry much, but she was crying hard now. Through the kitchen door I could see Lyman glaring at me from across the length of the house. He was standing in the parlor doorway as if he would fight anybody who tried to get past him. He looked wild. That travel clerk's visor of his was tilted lopsided on his head, and his eyes looked flat crazy, insane, bughouse.

"What's going on?" I said.

222

Rena was crying something into Edith's shoulder; it came out muffled and wet.

"What? Honey, I can't understand you."

"Never mind now, sweetheart," Edith said. "It'll be all right now. Your daddy's here. Don't you know it'll be all right? It always is, isn't it?"

Rena looked up into Edith's pale wrinkled face. "But Lyman hit you," she said. "I saw him hit you with that cane."

"I know. But never mind now. It's all over."

"And he hit Nancy too. I tried to make him stop but he wouldn't."

"Nancy will be all right too. You'll see. Look, she's over there in the corner on her rug. See how she likes it there where it's warm. Why, she's asleep already, so don't you worry about Nancy—no, now don't cry anymore. Just lean your head back. There, that's my girl."

"Edith," I said, "what happened here?"

Edith didn't say anything for a while. She was caressing, calming my daughter. Finally she said, "I don't know really. I think it's just too much for him sometimes. He doesn't know what he's doing, and then something happens and—"

"And he hurts you."

"Not very much. I'm all right. It's just that I don't know right now what I'm going to do with him. I've got to think."

"Will you tell me what happened?"

She was still holding Rena on her lap, petting her hair and smoothing the collar on her school dress. After a while, when Rena stopped crying, when the hiccups too had stopped, Edith told me. From her account and from what Rena was later able to say, I've pieced this much together:

They were traveling in the parlor together as usual. The boxes of travel stuff were spread around them; the maps of the country were on the wall. In front of them on the desk they had their work papers and charts and Crayolas and pencils, the two of them sitting there in the travel bureau in their matching green visors, that old man and my daughter, getting up another trip for themselves. They had decided, it still being late winter in Colorado, that now would be a good time to take the sun in Phoenix because it would be full spring there, and Rena said she was getting tired of this snow and rain dripping all the time so they had to stay in the gym for recess, and Lyman said: "Phoenix." Well, that turned out to be a mistake: the train connections were too difficult. They would have to get on in Denver, go north to Cheyenne, cross over to Salt Lake, track west to San Francisco, change trains for Los Angeles, and then come back eastward into Arizona. Something like that, anyway. And Lyman couldn't manage it. It called for more sense, more figuring, and more understanding of time changes and layovers than he was capable of. He had to call Edith in from the kitchen three or four times to help him. So he was getting hot. It set him off.

But he wouldn't change his mind either. Not that he had a lot of mind left to change, you understand, but it had to be Phoenix, so leave him alone.

Of course it didn't matter much to Rena where they went; she didn't care; she had only said that about the snow and rain because she preferred slides and playground swings to a constant ration of dodge ball in the gym. Parlor travel was a game to her, a good reason to draw more and more elaborate figures on yellow paper and afterwards to cut them out, a chance to wear a green visor and pretend. But it was never any game to Lyman. He took it as hard as if his life depended on it, and I suppose in some ways it did. So he was beginning to fume now. He was mixed up, mad, losing control. He didn't know where the hell he was.

Meanwhile my daughter had finished coloring their train tickets. She wanted to start. She was ready for the pretense of seeing the country. But Lyman wasn't ready yet. Far from it. So finally, out of boredom I suppose, Rena called Nancy—that's what they called the dog—into the mess of the travel bureau to play with her while she waited. And that was too much for him. He thought he had reason to dislike the dog anyway. He came unhinged. He started shouting.

"Get that damn thing out of here! She don't belong here with us."

You understand he was like a frantic kid now, screaming and shouting. And Rena was saying, "Well, Nancy can stay in here if she wants to."

"No, she can't. She stinks, damn her. Get her out."

"Nancy doesn't either stink."

"She does too. Don't tell me, by God . . ."

"Do you, Nancy? Nooo, her doesn't stink. Her's a good old poochy."

Rena was kneeling in front of the dog, talking baby talk into its grizzled face, patting its old head while the dog shut its eyes, shivering in pleasure, and then Lyman hit Nancy on the spine with his cane. There was a sharp crack, a yelp.

"By Jesus!" he yelled. "I bet that'll move her."

The dog did move too. It even managed a kind of waddling gallop; it ended up in the kitchen cringing and whimpering beside the stove. Rena, I gather, was just shocked at first. She had never seen an animal mistreated before; it was something new to her. Then she was mad, as outraged as any six-and-a-half-year-old girl can be. She began to shout back at him, crying up into his face that he was mean and old, that he was the one who stinked; she was not going to play travel with him ever again. She took off her green visor and threw it at him.

Then Edith was there too, in that crowded box-filled room at the west end of the house. But it was too late. Lyman was gone now, the poor old bastard; he was crazy with frustration, his eyes like new copper, red and insane, out-sized; he was flailing his cane around in the room, hitting anything, the desk, the boxes, the lamp, and before Edith could get Rena and herself out of the way he hit his sister sharp blows on the arms and back. "Get out!" he was screaming. "Get out of here." They retreated to the kitchen. That's when she called me in from the machine shed. You know the rest.

After that much had been told, when it was all accounted for, even if it didn't make sense, because it wasn't a question of that, we sat there on kitchen chairs staring at nothing for a while. The radio was playing the top forty from Denver, and there was the slow drip of rain outside. Finally Rena got up off Edith's lap. She came over and stood between my knees. "Dad, I want to go home now," she said.

"Yes," I said. "Mom will be waiting supper for us."

Rena went into the other room, put her coat on, and we could hear her saying good-bye to Lyman. Lyman was still standing fierce guard in the far doorway. He didn't say anything. Rena came back into the kitchen and gave Edith a long hug.

"Go on out to the pickup now," I told her. "I'll be right out."

"I want you to come too."

"I am. Go ahead now."

"Good-bye, Edith," she said.

"Good-bye, sweetheart. Lyman didn't mean to scare you. He loves you too, you know. We both do."

226

"I guess he's just sick," Rena said. "Probably he'll feel better tomorrow."

Then she went outside. Edith was staring at the closed door; she looked small and defeated. Her face was white, colorless, pained; her gray hair had become dislodged from its knot. I felt as bad for her then as I ever have for anyone in my life.

"He just can't help what he does," she said.

"I know it," I said. "But that's the point, isn't it?"

"Yes, but it's not that simple. What am I going to do with him, Sandy? I won't have him strapped down to a hospital bed. Or whatever they do now—sedate them with pills and shots to make them sleep all the time. I couldn't stand that. And he's mine to take care of."

"There aren't a lot of options," I said.

"There must be something," she said. "I've just got to think of it."

I sure as hell didn't have any answers. So I left then and Rena and I went home for supper. Rena didn't go back to the Goodnoughs' again by herself. In the next eight or nine months Mavis or I took her often to see Edith, to visit in the kitchen or to do things outside in the yard during the summer, but she didn't play travel with Lyman anymore. Lyman had almost stopped playing travel himself. He managed, I think, to take a few brief imaginary trips to Denver, but that was about all. Of course all that time Edith was still taking care of him. With patience and kindness, and yes, love, too. Only you'd have to have seen that yourself. I don't know how to tell you about it.

· 11 ·

ALL I KNOW how to tell you is that sometime between March and December Edith Goodnough decided by herself what to do with her brother. She didn't consult anyone. It isn't the sort of thing you can discuss with anybody else. What in the hell are you going to say?—look here now, if I do this and this, do you think it'll turn out all right? No, Edith made up her own mind. It had to be her own private, solitary decision.

But I can tell you what it was she decided. I was there for the ending. And in these past three and a half months she's had time to tell me the rest, to tell me how she filled those hours that led up to the end. We've talked a lot about it in that hospital room in town since the beginning of this new year. I've held her hand, watching that slow drip pushing life back into her through a sterile needle in her other arm, life she didn't much want or care to continue anymore. I've seen her sleeping with her gray, troubled face turned toward me on a white pillow, been there too when she woke and asked, "Are you still here, Sandy?"

And I've said, "Yes. I'm still here. I'll be here for a while."

So I didn't leave her and we would talk. She seemed to want to talk about it. Of course I was interested.

She said she woke that morning later than she wanted

to. There was already more than enough light in the living room for her to be able to see Lyman clearly over there against the opposite wall in his cast-iron bed with the yellowing postcards pinned on the walls above him, the wallpaper itself discolored now behind the curled edges of the old postcards. She said she was a little panicky when she realized the hour. She had a lot to do. She got up out of bed in a hurry, dressed in house clothes, and went out to the kitchen to start coffee. When the coffee was going good she returned to the living room and woke her brother. Ordinarily she let him sleep until he woke on his own, and by December it was not unusual for him to sleep until noon when he would rise and shuffle about the house until she fed him and found some task for him to do, but that morning she woke him early so that they could eat breakfast together. Also, she wanted to be certain that he would go to bed promptly after supper. She had it all planned. It should have worked, too.

They ate a breakfast of poached eggs, buttered toast, and coffee. Afterwards she did the dishes while Lyman shaved himself in the bathroom. When she went in a little later to lay his clothes out she found that he was still in the bathroom studying himself in the mirror. He had cut his neck along the gray folds of loose skin under his chin, and he seemed to be amused by the trickle of blood dripping onto the whiskers and gray lather in the sink. It wasn't a bad cut, but it was bleeding enough to entertain him. She stanched it with toilet paper. Then she cleaned him up and got him dressed in his customary white shirt, dress pants, and slippers, and sat him down in a chair under a lamp in the parlor so he could look at pictures. She had planned that too. Several months earlier she had taken a subscription to *National Geographic* magazine with those colored pictures in mind. When the issues had begun to

229

arrive she had kept them for a later date, and that morning she gave him two magazines to look at. Like a bald-headed child, he sat in his stuffed chair with a good light behind him and studied the pictures of Eskimos and marine life and wide-hipped Hawaiian women dancing for him in color on the page in his lap. He was satisfied for a while.

So Edith put on her winter coat and scarf and went outside. She took the old mongrel dog with her. The dog waddled around the corner of the house to its usual place and scratched feebly at the frozen ground to cover its dump. Edith went on under the bare elm trees, through the picket gate, and out across the gravel to the chicken house, where she poured chicken feed into a trough. There were no eggs to gather, not now in December, so she merely stood there for a few minutes in the dim close air of the chicken house watching the six or seven chickens scratching in the hard dirt, pecking at old frozen food scraps, their loose tomato-colored combs jangling and tossing. When she went back to the house the dog was whimpering on the porch steps. It was a cold day, dry and cold and bright.

Inside the house again, she sat down to catch her breath. Lyman was still bent in satisfaction over his *National Geographic*s. When she felt rested she took him a cup of strong coffee. She asked him if he liked the magazines.

"Huh?" he said.

"The magazines, Lyman. Are you enjoying the pictures?"

He looked up at her out of his faded eyes as if he was coming out of some fog, as if she had interrupted some deep thought of his. His spotted head shone like water.

"They got a lot of pictures."

"Yes," she said. "I saved them for you. But maybe you should go to the bathroom now."

"What for?"

"All right, later then. Remember to drink your coffee before it gets cold."

So the morning passed quietly for them. Later she made a pie, rolled the thin crust out onto the counter in the way her dead mother had taught her seventy-odd years ago, and filled the crust with pumpkin batter. She was well pleased, she said, with the result. Pumpkin was Lyman's favorite—not that it mattered much to him what he ate now, or if he ate at all; I suppose it all tasted like oatmeal mush to him by this time. But she was pleased nevertheless. She wanted things done right.

Then the phone rang, and that turned out to be a good thing too. It was Mavis calling from town. Mavis said that she and Rena were at the grocery store and they wanted to know if there was something Edith needed. "They'll be closed tomorrow," Mavis said.

"That's right, they will."

"So Rena said we had to check with Edith."

"Wasn't that nice of her?" Edith said. "Well. Let me think. Let's see—yes, if they have some fresh cream. I forgot that."

"Anything else?"

"If there is, I can't think of it right now. I guess not."

They talked for a minute more and hung up. Edith said later she didn't mind lying about the cream. It was a lie, though. In the refrigerator on the top shelf she knew very well that there was already a full, unopened half-pint of cream, more than enough to whip for Lyman's pie. But now she was glad she had lied. She said she was even a little bit proud of herself for having thought so fast on the phone. It meant that she would be allowed to see Rena and Mavis once more. That had been the one thing she hadn't been sure of accomplishing—and she wanted very much to see Rena again. Now that too was going to happen. So she went directly from the phone to the refrigerator and took the half-pint of cream and poured it into the sink. Then she made lunch.

Lyman was not at all hungry, she said. Stooped over his bowl of tomato soup, he played with his spoon, stirring the red stuff around in the bowl, and ate only a bite or two of his cheese sandwich. He was tired, wilted, glassy eyed; the early morning had exhausted him, she knew that, and he was ready now to lie down on his bed in the living room. But she just couldn't permit it. Not yet, she couldn't. She told him she had two more magazines for him to see.

"What magazines?" he said. "I already looked at magazines."

"No, these are different. You've never seen these before."

"I did too," Lyman said. He pushed himself up from the table and shuffled into the living room. Edith followed him.

"Wait," she said. "Lyman."

"What?"

"You can look at your postcards."

"I don't have no postcards."

"Of course you do. Why, the ones you sent me when you were gone all those years."

She went over to the wall above her bed and untacked the first postcard he had sent her, the one from California, during that other December, that December in 1941 after they had bombed Pearl Harbor. She brought it back and showed him the picture he had chosen.

"See what it says up here in the corner? Los Angeles, California. And on the other side this is what you wrote me:

"Dear Sis,
Well, I made it out here. Now they all say I'm
not right for soldiers. So I'm working a job in a
airplane factory. It beats farming anyhow.
                              Love, your brother,
                              Lyman."

"I wrote that," Lyman said.

"That's right. You do remember, don't you?"

"Give it to me," he said. "It's mine."

She gave him the postcard to hold in his own old farm boy's hands, to peer at and turn over, to remember even if it was only dimly; and so he was perked up again for a while. He sat down once more in the stuffed chair in the parlor under the lamp, while his sister removed the remaining postcards from the walls in the other room. But Edith didn't know how long that semi-alert condition would last; she said she realized then that she would have to move her plans ahead by at least an hour. But that would be all right too; afterwards such things as time and tiredness wouldn't matter. There would be something like rest, afterwards.

So she began immediately to clean and stuff the chicken. A month ago she had thought of having turkey for supper, but in the past week she had decided against it because there would be too much left over, and besides, chicken was turkey to Lyman. So she made that one compromise, and when the chicken was ready, stuffed with its legs secured, she put it to bake in the oven in time for an early supper. Then she peeled potatoes and got out a jar of canned beans to have ready. Chicken and potatoes and green beans and, afterwards, pumpkin pie—it would make a satisfactory meal.

That's exactly what she said, a satisfactory meal. You see what lengths that old lady was going to. If you don't it's my fault; I sure as hell mean for you to see it. Because she had thought about it for a long time—I don't know for how long exactly, but for long enough anyhow—for God only knows how many nights, lying there in that dark room in that yellow house, listening to her brother snore and whistle and mumble nonsense in his old man's sleep, while all the time she was trying to think, trying to know what to do with him, until finally after enough nights and enough troubled hours there seemed to be only one option that might work. An option, of course, that concluded with a satisfactory meal. Only she didn't tell us that. Not at the time, she didn't. Over here, we were still just hoping that he would die, that he would go to sleep and not wake up. It didn't happen, though. You know that. It just got worse and worse, without ever quite becoming impossible. And all the time she was tired.

She said she was so tired in fact that she permitted herself a short nap that afternoon. She folded her arms on the table and put her head down. It wasn't a long nap she intended to take, but she didn't wake until almost an hour later when she heard the car on the gravel outside the house. It was Mavis and Rena, bringing the cream. She stood up and met them at the door. Rena, my green-eyed, black-haired daughter who loves that old lady, was full of a little girl's news.

"You know what?" she said.

"What, sweetheart?"

"I'm staying overnight with Sheila Garfield. At her house."

"Are you?"

"But you probably don't know Sheila Garfield, do you?"

"No, I don't think so."

"Because she lives in town and goes to the second grade with me. Well, we're going to stay up past midnight and have a party and everything. On account of it's New Year's. That's tomorrow."

"I know. And it sounds like a wonderful idea."

"Oh, it is," Mavis said. "It's strictly a big deal. Definitely groovy."

"Mom," Rena said. "We don't say groovy anymore. We say stud."

So Edith hugged my daughter close to her that afternoon, and then she whipped up the new cream from the store and the three of them sat down and ate at least a third of Lyman's pumpkin pie. They had a fine time for a while, visiting and chatting, talking about nothing as if there was nothing particular to talk about—and all that time, you understand, Edith still had in mind what she was going to do later. When they left, having wished the season's greetings to Lyman and listened in turn to his mumbled confusion about postcards, Edith thought it was for the last time. According to her plan she wouldn't see them again. But, in the iron manner in which she had done everything else in her life, she pushed that thought away from her—or accepted it—and just put her coat on.

Now I think I told you when I first started talking, telling you this story, I believe I mentioned that business about the chicken feed and the tied-up dog. Well, I haven't forgotten. And not just because it was after my wife and daughter left her that Friday afternoon that those things happened, but because they seemed to clinch the matter, to finish it. What I'm saying is, she took the dog outside again. It didn't want to go; she had to force it, to take the dog by the collar and lead it, its back legs dragging in weak objection while she talked to it, coaxingly, out to the garage. There she tied it to the latch in the open doorway with a length of rope, with enough food and water to last it a day or two. Then, ignoring that pitiful whimpering and complaint behind her, she went on to the chicken house, to leave food for the half-dozen red chickens. I mean she lifted or dragged—don't ask me how—a fifty-pound bag of chicken feed into the center of the dirt floor and cut it open so that they too would survive until somebody happened to remember them afterwards. And that clinched it. It was then, while walking back to the house under that late purpling sky, that she understood for the first time that what she was doing was a real thing, a certainty. Up to that point it hadn't been real, even to herself.

"But I knew it then," she said. "Nancy was crying at me from the end of the rope. I kept hearing her all evening—or thought I did. And I wanted to release her, I wanted to let her go, Sandy. But I didn't. I went back to the house and shut the door."

So there was really only one thing more for Edith Goodnough to do before she put supper on the table. She wanted to iron Lyman's shirt. And she did that then, while the potatoes and green beans boiled, pressed his best white shirt out neat and clean on the ironing board so that he would appear gentlemanly. When she was satisfied she took it in to him where he still sat in the parlor, fumbling with faded pictures of Memphis and Mobile, New York and Boise, and somehow persuaded him to not only put on a different shirt than the one he'd been wearing all day but to also get into a blue suit jacket that matched his dark pants. He didn't know why. It didn't matter. I suppose all he understood was that it was an imposition, a damn bother, but like I've already said, she managed that too, somehow. And afterwards, when he was dressed to her satisfaction, she herself changed clothes, put on a fine dark skirt and pink blouse and brushed her hair. So they were ready for supper now. They sat down in the kitchen across the table from one another, looking, I fully believe, as if they were contented, even happy.

They didn't talk much. Edith said she hadn't expected that they would. It was enough to be dressed up, to be seated at a table with red candles flickering, to be eating a satisfactory supper of baked chicken and pumpkin pie. The only thing she remembers saying was, "I'm still glad you came home, Lyman."

Lyman was nodding in his chair, almost asleep.

"I know you don't understand. But I am glad you came home when you did. It was worth the wait. Can you remember all we've done?"

"I'm too tired," he said.

"You want to lie down now, don't you?"

"I want to sleep."

"Yes, it's been a long day. Come on then, I'll help you."

She lifted under his arm to help him rise from the chair, and together they walked into the living room. She laid him down on his bed in his suit clothes, took his slippers off. When she pulled a blanket up over his long quiet body she saw that he was already asleep, the blue veins and age spots at his temple showing dimly in the fading light, his chin fallen onto his bow tie. She ran her hand over his forehead once and bent to kiss him, then she went back to the kitchen and put the candles out with moistened fingers and locked the back-porch door. She had thought she would clear the table, put things away, but that seemed excessive now, and so she returned to the living room, where she locked that door too, that outside door that opened formally into the house but was never used, and finally she sat down in the rocking chair between the two beds. Rocking a little, she watched the dark collect in the room while she waited for the moment when she knew she would rise again and strike a match to the old dust-coated travel papers on the stairway, which her brother and my daughter had allowed her to store there on the steps in the past years. But that moment hadn't arrived yet. For a time, for a while longer, she was content to sit and rock quietly, with the matches in her lap. She looked past her brother and out through that south window toward the elm trees that stood in the yard, bare and clean and dark, against a sky that was lighter only by comparison to the dark trees. Still she waited, thinking: *In a minute now. Soon, soon I'll stand up.*

I T WAS a dog's barking, something as simple and ordinary and yet as unpredictable as that—that's all it was— just the loud and persistent barking of a neighbor's dog that prevented Edith Goodnough's plans.

"What the hell's got into Jack?" I said.

Mavis and I were upstairs in our bedroom getting ready to go out for the night and Rena was already downstairs with her coat on, waiting by the front door for us to take her to Sheila Garfield's house. Then Jack, our blue heeler, started barking. His nose was raised into the night, and he was howling.

"There must be something in the yard," Mavis said.

She looked out the east window.

"Come here," she said.

"What? Is it another skunk?"

"No."

"It better not be a calf out, not tonight."

"Will you just come here and look?"

So I looked.

"Good Christ," I said. "Call town. I'm going over there."

I ran downstairs and on outside and jumped into the pickup, spraying gravel out hard behind me entering the road. As I raced on toward the Goodnough place, I began to see bright flames through the second-story windows, where fire was already burning the old dry wallpaper in the empty bedrooms. Above the house there was yellow smoke rising in the updraft, and the whole place was lit up in that strange flicker of light so that the trees and the picket fence seemed to waltz on the brown grass. I braked the pickup beside the gate and ran up onto the back porch. Only of course the door was locked. Except I didn't know that. *They never lock their doors. What in Christ's going on here?* I ran off the porch around to the side to try that other door that opened onto the living room and found it locked too, solid and brick hard, one of those old-fashioned oak doors made before anyone heard of constructing doors with hollow cores. *What in hell is this?* So I was going to break the window, that south window in the living room, smash it in, and enter that way. And then I saw Edith.

Beyond the window Edith was sitting in the rocking chair. She was looking at me, sitting bolt upright and staring at me as if I had startled her, as if she thought I meant to cause her harm. I could see her eyes, her white face, and white hair. And then, while I stood there peering through the window, she did something that I will never forget, something that stopped me from kicking that window in and that—if you think about it—has altered everything else: she raised one hand from the arm of the rocking chair. That's all she did. But do you understand what I'm saying? She lifted one pale blue-veined hand up from the rocking-chair arm, not to motion at me for help or even to show that I should hurry, but to warn me, to stop me. It was as if by that one open-faced hand, lifted so I could see it, that she was telling me to stay away. She didn't want my help. She desired that I do . . . nothing.

And just then I understood that. I understood too, all at once, why the doors were locked when in eighty years they had no doubt never been locked before. It all came together for me as I stood there on that side porch watching her through the window. Gradually she relaxed back into the rocking chair; she lowered her hand and shut her eyes. Then I saw that Lyman was asleep on the bed just below me, his face turned toward the window, pale and speckled, and his bow tie dark against the white of his best shirt. So I stood there. I stood listening to my neighbors begin to cough while their living room filled with the smoke that was curling in past the closed stairway door and while the rooms over their heads burned on. And you can think what you will. Perhaps you would have been able to break that window and to drag those two people out into the yard, but I couldn't. I didn't. I had seen Edith Goodnough raise her hand. That's all.

ONLY THEN, the fire department and the ambulance got there. With Bud Sealy, Holt County sheriff, in tow. Because the fire department and the ambulance and the sheriff all pride themselves on speed and dispatch. Besides, it is only a short seven-mile drive from town, and Mavis called them at my instruction almost as soon as we understood why the dog was howling. Call town, I said. And she did. So it was within fifteen minutes—no more than that—after Mavis made that hurried call from our house that the local boys in the red trucks arrived. Long before they raced into the yard I could hear the trucks out on the blacktop, the sirens in full alarm.

So I tried to keep them away. That's true—I tried to prevent them from entering that burning house. Not that I blamed them; it was their job. But I fought them anyway on the porch in that flickering, waltzing light with the roar of burning timber above us, and they thought I was crazy when I hit Irv Jacobs as hard as I could in the face when he ran up onto the porch. He stumbled back off the steps.

"Goddamn it, Sandy. What the hell you doing?"

"Get out of here," I yelled. "All you sons a bitches."

"What's wrong with you?"

"Get out of here."

"We're coming in."

"Like hell you are. You miserable—"

They rushed me. I was hitting anything I could, Bob Williams in the throat and Tom Crossland over his eye, somebody at the side of his head, then they had me lifted off my feet and my boots up in the air, kicking somebody in the chest before they slammed me against the wall of the house and then carried me off the porch in a rush with my arms twisted behind my back, and somebody was hitting my ear to stop me kicking anymore, and I was shoved hard into the back seat of the county cop car, where Bud Sealy watched that I didn't get any other wild notions while I sat there sweating with the doors locked and that protective grille between Bud and me. The weight of that badge of his was tugging at his shirt pocket.

"By God, Roscoe," Bud said. "You just about done it this time. I ought to take you in for obstruction."

"Go to hell," I said.

"Sure," he said. "That's right."

He was turned around in the front seat talking to me through all that iron grillwork. His heavy gut was squashed against the steering wheel.

"That's the ticket," he said. "But you keep it up and I'm not going to give a good goddamn how long we've been knowing one another—I'll take you in."

"You can take and fuck yourself too," I said.

"Just keep it up," Bud said.

So he went on talking, saying something official to me from the front seat, but I couldn't hear much of it for the ringing in my ears where somebody had hit me, and anyway I was more interested in what they were doing to the oak door with axes, making the oak kindling fly, and now they had it smashed open and the smoke was boiling out, and they went in through the smoke and brought Edith and Lyman out of the house in blankets, carrying them down the steps and across the yard to the ambulance. They were both unconscious, their arms dangling loose like rags. The ambulance roared away towards town.

The rest of us stayed there until the house was gone. They couldn't save it. In the end they managed to contain the fire by soaking the well house and the outbuildings and the nearby trees with their hoses, but the house burned down to the old square limestone-block foundation. When the roof caved in, the sparks exploded into the sky like fireworks and then were shot away in the updraft into the dark. After that they unlocked the cop car and let me out.

AND SOMETIME that same night Lyman died. He never regained consciousness. After his sister fed him pumpkin pie with a dollop of whipped cream on top and after she laid him down on his bed in the living room for the last time, Lyman went off to sleep and never woke again. The next day, at the hospital, they told me it was due to severe smoke inhalation. They said it was not possible to save him. For my part, I believe there must be worse ways to die.

Two days later, on January third, a Monday, I helped bury him. I was one of the pallbearers. He was still dressed in his good dark suit, and we lowered him in his silver coffin into the frozen ground beside his mother. I had instructed John Baker to dig the hole in that place. It seemed fitting to me. There would be at least that much distance—the width of his mother's grave—between him and the old stump-armed man that Lyman had spent a good fourth of his life running away from. I figured Lyman would appreciate the head start, in case he ever had to run again.

Edith didn't attend the funeral or the graveside rites, though. She was still too sick. In fact, she almost died. They had her in an I.C. unit with machines attached to her everywhere they could think to attach them, monitoring her round the clock, and I admit to you that there were times, particularly in that first week or two afterwards, when she was lying there with that damn tube shoved up her nose, when she was still unconscious and coughing, her thin throat wracked with the awful effort and the yellow spit brought up and bubbling on her cracked mouth—there were plenty of times when I wished she would die. I wished that she would just give up. But she didn't. Edith hung on and hung on, like she didn't know how to let go or stop even yet.

And now I'm afraid she's getting better. I'm afraid Bud Sealy and these imported lawyers will be able to drive her over to the courthouse after all and make her endure a trial for something they insist is murder. There is not one son of a bitch amongst them that understands a goddamn thing.

So, IN THE PAST three and a half months, I have gone up to see her almost every day. Of course, Mavis and Rena have gone with me. We went up there last night. Because of that front page *Denver Post* newspaper article a week ago, they have begun to position a deputy sheriff outside her room in the hallway. And the hell of it is, I don't for a minute believe that anything would have come of it if it hadn't been for that damn newspaper kid poking around. Bud Sealy had forgotten any notion he had of charging me with obstruction, and folks were calling the fire itself just an accident. At least in public, for the record, that's what people were calling it. But then, somehow—I still don't know how—those Denver people got wind of the thing, discovered a wild hair up their ass, and sent their kid out here to sniff around. He talked to enough of the wrong people, and now it's all gone to hell. Last night they even had a new guy stationed at the hospital, somebody I never saw before. He had a cop's revolver on his hip, and the son of a bitch wanted to frisk us before we went in. I told him to keep his damn hands off us.

"I'll have to call Bud Sealy," he said.

"Call him then, goddamn it," I said. "But you ain't touching us."

We walked past him on into that white room. Inside, as usual, there was nothing but quiet and pulled blinds and some flowers on a bedstand. Edith was asleep. One arm was outside the covers with that steady flow of liquid still pumping sugar water through a needle into her hand. She woke up when she heard us enter. Rena went over and sat down on the edge of her bed and cocked her feet on the bed rail.

"How do you feel now?" Rena said.

"I've been asleep, sweetheart. I can't tell yet."

"Do you think you feel any better?"

"Why yes, seeing you always makes me feel better."

She took Rena's hand, and Mavis and I pulled up chairs beside her bed. We talked together for about an hour. A nurse came in once to take her temperature and her pulse and to check the drop chamber, while we waited for her to leave so we could go on talking. Then at eight-thirty another nurse stuck her head in the door to tell us visiting hours were over. We stood up to leave.

"Is it nice outside?" Edith said.

"Not bad," I said. "Looks like another clear night."

"I can't always tell," she said. "They won't let me open any windows."

"Why not?"

"They say the bugs will fly in."

"There aren't any bugs in April. Do you want me to open it?"

"If you would," Edith said. "I was thinking maybe I could smell something."

So I pulled the blinds and cranked the window open for her. Then Mavis and Rena hugged her and we left, with the promise that we would come back today, this Sunday evening. Outside her room the new deputy was still on guard in the hallway. Somebody had brought him a cup of coffee. We pushed past him and walked outside to the car. When we looked back at Edith's room we saw that a nurse was there, shutting her window again. They weren't going to let her breathe.

I'M DONE talking now. I've told all I know.

Only, before you leave, before it gets full dark, you have time to drive over there a half mile east and see what remains of that yellow house. Poking around, you might find some charred travel brochures and some heat-twisted forks and a cracked plate or two, and then, depending upon how long you stay there, you might still have time to go on into town and notice Lyman's last green Pontiac rusting in the Holt junkyard with the weeds growing up around it, before you drive on to the cemetery, where you will find the three Goodnough headstones over there at the far edge across the fence from Otis Murray's cornfield.

You go ahead and do all that. But I can't go with you. I've promised to collect my wife and my daughter in town, and then we're going back to the hospital to visit an old white-haired woman who, though she will be eighty years old on Thursday, is still in the ways that matter just as fine and beautiful as she must have been in 1922 when she was twenty-five and went riding out in the sandhills in a Model T with my dad and the windows were rolled down and the night air was blowing fresh in on them—all of that and it almost fifty-five years ago now without her ever understanding how to say anything like a continuous yes to herself.